THE RISE AND FALL OF THE SACRED BAND OF THEBES
G. A. HAUSER

Chaeronea in the year 338 BC

CHAPTER 1

Through his dust-caked eyes Nikanoras could see the spray of the sun spilling out from the cloud filled heavens like the mist of sea-foam crashing into rocks from the Mediterranean. One thing plagued his mind. Was he dead?

If one is dead, could they hear the last fatal gasps of their fellow comrades in arms all around them? Would the blood flow from his sliced skin? Perhaps not. Perhaps he is still alive.

Last he remembered he was on the battlefield of alongside two hundred and ninety-nine of his deeply committed corps of elite fighters. Yet now, all that was dear to him lie dead or dying on this body-riddled field of weathered grass and horse dung. As he struggled to see, with blood, dirt, and sweat hindering his sight, in his heart he knew they had been massacred. Philip II of Macedon and his glorious golden-haired son had been their doom.

If he moved, would they find he was yet alive and spear him through the heart?

As best he could he listened for footfalls. Someone was drawing near. He dared not look. But, what will living bring him? Slavery and hard labor no doubt. Surely now would be a very good time to die. Then he can join Meleagros in the afterlife. He had seen his lover cut down by Alexander's cavalry. A devastating blow he did receive that knocked him down in his path. What hope had he that any life was left to his earthly body? It had been at that point in battle that he had gone mad, slashing and hewing at everything in his way. Killing more than thirty men, he finally felt the crash of steel

4

himself, cutting across his chest armor, slicing his right biceps so he no longer could hold his blade. As it dropped from his useless limb, another forceful strike of a spear deflected off his chest plate, sending him to where he lay, choking to catch air into his lungs through bruised ribs as blood flowed from his arm. Indeed, he wished he were already dead.

As the crunching of metal approached he decided to take his execution with honor. Meleagros had. Never would he feign death and shame his lover or himself.

Forcing his eyelids to open against that brightness in the sky, he faced his enemy.

He struggled to focus as a shadow crossed his brow. He met his eyes. The brilliance of their color startled Nikanoras, for they were as blue as the sky behind his halo of golden hair.

"One is alive, Father," he called to someone behind him.

"Then kill him!"

Nikanoras heard that roar of what he could only guess could be the King of Macedon. Having heard it once before in this battle, he never forgot it. So, this is Alexander, Prince of the World.

As this young prince knelt down near him, he never released contact with his gaze. With gentle hands Alexander removed his helmet of silver and bronze with the white crest of horse mane, and petted his damp hair back from his face. Once again to his father he did shout, "I cannot. I will not. Not one so brave as the Sacred Band."

In his irritated grumble, the father-king, replied, "As you wish." The pounding of hooves Nikanoras heard soon after as he left his son to his own.

Alexander's smile was disarming. They had all thought he was an enemy, a barbarian, hated by Athens and Thebes. What was this? Compassion? Kindness?

In formal Greek Nikanoras asked, "Will you not do me the honor and kill me now lest I be ashamed that I have not died valiantly? I am no slave."

Alexander urged him to use his lap for a pillow. "No, you are no slave. Who are you, noble warrior?"

"I am Nikanoras, son of the Theban statesman Saliukos."

"And you will be cared for, and your wound treated." With that, Alexander raised his head and shouted for another of his comrades. "Hephaestion, help me get this wounded man to our camp so we may tend him."

When the two righted him, Nikanoras was able to witness the carnage. It took everything he had to not wail in agony at the sight of his companions cut to ribbons and still as stones. Averting his gaze once again to Helios in the heavens for the last thing he dared find was his lover, Meleagros, somewhere among this mass of grisly corpses.

Though he tried to prevent it, a moan of anguish did pass his lips.

Both men squeezed him tighter around his waist in comfort and almost had to carry him to their camp.

A prisoner was he. Though he was treated kindly and his wound cleaned and dressed, he knew his fate.

Alexander himself brought him a bowl of beef and broth then sat at his side and urged him to eat. Nikanoras had not the stomach for it. Seeing this, Alexander had a slave pour him wine. Of that, Nikanoras drank down to the bottom.

"Father is burying the men of your Sacred Band with honor, Nikanoras. Two hundred and fifty-four of your men will be given proper funerals. And he will see to it a monument is erected to watch over them."

With tears rolling down his cheeks he asked, "Why are you being so kind to your enemy?"

"Because you are known as the boldest of adversaries, committed to one another like a lover to his beloved. All who stood before you were in mortal fear of your power and skill. You have been a thing of wonder and worship to me all my life."

Of that, Nikanoras guessed, it would be no more than twenty years, his own age. Like a shade passing in his mind, instantly the face of Meleagros appeared before him. His beauty and grace, his warmth and intelligence, gone from him forever, like a feather to the breeze. Gone while this enemy, the crown Prince of Macedon tells him he was worshipping them at the same time as his army had extinguished them.

As gentle, and with as little condescension as possible,

Alexander again handed him the bowl. "Eat, Nikki, eat."

When Nikanoras spun quickly to see his face, Alexander knew that pet name had been used before. Nikanoras gaped at him in horror and said, "Do not call me that again. I beg it of you."

"I am sorry." The adoring smile remained on the prince's face, however.

After thinking carefully, Nikanoras asked, "You said, only two-hundred and fifty-four graves shall be dug. Do you mean that forty-five more of my band have been taken alive?"

Handing the bowl off to a servant, Alexander studied Nikanoras' bright brown eyes. "Yes. We are keeping you separated. You understand why. For now." As if he were a doting mother, Alexander caressed his hair reassuringly. Though he tried to take comfort, and Nikanoras knew they were being cared for as was he, he could not help but wonder, to what end? What hell? What sacrifice? This he did not know.

He knew only one fact: It was the end of an army that had never seen a loss. One that had always been triumphant for over the last forty years. And to his own private nightmare, it has been defeated whilst he was a part of it.

Thebes never again could claim any power. This was the time of Macedon.

CHAPTER 2

As a six-year-old lad he was taught the long violent history of Thebes by his father. Part of the New Boeotian League, which had at least seventy members banding together in a precarious agreement of peace and cooperation, they hung on tenaciously to any hope of remaining unconquered. Their common enemies in those days were many, among them, Sparta, and to their dismay, Athens. They were so close to Athens geographically, they should have been their sister city. But, one has to understand those tyrants and theologians of that powerful state. Their egos surpassed reckoning. It was the Athenian way, or war. His father, Saliukos, one of Thebes' aristocratic statesmen at the time, filled him with hatred and propaganda against anything Athenian. It is no wonder, for decades, peace talks with them failed. Not to say they did not try and reconcile with them. At one time they managed to band together to fight off Sparta's naval fleet. But, that was short lived as loyalties were traded like silver mina coins.

His stately, tall, lovely mother, Thessenike, daughter of a Caria regent, regrettably bore nothing but females for the first few years of their marriage. Of these his father kept one; the first, his sister, Euridises, and exposed the others in the wild wood. In the quiet of his bedchamber, Sister informed Nikanoras if he was yet another female, father would have banished their mother into the hills and re-wed. It was Nikanoras' understanding later his father had a list of concubines in waiting. He'd no doubt he'd bastard brothers

8

wandering the streets.

But then, after another difficult pregnancy, came Nikanoras, kicking and screaming into a world he had no power to even understand, least of all, defend.

Ten years his elder, beautiful Euridises babied him and brought him up as if he were her offspring and not her sibling. Their father soon put a stop to it, complaining he would be too soft for his purposes. Of this he would find out very young, he was to be groomed as an elite fighting machine. A warrior of the Sacred Band. An honor only few held in their lifetime.

From the moment they knew he would not die in infancy, seemingly healthy enough to survive the diseases of childhood, discussions took place in the dim halls of his father's huge gilded palace.

Over blood red Thessilian wine, Saliukos would hold council with his best friend from childhood, the noble Arybos, son of Hellious. Having grown up as children and been in battle together, the two were as close as brothers and ne'er did Nikanoras ever see them fight, or at least have anything more than a heated debate. But, it was Arybos' constant pressure that had guided his father's choice. With tactics and logic that he would never learn of, or hear whisper to, Arybos declared Nikanoras should be one of the chosen.

"Saliukos," Arybos glared at him from over his gilded cup, "You must force the boy into service. Make him one of the honored guard."

His frown causing deep furrows in his worried brow, Saliukos paced, his hands drawn behind his back. "My only son? Think, Arybos, my friend, if he were to perish. What of my estate? My riches?"

And Arybos thought of nothing else. The wealth of his childhood friend was always at the forefront of his mind. "Of this he can share after. Allow him the distinction of being a battle hero. What fear is there? The Sacred Band has never been defeated."

Stopping, dropping his hands to his sides so his robe hung properly from his broad shoulders, Saliukos said, "A male lover is he to have? A lover? Not a wife?"

9

A tight wry grin under his beard, Arybos replied, "Yes. A lover he will have, to join the ranks. But, I shall be his erastes, dear friend, to teach him how to enjoy the touch of a man." When he found Saliukos gearing up for a comment in defiance, Arybos reminded him, "I hold a grave secret over your head, my brilliant statesman. Do not tempt me to use it in anger."

Knowing that secret could not only cause him to lose his position at the council, Saliukos knew clearly, he would lose his life, and his family would be executed as well. In tacit understanding of the strangle hold this man held, Saliukos bowed his head in defeat.

And so it was decided. Nikanoras was destined to be one of the Sacred Band. Against his father's wishes, for in his mind he would marry young and inherit the vast wealth of his vault. Arybos convinced him glory first, marriage later. Little did his father know of Arybos' true intentions. For delaying Nikanoras' right to his family name and riches were foremost in his plans. With wicked fire in his black eyes, Arybos drew a vision of heroic proportions in whose shoes Nikanoras was meant to fill. Agreed, like a contract with Hades, Nikanoras was sold and given to Arybos to shape into a legend.

****

The year Nikanoras turned nine, his father hired a personal trainer for him and after his lessons with the other nobles of his peers in writing and mathematics, he would work him until dusk, placing a sword in his tiny fist and a tortoise shell shield on his elbow.

Though it was all games to him, it did wear Nikanoras out so he fell asleep without a nod in his sister's arms. Euridises made sure he was fed extremely well for she had heard horrible rumors of young boys who were worked too hard by their tutors, only to not grow to their potential height. Their father was a very large, muscular man so she had hopes of the same for her brother. It seemed her hopes were to be realized.

It didn't take long for Nikanoras to understand that their family was one of the privileged few that could afford several slaves and clothing bought at the agora. While other females of lesser wealth had the task of weaving their own linen and wool, his sister and mother were solely in charge of running the slaves. He was certain that this was a much preferred way of life to that of weaving at the loom night and day. Like a queen, his sister would spend her silver staters on fine cloaks died brilliant colors at the marketplaces near the palace. Most she would bring back for him. Spoilt was he, giggling, dancing, carefree, having run of the grand house, naked, until he was seven.

But, as she tended her chores, Euridises caught many a roving eye. It was surely her hope to attract a man of as much wealth and status as her father. Nikanoras had no doubt she would. Her beauty and charm would see to it she could enslave any man. Loving her more than his own mother, who ignored him, he adored his sister, and imagined his own future wife not far from her image.

His carefree existence was about to alter drastically. The passing of time was what they had been waiting for. It was then he was to be treated differently. The spoiling would cease, the serious training would begin.

Never one to explain his deeds, on the night of Nikanoras' thirteenth birthday, Saliukos brought him with him on his evening stroll.

In awe of the sights and smells around him, Nikanoras' eyes were wide as he lavished in Thebes' beauty. A city walled for its protection, lovely temples towered over their heads, their columns adorned with statues of great gods and goddesses of history. As they passed the Mycenaean Palace he imagined the wonderful murals on its interior; tiny tiled images of women bringing offerings to the god Apollo in brilliant blood reds and wheat yellows. Having been inside, he knew it well.

The watch fires were lit on the streets and towers as the homes glowed orange from their own internal flames. A special occasion he assumed it was to be, for Saliukos had him dressed in a new red chlamys cloak the slave had just purchased the day before, and he had tasted the fruit of the vine on his lips for the first time with their meal of seafood, figs, olives, and goat's cheese.

When his father left him off at a strange building, doing nothing more than nudging him inside, he was more than a little confused. Wasn't this their evening together? He had waited years for the chance to be by his side with his colleagues. He felt he was man enough, and educated enough to carry his own in conversation. He imagined they would discuss this new threat to their world known as Macedon. How even Athens was considering a peace treaty with them to form a league against this new gluttonous king.

Always at the council meetings, his father was never home for his dinners. It wasn't as if they had spent their nights speaking together over the oil lit lamps and sipping from their chalices. The demands of his time were too great. It was his intention to entrust his son to his tutors, his trainers, and now...some kind of mentor of sorts. Nikanoras' questions were not to be answered, but his obedience was to be expected. He knew what his father's mind was like. Euridises had made sure he was aware that three sisters had perished before they had even been suckled by his mother. A man such as this may decide his son was not good enough, and then go about harvesting yet another. It kept him in line, as one can imagine.

"Father?" Nikanoras tried not to yell as his father abandoned him, in what seemed disgust, leaving him feeling lonely and afraid. With his father's footfalls dying out behind him, he inhaled for courage and stood tall. Spinning around to face the doorway, he braved the foreboding darkness of the marble columned halls and shadowy corners until he could indeed see a flickering fire and hear light chatter and laughter. As he made his way around a bend, feeling not unlike a Spartan thief in the night, he was hoping his father had at least informed those inside he was expected. The idea of being caught spying mortified him.

Indeed he had. A dozen men of his father's age and standing in the community, of whom he would guess were in their mid-thirties, were lounging on cushioned benches, as young boys his own age, sat at their feet and listened to the gentle hum of the sharing of ideas and hypothesis. One of these bearded noble intellectuals he recognized immediately. Yet, he was the only one on his own. The moment this man spotted him, hovering shyly like a butterfly near a buttercup, he rose to his feet and reached out to him with both hands. Nikanoras could not believe the sight. His heart stopped knowing in humiliation he was to come to this man's embrace in front of so many strangers. It was the dark-eyed Arybos who was beckoning him. Even more shocked would he have been to learn this man had visited his home numerous times whilst he was absent, discussing this part of his education with his father in crude detail.

"Nikanoras. Come...Come. We have already started." Irritated at his reluctance, Arybos expected to be rushed and embraced, not feared as a leper.

Drawing closer to this beast a step at a time, Nikanoras thought to himself, *Started?* He puzzled at what was not told to him. Started what? What kind of debate group was this and why didn't his father at least allow him to prepare himself for it?

As he moved slowly across the dimly lit room, the other boys were riveted to his progress. A snicker caught his attention and in no time did he glance over at two of his peers' smirks, did their mentors give each a bop on the head in punishment.

After the stiff embrace, which he broke quickly, Nikanoras sat down in what he assumed was his proper place, at the floor on cushions before Arybos' lounge. Immediately, he was handed wine by a slave boy who was no older than ten.

Instantly the debate resumed. Handsome, dark Sostios with a fine short beard said, "Do you think the newly elected Ephor of Sparta is once again planning war?" he continued, "We had so savagely defeated Sparta in the last Mantinea battle, no one thought they could gather enough men to fill an army, ever again. Their last thousand standing to fight, we almost eradicated them from the soil thirty years ago. A barbaric way of life, the Spartans." He rubbed his hand over his beard. "They seem to hold women in such high esteem that they give them power and allow them to own land. A very shocking thought, don't you think?"

Out of the shadowy corner, one of the mentors, Eronimos, said, "As one of those men who lived around that province of feminism, let us hope the idea will never catch on here."

Sostios laughed softly at the comment as a pause appeared in the debate. At this handsome man's feet was another young boy. Though Nikanoras was shy to catch his eye, the youth was not as timid. Boldly he stared at Nikanoras as if he were some kind of whore dancing the erotic kordax. It was unnerving Nikanoras so much that he could not concentrate on what he knew was the reason he had been sent by his father. Obviously something in this conversation was of the utmost importance. Why else was he placed there like the dozen men and their young charges before them? Of this he was soon to find out. And he would be none too pleased.

The conversation spun and veered as if it were a chariot at the Olympic tethrippon race when it finally rested on a topic he was very learned in. The life of Pelopidas. Arybos' turn had come and he spoke softly to the group, "Though he died six years before your births, my young friends, this man had immeasurable wealth and was always giving to the poor and crippled. He had become a legend, even whilst he was yet alive. But, the reason this man and his elder friend, Epaminondas, are given top priority in your education is quite simple. They had begun the elite corps you," he nodded directly to Nikanoras, "and all the rest of the boys in this torch lit room are being groomed for."

As he heard those words, and for the first time understood he was not to be a statesman, but a warrior, Nikanoras gasped out loud before he could prevent it. Covering his mouth at the idea of a lover who was to be male and no woman to marry, he could not help but look again at all the others around him who had similar fates in store.

Waiting until he had their complete attention, Arybos said proudly, "The Leros Lochos. The Sacred Band. That is how you will honor Pelopidas' memory. No one loved Thebes more than Pelopidas, and his selfless giving to make it strong and honorable, rivaled only Athens in its jingoism. His victory against Sparta at the battle of Leuctra, with his newly created Band, had so much exceeded all expectations, that new chants and dances by Pindar were made up to tell the tale."

Then to his astonishment, Arybos gestured for Nikanoras to speak. He'd done all he could to blend into the dimness and disappear. Suddenly he was center stage and knew he had to perform or be booed off the dais with rotten tomatoes thrown at his head. Of what Nikanoras knew of Pelopidas' life, he gave when asked to share by Arybos. Knowing better than to act a fool or a coward, he said, "His greatest friend, Epaminondas, who valiantly rescued Pelopidas in the war with the Arcadians, after Pelopidas had been wounded seven times, had proven again and again the loyal friendship between them." Nikanoras caught the eye of the young boy staring at him as he continued, "Epaminondas was there to bring Pelopidas to safety risking his own life. Thus the idea was sprung of the coupling of warriors to bring out the best in them all."

When Nikanoras' voice died in the stillness he noticed the glittering of eyes on him, young and not as young, a source of pride for him, not intimidation. His father was an orator, so he dared not quiver at the task. All would be reported back to him in detail, he had no doubt.

"Well done, Nikanoras," Arybos whispered, petting his hair.

Later, as the wine in his belly made him sleepy, and the voices became a jumbled hum in his ear, the seductive caress on the back of his head woke him out of his stupor. Tilting over his shoulder to see Arybos' leering gaze, he caught his sensual whisper in surprise. As he leaned down so only he may hear, he said, "For a lovelier eromenos I could not have hoped."

It made it difficult for Nikanoras to swallow suddenly. Arybos was like an uncle to him, one almost part of his family with his kinship and familiarity. How could his father have arranged this embarrassment? Was he not old enough to have a say in his selection? Obviously not.

With this distraction behind him, he made eye contact with the still curious gaze of the young one at Sostios' feet. His name he had finally heard and remembered, was Meleagros. They were the same age, same height, and both sons of politicians, not generals. Though they had not been educated together, Nikanoras felt as if he knew him. Maybe it was his intense gaze on him that was growing comforting as the oil lamps flickered and dimmed, he did not know. But they were kinsmen in an instant if not solely because they were both in identical situations.

The slave boy refilled their goblets and the debate had evaporated. It was nearing the middle of the night and he yearned the comfort of his bed.

As soon as the boy had topped off all twenty-four cups the young slave began to dance for them directly in the center of their circle of benches. A kithara was playing for him somewhere out of Nikanoras' line of vision. As he watched this talented young male perform, a hand once again touched his long brown hair.

Torn between the caressing of the man behind him and the sensual gyrating of the boy before him, Nikanoras froze.

When that strong hand urged him to the couch he did his best not to resist. Something told him this was what he was brought here for. Some odd initiation of sorts.

Whatever it was to be, he was not to run away from it like a coward. Not only would Arybos be angry but his father would be obligated to punish him.

With the music and movement filling the room, odd fragrances of musk and fruit followed. One last time Nikanoras tried to see Meleagros from across the increasingly darkened room. No longer did he meet Nikanoras' gaze. With his body boldly lying over Sostios, something in Nikanoras twisted and spun out of control.

As his attention to Arybos was not enough, Arybos gripped Nikanoras' jaw and urged him to stare at him. "Come here my lovely boy. Let me make you a man."

Holding his breath to prevent a full blown cringe, Nikanoras was forced to kiss his bearded lips. A shiver-like sickness rushed over him. Closing his eyes Nikanoras imagined Meleagros caressing him. Only then was it possible to tolerate.

CHAPTER 3

The following day his father did not discuss the events of the night before. In reality, he shunned him as if somehow the evening had been unbearable to *him*. The irony was lost on Nikanoras. Yet, it was up to him to understand the things that passed, and with the help of his sister easing his anxiety, Nikanoras learned that this was pederasty. Arybos was his erastes, or male lover, and he was what he had called him that night, his eromenos, or his beloved. There to develop his mind, train him in customs, morals, politics, as well as learning to be a responsible member of their society, while Nikanoras was there to fulfill him sexually. It had been done the same way for centuries and it would be done a hundred more years. It did not matter what Nikanoras thought of it. Some things were what they are, regardless of one's input. When you are born into a custom and time, you simply live it without more than a thought as to how it has come about. But why the close friend of the family Arybos?

Wouldn't his contact with Arybos taint every other visit? Of this Euridises had no answer. They followed their father's wishes with tacit acceptance. No one was to question his authority in that house, not unless you wanted to be on the street begging for crumbs.

Leaving early in the morning, dressed in his bleached white chlamys, Saliukos strutted through the narrow whitewashed alleys to the dikastery, or courts of law, where he would either witness or participate in the hearings.

As Nikanoras stood in their doorway, watching as he vanished slowly from his sight he wondered why he had chosen this course of war for him when so clearly he could have followed in his footsteps. His education was beyond reproach, his intelligence, he had hoped, beyond what they had anticipated. Yet, a sword he had placed in his hand. Did his father want him to die young?

He should not complain of this out loud, for so many of his peers were offspring to the military. It was no shame, and on the contrary, worthy of praise to be victorious in battle. His father had served his time, he knew, but he had not been in the military long. With friends in very high places, he had quickly been brought off the lines of warlords and into the courtroom and senate.

A prouder son he could not be. And still, the yearning Nikanoras had to question his father's decision he had to keep behind his sealed lips. But, his father had the power to change things. He could be schooled for politics instead. Not war. Not a male lover.

Of his mother he did ask it. After a look, which was of so much disgust Nikanoras could never have anticipated it, she shoved him out of the house and threw his practice shield and sword behind him into the dirt.

Brushing off his pride and shield, Nikanoras knew he was no coward. War did not frighten him. Dying is not to be feared if it is a noble death. His only question was, why was he being educated as a scholar then? Could one truly be both? Was his father planning to pray he survived until old age, when he would be too feeble to hold a saber, and then have the wit and wisdom of his schooling?

Maybe so. Or maybe the Fates had in their plan that he would never lavish in the wealth that surrounded him. He was destined to be a visitor in these halls, never an owner. As if the prophets at Delphi had predicted his future, truer words had not been spoken.

Kissing his fair sister good-bye, he made his way to the palaestra for his exercise. Completely preoccupied with his thoughts, dreading contact with Arybos, and asking the question 'why' over and over in his mind, he didn't even notice when Meleagros was stepping along beside him. How long he had been there, he had no idea.

When he finally turned his way, the stunned look on Nikanoras' face appeared to please the young noble.

"Lucky for you I am no paid assassin."

"Meleagros. I do not know where my head is." The very sight of his dazzling grin and long flowing hair electrified Nikanoras.

"Not know? Why, it is with the bearded goat, Arybos. My guess is that you are reliving your night with him with much joy." With that, Meleagros burst out into laughter. "You do not like him? Perhaps you have another in mind?" Meleagros purred like a kitten and wrapped his arm around Nikanoras' waist so their shields were framing them.

What was he to say? Though educated in many subjects, love and attraction were still as foreign to him as Persia's exotic temples.

Meleagros said, "I think Sostios a fine man. I could do worse...as you have." His bright eyes emitted an impish twinkle. "Is it just me? Or does Arybos give off an air that is unwholesome?"

"Oh. No, it is not just you. There is something sinister about him and I do not know what." Nikanoras shivered as he remembered his touch.

"It is his forked phallus that gives him away." Meleagros snickered wickedly.

Stopping short to see his explosive laughter right behind his wry smile, Nikanoras said, "You enjoy teasing me."

"Teasing is the very least of the pleasures I would enjoy doing with you, you lovely thing." Meleagros' eyes seemed to mist over. His voice had changed to a breathy sigh. The seductiveness of it made the gooseflesh rise on Nikanoras' arms.

"We are on our way to training school."

That wonderful full laughter of his once again burst out of him as if he were an overflowing goblet of wine. "Not now, Nikki. You certain you are the son of Saliukos? For you are acting as if you were more like the son of Pan."

The blush ran hot on his cheeks as they continued on their way, jumping and skipping with their youthful excitement.

It was their day for training in both the stadion race and the pankration bouts. The running Nikanoras loved, the violent fighting in the sparring he detested. Though their erastes, who were acting as instructors at the palaestra, told them to fight half strength, inevitably someone got hurt. Dreading the fights, Nikanoras did not mind the act of kicking, punching, and taking a man to the ground. There was nothing he enjoyed more than a good battle, but, not against his own brothers.

How was he to hold back when the purpose of the contest was to win? Pit against Meleagros, for example, he would sooner allow him victory than harm a hair on that pretty boy's head. So, he knew, since he was too kind and loving to cause pain to his companions, that he would most certainly be the recipient of several painful bruises.

His partner, Meleagros, did not have the same compassion. To him it was about winning. As their luck would have it, they were about to find out who would be the stronger.

In the brilliant hot sun, on the playing field of green, with only a leather strap around their knuckles for protection and were naked as a newborn, they circled one another warily as the rest shouted and urged them to fight. Nikanoras was certain Arybos and Sostios had wagers on their outcome as they stood together shoulder to shoulder and shouted rude things to spur them on.

Twice Meleagros struck out at him, and Nikanoras deflected both. If anyone expected Nikanoras to bruise Meleagros' lovely features, they were mad. Somehow he would get the best of him without making him bleed, outside his skin or under.

Angry Nikanoras was backing from the battle, Meleagros began taunting him. Shouting, "You are too timid for me. Why aren't you even throwing a real punch?"

Catching sight of Arybos' red, angry face behind Meleagros' back, Nikanoras knew he would be sorry if he allowed Meleagros to win. A purse of drachmas was wagered and severe punishment awaited him for losing.

When Meleagros planted his left fist into Nikanoras' jaw, it was obvious Meleagros was not as careful with his beauty as Nikanoras was with his.

The teasing from the rest of the group was getting just as painful. What else could he do? Nikanoras charged Meleagros, gripped him around the waist and threw him to the ground. As they grappled together on the cool grass Nikanoras felt Meleagros' chest shaking oddly. He leaned back to see Meleagros' expression. He was laughing uncontrollably. When Nikanoras tilted his head in confusion, Meleagros grabbed his face in his hands and brought him for a kiss. The jeering surrounded them instantly from their peers as their erastes shouted in anger.

As Nikanoras pulled back from him with astonishment, Meleagros whispered, "That's for growing excited for me."

The fiery rush of humiliation was impossible to hide. There was no doubt he was blushing from his ears to his chest. Hopping off him quickly, Nikanoras backed up to the outer ring, both his hands crossed in front of himself. Instantly, Arybos grabbed him by his ear painfully so he may get the full extent of his anger.

No time did the other erastes waste on their foolishness, as two more were selected to fight. As their punishment he and Meleagros were to run laps around the arena in the heat. Something Nikanoras preferred.

He sprinted off before Meleagros could as much as turn his head. When the boy did manage to catch up and with puffing breaths, he said, "Do not worry. It is meant to be."

With his frown firmly in place, Nikanoras didn't even grant him his sideways glance. He knew word of this punishment would reach his father, and he'd yet to get the full tongue lashing of Arybos. Immediately he thought Meleagros arrogant and irritating.

Passing one of the entranceways cut into the surrounding stone stadium, Meleagros grabbed Nikanoras' arm and off-balanced him with such force, he started tripping over his own feet. Meleagros held him, dragging him off the track where Nikanoras knew only more trouble could follow. Backing him against the wall in the darkness of shade, Meleagros pressed his length against him with a hunger he did not even try to disguise.

When his mouth contacted Nikanoras' he felt he could not gain enough air for his expanding lungs. Nikanoras pushed him back furiously. "What are you doing?" He knew full well, Arybos and Sostios would be watching them like hawks.

With their sweat mixing together on their overheated bodies, Meleagros slid his smooth chest over Nikanoras' skin and slowly, softly, said, "I am making you mine."

Stunned and horrified of their punishment to come, Nikanoras shoved him off and rushed back to the track. As he looked over his shoulder he found both Arybos and Sostios in the process of hunting them down. Feeling as if he were caught like a spy before battle, Nikanoras increased his speed to get away from them, with the pretext of running as ordered.

The soft pad of Meleagros' feet fell behind him. As he caught up Nikanoras said, "You will see to it I am whipped!"

"Do not worry, my lovely. Just let me do the talking."

Rolling his eyes at the insanity, Nikanoras thought his companion was truly crazy. Nikanoras shook his head, knowing that no amount of talk would get them out of this mess.

When they had finished their meted out punishment, Nikanoras stopped to catch his breath leaning over his knees to come back to normal breathing, sweat dripping from his every pore. As Arybos approached he didn't flinch. Whatever he would do, Nikanoras knew he deserved. To his astonishment, instead of a beating, Arybos smiled at him. When he and Sostios exchanged knowing grins, Nikanoras was left to his own confusion until he deciphered the riddle.

****

On the long, lonely walk home through the back alleys, Nikanoras thought about what Meleagros had done and the fact that it had gone unpunished by their erastes. Knowing his history lessons, he knew what was expected of him. At thirteen and eight months, he was not so unworldly as to think reality was but a fantasy. It was plain. His father had ordered it. He was to be one of the Sacred Band. And that meant...he had to have a lover to fight along his side. That exchanged smile from teacher to teacher, was a hint that they were moving in the right direction.

Though it should have made him proud, it did not. It worried him. In his dreams at night he envisioned his future wife, the sons she would grace him with, and how he would not be a stranger to them as his father had chosen to be to him.

He wondered if there was a reason he could not marry. What if he chose, before he left on his march to war, to quickly make a vow? Would his father approve? Or would he, with an angry snarl, remind him that he would never see her again until, if he lived, he was sixty and could retire. This course of military obligation was not for him to decide. As if it had been chiseled in stone for all to see, he was to become one of Pelopidas' legacy. And a lover he must have. This man would be expected to mean the world to him. To fight with him with unmatched courage and devotion. He was to be like his very own bride.

His head lowered, his body exhausted, Nikanoras scuffed his sandals to his parents' house, the one of wealth and prestige that he had been born to. It was the first time in his life that he realized his sister Euridises, had more freedom than did he.

She was the first to see his entrance inside their home. Compared to most, it was a palace, with a kitchen, men's dining area, and a ladies' sitting room. Alongside the baths and sauna was the courtyard, where his mother could be seen sitting in the shade of the olive tree.

Nikanoras threw down his practice sword and shield in disgust as Euridises watched him with careful attention. She alerted their male slave, Nazabine, that Nikanoras should be assisted with his clothing and bathed.

Overhearing her, Nikanoras managed a smile in gratitude and followed the well-worn path to the luxurious mosaic encrusted bath. There he was stripped and sank into heated water as the slave scrubbed scented herbal soap, purchased from the markets, into his long brown hair.

Hearing the scrape of a slipper, he watched Euridises bring him a glass of wine herself.

She handed it to him and before she took her leave Nikanoras called her back. "Please. Stay."

That sweet smile appeared on her ruby colored lips, one that could melt Medusa. Setting the wine down, Nikanoras dismissed the slave and waited for him to leave. As he rested his arms on the side of the recessed pool, he stared at her with the contentedness of a lover.

"How was your practice?" She sat on a carved marble bench so close to him, she could have touched her toe into the water beside him.

"Very hard, sister, but, rewarding." At twenty-three he was sure he would lose her to her own house and marriage soon. He had overheard their mother as she spoke to her about a possible match. His sister had stayed longer than most, not wanting to give up her loving place in the household. In his head, Nikanoras believed it was because of him she did not want to leave. In this too, he was right.

Again she lifted the wine to him.

"Do I seem worn?" he asked, wondering why tonight she was prodding him to drink.

"Yes. And worried. I'll not ask it if you do not wish to share it."

After taking a generous gulp he handed her the empty cup, catching her hand as she reached for it. "I had always thought I would have a soft enchanting woman to care for me." The pain his words revealed made her listen with great concern. "But, I have instead an erastes in the form of the revolting Arybos, and a pawing, aggressive lover of my peers who thinks I am his virgin maiden to deflower. It is as I am destined. And you ask why I am worn? Oh, Euridises, I yearn for a woman to love and marry. Why did Father choose this for me? Does he hate me so?"

****

Releasing his hand she caressed his cheek gently. About his decision to place Nikanoras into the Sacred Band, she knew more than she wanted to know. Though she yearned to reveal the plot to him, she did not. Fear was a powerful influence on one who is fragile and so easily can be sent off into poverty or slavery. Only three nights earlier she had heard Arybos and their father speaking to each other about his future. And though her father again and again worried for their wealth and family name, Arybos denounced any change in plan and forbid him to marry before he left for training with the Sacred Band. Knowing she was helpless, and that this information could only enrage him, she kept it inside, all the while, yearning for Arybos to leave them alone, and to make things right again.

And it was not only her father that Arybos held sway over. Euridises had confronted her mother after spying her flirting with the distrustful man.

Waiting until Arybos kissed her mother's hand and left, Euridises entered the courtyard to voice her anger. "Why do you speak to him as if he were an oracle? Do you not see his intentions?"

Rising up to her feet, her white robe shimmering with gold thread, her hair wrapped in layers atop her head, Thessenike glared at her daughter. "His intentions, though it is nothing of your concern, is for the pride and good name of this family."

Unable to hide her sneer of contempt, Euridises replied, "And you have given Nikanoras to him. Like he is a king and must have our most valued possession. Oh, Mother, how can you be so blind? Our only male child and you sacrifice him like a lamb to Apollo."

Preparing herself for a slap from her mother, Euridises never flinched or turned her gaze.

Thessenike lowered the hand she had almost used to strike with, and said, "Do not speak as if sending him to war is on a par with slavery. Do you realize how much of an honor being a part of the Sacred Band of Thebes is to this family? You know nothing of what you say."

"But, you place him before all the others in battle. He will be the shock-force who will go into the most volatile and bloody action. You will lose him. And what then? Who will you give your estate to? Greedy Arybos? As he intends.?"

This time the strike did fall. Smacking her face in fury, Thessenike shouted for her to leave her sight. "Quickly. Before I ban you from this home."

Her hand on her sore cheek, Euridises saw through the plot. If she told Nikanoras, both of them would be sent away from that house. Either way, she knew her days were numbered, and she would be married off in haste.

Pushing those intruding thoughts from her mind, she said to her brother, "In time, you will learn to love your partner. You are but Achilles in search of his Patroclus."

She spoke softly, trying to convince him. "Open up yourself to him. Allow yourself at least the Platonic relationship, one of true love, even if you cannot give him the physical love."

She knew he had no choice in this matter. Instead of commiserating with his plight, she was urging him to accept his fate.

And it was not a horrible destiny that awaited. He was not a slave, or born to the madness in Sparta. He was blessed and cared for, his father giving him a chance at greatness. Wasn't he?

****

Pressing both his hands on the tiled edge, he elevated himself out of the water to get near her. "Why did you have to be my very own sister?"

In a moment less than a blink, she had left him, still bracing himself over the edge only to slowly sink back into the water. In the hollowness of the room, he tried to think of Meleagros, for he was, for better or worse, his future.

****

Not long after Nikanoras' entrance into his home, Arybos had followed. Unknown to Nikanoras, Arybos was making himself at home more and more within the confines of their palace walls. In the night, when Saliukos was away, Arybos ingratiated himself to Thessenike. Only Euridises witnessed him wooing their mother like a lover. And to his sister's disgust, their mother would bat her lashes and accept his flirting.

"Does he treat you well, Thessenike? For I would worship you as a queen," Arybos would whisper in the dimness.

And their mother would coyly tilt her head like a child. Shying away from his leer with such false modesty it disgusted all who witnessed it.

If Nikanoras had known at the time, he would have slain him on the spot. But, cleverly Arybos knew his schedule and when Saliukos was to come through the door. He would either have vacated or been seen innocently to keep the lovely Thessenike company, whilst her husband was away at the senate.

And Saliukos, he was boasting, almost too loudly, like he was on a stage, how eternally grateful to Arybos he was for accepting the position of his son's erastes. So wrapped up in his world of politics, could their father not see treachery in his own home? His wife was being seduced by the snake, his fortune eyed hungrily, his daughter hated like an enemy, and his son he handed over as if he were a whore. It was inconceivable.

What earthly curse could Arybos have over him? Would he ever find out?

CHAPTER 4

Two years had passed excruciatingly slow as he was trained physically, mentally, and used sexually by Arybos. Honed like a sword of the purest metal, fed information as if he were a hungry shark, and caressed and stroked like the finest silk, Nikanoras was being groomed like no other soldier in the land. Night after night the boys had met with their erastes, being taught the art of war and love.

Though he found his touch revolting, he was growing used to the ways of Arybos, sadly, as was his mother. But of this he had no idea. His father urged him to appreciate Arybos' dedication and loyalty to him and his family and find it honorable. Honorable. The distaste Nikanoras had for this man was closest akin to hatred he had ever felt in his sheltered, pampered life.

Known for being the oldest friend of his father and giving his mother his doting attention when he attended their home for dinner, Arybos attempted to endear himself on the growing Nikanoras, whilst he, himself, had no wife or family to go home to. No kin, no ties. Nikanoras would eye him with suspicion more and more every day. Mysteriously, no one would answer his questions as to why Arybos had no spouse of his own.

Only years later, was he to learn it was only because he had always been in love with his mother. Though other erastes were as close as a lover physically and mentally to their eromenos, Nikanoras kept distant about personal things with his. It was improper for him to ask Arybos the things he had in his mind. And

28

he very well could not expect him to reveal his carnal cravings for his married mother or his strange power over his father. Questions from the eromenos were to be related to their studies, nothing more.

Nikanoras was jealous of Meleagros for his relationship with the noble Sostios, for he was handsome and extremely intelligent, keeping himself very well groomed. With his lip curled in revulsion, Nikanoras could not say the same for Arybos. A body far from ideal, breath that smelled of too much wine, and a grunting from him when he was in orgasm that reminded him of goats rutting. He shivered merely at the thought, coming home to the baths to scrub and soak for hours to rid the sensation off his skin. Only Euridises kept him from ingesting too much wine in an effort to forget, or numb his senses.

And in his own sweet way, Meleagros was doing his best to groom Nikanoras as well. Unknown to him, Meleagros had fought bitterly for the title of his lover.

After training, only a week had passed since their first kiss, Meleagros caught sight of one of the other boys eyeing his prey.

Rushing him like a panther on impala, Meleagros had him by the throat and pinned to the stone wall of the stadium. "Who are you looking at?" He snarled, squeezing the boy's throat tighter.

Struggling to shove him back, Callastines choked and wrenched Meleagros' arm away. "What is it to you whom I stare at? You think you own someone who cares not for you?"

Hearing a comment that nearly snuffed out his burning heart, Meleagros went for Callastines' face once more, this time with more fire. "He is mine! Do not think you know what is in Nikki's soul. It is claimed. You do best to find a beast, such as the likes of you." With his right palm he shoved Callastines' jaw upright painfully, smashing the back of his head into a bulging mortared stone.

With the harmed man's cry the instructors rushed over, separating them. As he was admonished, Meleagros never took his eyes off the injured boy. "I will never let another have him!" he roared in defiance as he was shoved to the next group to continue his schooling.

Brooding and preoccupied, Meleagros' possessiveness over Nikanoras was becoming well known among the group, to all but the boy he loved.

After several more rivals for Nikanoras' attention tormented Meleagros into battles and some of these were not in the training arenas, but the back alleys of Thebes, Meleagros finally succeeded in defeating any who attempted to get a foothold. Why Nikanoras was so naïve to them he could only put down to apathy. Yet every time Meleagros showed up with a new bruise Nikanoras did notice and questioned him. Some of the excuses he came up with would have amused a comedian. His sense of humor was lost on one so self-indulgent. Falling off a wall and onto a boar? Tripping over a rat and into a basket of apples? Was he testing to see if he was paying attention?

It pained Nikanoras to think back on those years. His neglect of Meleagros was nothing short of callous. Though he adored Meleagros like a god, he mistreated him as if he were a scorned pup. Not long did it take Nikanoras to learn his lesson, and learn it well. And the irony of it was that Meleagros was by far the most beautiful boy in their group. As lovely as a goddess, he inspired jealousy as heated as a poker, for his mind was so made up on having Nikanoras, he hardly met eyes with another soul. The anger he inspired was slow to cool. And only with the help of their erastes did they not kill one another outright.

"Where on earth did you get that one?" Nikanoras pointed to a scratch along Meleagros' cheekbone.

"Ah..." Meleagros remembered the scuffle well, right after practice, changing for the baths, he caught yet another ogling his beloved as he washed. It was tiresome work, but he felt obligated to protect his interest. "An alley cat. I tried to feed it and it jumped on me."

Tilting his head at another unlikely tale, Nikanoras could only shake it in amusement at the bizarre life of strange accidents his companion suffered on a daily basis in his absence.

Try as he might Meleagros could not get Nikanoras into his bed. Not that Meleagros was unappealing to him, for he was ideally proportioned in every sense of the word. Not only was he beautiful in his features, but, his physique was the model for Adonis as far as

Nikanoras was concerned. Of his physical being, he had no complaint. It was his pressure he did not take kindly to. The way he would handle him as if he were some little girl whore. Grabbing him, forcing him to commit his body to him, begging and crying when he resisted. Nikanoras was already playing that role with Arybos and found it offensive. What Meleagros did not understand and what Nikanoras failed to communicate was that he was a man. It was not up to another to be aggressive. It was up to him. Bad enough was it he had to submit to Arybos' constant groping advances. And that service must be done without hesitation, and with gratitude. All he wanted was to be left alone. If, perhaps, Arybos was in his early twenties and lovely, he may not argue. But, as it was, he felt as if he were bedding his own father. The revulsion was almost too much to bear. But, bear it he did. So when finally rid of the sensations to his skin, to have Meleagros anxious for a taste of him, was infuriating what little pride he had left.

"Why do you tease me?" Meleagros would whine, his hands once again being batted away. "I yearn for you. I am mad for you."

"Not now, Meleagros. Not ever." Nikanoras would say, quivering back from his advances.

And the pain would brush across Meleagros' face like a wet broom. Defeated again and again, he refused to give up, knowing it was the fate of the gods that they must be together.

Dreams plagued Nikanoras of cradling a delicate beauty and how she would succumb to his arduous advances. Dreams he had not of a strong male shoving him to the ground and smothering him with his kisses. So again and again, he would push Meleagros back and turn his face.

"Why do you not love me?" The tears would fill Meleagros' eyes. "I adore you, Nikki. You mean the sun and moon to me."

"But, I do love you." How was he to explain what he felt was platonic?

It was mere empty words to Meleagros. His fifteen year old desires were haunting him and it was Nikanoras who was the central specter. To Meleagros, physical love equaled emotional love. The pain and emptiness Nikanoras was creating in him made a happy, dancing soul into a tormented angry Fury.

In truth Nikanoras was in misery as well. In what felt like a flash of lightning from Zeus' armory, Euridises had wed, finally, and was taken from him. The hole that had left in his heart he shielded as if it were an open wound.

With flowers littering her long hair, her gown of crimson and white, she tilted her head to see her brother's tears. "Be strong. Be wise," she whispered, "You shall never stray from my thoughts."

"Dear sister-" he choked on his words as the mighty general snatched her from his presence.

He never lay eyes on her again. On strict orders from her mother, Euridises was not allowed to come out to see him. The man she had married had wealth, and power, and above all, jealousy. Nikanoras despised him. Bowing her head submissively, she claimed to love him.

He never believed it for a moment. Persepolos, that arrogant, lofty, graying general slammed the door in his face and forbade him access to see her.

What was he? A scorned lover of hers that he could feel threatened by? He was her kin. Alas, it was of no use.

Persepolos knew what they meant to each other and it angered him. In some sick way Nikanoras imagined it was upon his mother's instructions to keep them apart. And it was. So, Euridises was lost to him as if she had already passed into the realm of Hades. Of this agony he could not bear.

Trying to heal his heart which could never be mended, Nikanoras sought the help of the gods. Time and again Meleagros found him on his knees at the temple of Apollo Ismenios, tears gliding down his high cheekbones, having sacrificed a lamb, the blood still glistened on his hands and sword. As Meleagros stood silently behind him, pondering why he was as unhappy as he, he prayed to the gods to give him strength and find peace somehow in his heart.

Moving slowly, like he was still in a trance, Nikanoras went to the cleansing bowl to wash his hands. A servant stood by patiently with a towel. It was then he did find Meleagros' pout aimed at his own.

Without a word they walked outside to the cemetery of Aghios Loukas and located a place to sit in the shade under the soft pine trees.

The scent of needles was welcoming after the odor of blood and raw flesh. Nikanoras inhaled it to refresh his lungs, narrowing his eyes at the vast view beyond their city's seven gates.

"Rumor has it that this King of Macedon, Philip II, is hungry for power. He takes Thrace and Cardia as his own," Meleagros said, "He has a deadly army. One of long spears that they say cannot be defeated. But, he has not yet met the Sacred Band."

Rubbing his face tiredly, Nikanoras knew they were getting closer to being recruited to war service. One more year. Then they would see all this training intensify. Facing the King of Macedon was not something he looked forward to. Athens was terrified of him.

Meleagros continued, "What choice have they? They must ask for peace with the bastard. If they fight him, no doubt Athens will join him and leave us alone to battle. If they join him, we fight with him against Athens, only to be enveloped into his already greedy kingdom. Some choice, eh, Nikki?"

"Why can they not all leave us alone?" Tearing at a blade of grass as he spoke, Nikanoras had more important things on his mind than war and peace.

A sweet smile washed over Meleagros' lips. Gently, he urged Nikanoras to lie back. Letting out a long slow exhale of breath, Nikanoras rested his head on Meleagros' lap and closed his eyes. As if he were his pet, Meleagros caressed his face and hair tenderly.

"Has your father mentioned which way they will turn?" Meleagros asked.

"No. Has yours?"

Like the flicker of a passing cloud, a sad smile raced made its way across Meleagros' mouth. "No, he has not. He leaves me to gather my own information when he stands at the council and debates this himself. He and my brother, Ephisomines. Demosthenes begs him to back Athens, but I feel Demosthenes is a traitor and will use us as a pawn to win favor with Philip."

"I care not...enough." Covering his face, Nikanoras could not deal with it right at the moment.

It silenced him. "Please," Meleagros whispered, still lovingly running his fingers through Nikanoras' hair as it fell across his thigh. "You speak your heart to no one. Why are you aching, my love?"

He wanted to tell him. Who else did he have now to share his life and secrets with? Treacherous Arybos? No, no one. To himself, he had closed everything up, and from the time Euridises left him, he stopped sharing anything other than idle chatter with a soul.

Lowering himself to lie beside him, Meleagros cleared the pine needles from his hands and toyed once again with Nikanoras' hair. Raising it to his lips, he kissed one of the long brown locks, then met his eyes as his yearning once again tore at him like a lion shreds meat.

After releasing a long agonizing sigh, Nikanoras whispered, "I mourn the loss of my sister."

"But she is not dead." Meleagros enjoyed the silky texture of his companion's hair.

"She is to me. I am forbid to see her." Rolling to his back to gaze at the clouds passing by the sun, Nikanoras struggled to hold back his tears.

"But why, Nikki? What difference would a visit from you make?" Meleagros leaned up on his elbow to stare at him as they spoke. "Who has made this decision?"

"I believe my mother. Or the general. Or both." He laughed sadly. "If they mean to punish me, they have. There is no reason to keep us apart, other than our love for each other. And that is a very cruel punishment indeed, Meleagros."

Meleagros leaned against him, caressing his chest and then his throat gently, imagining a kiss to comfort him.

At what he perceived as groping, once again, Nikanoras grew upset and shoved his hand back. "It does not help me that you treat me as if I am a maiden." So long did Nikanoras need to tell him this it felt like he was unburdened to release it.

The insult ran deep. It was the only way Meleagros knew to show him his love. Scorned yet again, he tilted his handsome face away in shame. No words could he speak to hide his damaged ego and pride.

Finding that beaten mongrel expression once more, Nikanoras said, "Meleagros, I am a man. A warrior. I already suffer from Arybos' groping. Yet you caress me, handle me, as if I were some princess chosen for you to woo. It is offensive and not a means to seduce me."

Oh, the harshness of his words bit like a cobra's fangs. It was as if he were delivering physical blows with his saber, ripping and tearing his flesh off his bone. Meleagros felt he would rather die than suffer this humiliation. Making a move as if he would get up, Nikanoras stopped him, grabbing his arm painfully.

His obvious suffering angered Nikanoras immeasurably. Jumping over him, as Meleagros always did with him, he pinned him back to the earth and gripped his hands over his head, that act of submission Meleagros repeatedly placed him in. "How does it feel?" Nikanoras yelled in anger, "How do you like it to be dominated as if you were some weak female? Do you like feeling as if you were less than a man?"

With his chest heaving with his surprise, his brilliant grey eyes glued to Nikanoras', his mouth open with his gasp of complete awe, he whispered, "*Yesssss.*"

It took a moment for Nikanoras to hear it. It was the opposite of what he expected. In his mind he would grapple, fight for his right to play the aggressor, as he seemed to do for the last two years. "What did you say?" He was certain he had not heard it right.

After a dry swallow down his throat, and his glistening stare never leaving Nikanoras', Meleagros pressed his hips up to convince him, showing him how this excited him. "I said, *yesssss.*"

It was Nikanoras' turn to gape at him. In a complete reversal of roles, he grabbed Meleagros' beautiful face roughly in both his hands, used his knees to open his legs, then he ate at his mouth with a passion he had not known he contained. It was bliss, it was a release from his agony, and it was his duty to appease the gods.

In the heat of the midday sun, with seagulls circling overhead and the shade of the pine casting its round shadow, it was finally

Nikanoras' opportunity to make Meleagros his.

Under him Meleagros opened his thighs, allowing Nikanoras between them. Knowing the ways of man to man sex from his mentor, Nikanoras spat on his hand and used it for lubrication. With Meleagros' eager help, Nikanoras made his way inside his lover. As they connected they met gazes.

"Nikki." Meleagros cupped Nikanoras' jaw and drew him to his mouth. On contact, both men began thrusting against each other. The heat of the day, the friction between Meleagros' legs was like pure honey. Needing deep gasps of air as their bodies rose to the heavens, they parted mouths. Nikanoras braced himself on his arms and stared at his fabulous lover as he hammered into him. The sensation in his groin was by far better than anything he had experienced with the dreaded Arybos.

"Nikki!" Meleagros exposed himself from his clothing and fisted himself as Nikanoras watched in awe.

When the climax hit, Nikanoras gasped and drove hard between his lover's legs as creamy white ribbons erupted from Meleagros' length.

They huffed deeply to catch their breath and Nikanoras pulled out of Meleagros' body, on his knees, recuperating.

"My love. My partner." Meleagros had tears in his eyes.

Nikanoras fell on top of him and held him tight, knowing his fate was sealed.

****

Waiting outside in the shadows until Saliukos had left for the senate, Arybos entered the unlocked front door in search of the lovely Thessenike. Like a snake slithering in the grass, he sniffed out his prey, a gift behind his back of the finest gold and rubies his money could buy. Finding that lovely woman on her own in the courtyard, Arybos leaned on the doorway to gaze at her adoringly.

"Your beauty is unmatched, my lovely Aphrodite...."

Raising her chin to where he stood, she smiled at the flattery as if he were praising her as a goddess. "You speak such nonsense, Arybos. Really."

Moving across the stone masonry, Arybos made himself comfortable next to her on the cushioned bench. "He does not appreciate you. Why does he leave you alone every night?"

"He is busy with the senate. You know its halls ring out with debates late into the night. What a rascal you are." Though her words were condemning his actions, her thoughts were opposite.

"But, there is one who adores you. Who you mean the world to. Ever since I met you, so long ago-"

"Arybos...Please." Thessenike tilted her head away, but the smile was still on her lips.

"For you, my princess." He handed her the pouch with the golden necklace.

She hesitated to reach out for it. "What have you done? I cannot accept anything from you."

Think of it solely as a gift of appreciation to the mother of my eromenos."

She opened the pouch to peer in. When the glittering reached her eyes, she gently poured it into her palm. "Oh, Arybos...I have never seen rubies so fine."

Taking it from her delicately, he opened the clasp and placed it around her neck. "Fit for a queen, my lovely Thessenike. With all my devotion."

Fingering it gently as it lay around her throat, she met his gaze. "You dabble in impropriety, Arybos. What shall I tell Saliukos?"

"Tell him anything you like. Do you really believe, my love, he will even notice it on you?" Arybos shifted closer to take her hand in his.

Lost on her thoughts, Thessenike wondered if it were true. Maybe her husband would not even see it through his preoccupied sight.

"Where is Nikanoras?" Arybos raised her hand to his bearded lips to kiss.

As his question found her ears, she woke from her thoughts to meet his ardent gaze. "I believe he is out with Meleagros."

The grin lit up Arybos' face. "Your son has remarkable taste. You realize he has the prize of the group. An outstanding young male. Have you met him?"

"No." She turned away as if this talk was distasteful. "Only what

Nikanoras has mentioned."

Using his finger to turn her chin back, he said, "Don't be sad, lovely Thessenike, your son's fate is with the gods." As she met his stare, he added, "And he gets his delicious innocence from his mother."

"Arybos." She giggled. "You silver-tongued gorgon." Batting her long lashes at him, both knew only the servants were left in the house.

Starting at her wrist, Arybos began running kisses up her forearm to the inside of her elbow. Loving her on first sight, he recalled the very day. Home from one of the many battles to keep Sparta at bay, he and his companion, Saliukos returned to a welcome feast. And standing shyly with her sisters and father, gorgeous Thessenike stood by with a pitcher of wine. As they raced to her, Saliukos did manage to muscle in line first. And from that moment, it was he who courted the lovely goddess, though her eye had forever been looking over his shoulder at another. Arybos knew it was Saliukos' family name that gave him an advantage. What was he but a foot soldier in a mass army? But, the tide was turning. Soon he would claim this beauty for his own.

****

Whilst the snake was in his house casting his spell on his mother, unaware sat he and Meleagros in the theatre of Apollo as a play from the Iliad was acted out before them. It was an old favorite they had seen before, but with nothing else to entertain them for the night, Meleagros convinced him to come along. Another couple from their training band also joined them. Fair Lysos and stocky Chasathenes, two boys born to generals who were also sworn to enter the Sacred Band, had formed a strong commitment to each other that Nikanoras and Meleagros tried not to envy. There was no fawning, yet a deep sense of devotion, exactly what they expected and nurtured in them. Destined to be the favored of the group, they seemed to complement each other in ways that one knew would be deadly in battle.

Nikanoras envied their faithfulness when sometimes in his heart he wondered if his was hollow. Though he loved Meleagros, it was perhaps not with the devotion he could with a wife. Or could he?

He had never had a female partner and unfortunately all he had to compare it to was his love for Euridises, and of that none could compare. It was a hard act to follow, as was the one he was witnessing on this grand stage.

It was three short one act plays; the first being the that old favorite of his tutors, which he was certain had an influence on the subject matter, for once again they were watching Patroclus donning his beloved Achilles' armor only to be killed in battle. Meleagros, in his new role as the weaker sex, refrained from gripping Nikanoras' hand as his eyes filled with tears at the emotion of the scene. As their roles were beginning to solidify, Meleagros knew it was up to his lover to play the dominant male, giver of comfort and strength. Appreciating that little fact, Nikanoras did indeed feel more like a man for it. Politely, he found and squeezed his friend's hand. In gratitude Meleagros leaned his head on his shoulder quickly, then dabbed his eyes.

Scene two jarred them completely as it was a parody of politics. Gotten up as clowns were the key players in the world around them. The Spartans portrayed as the lying thieves, snatching everything from everyone who dared turn their backs. The Athenians, all on stilts because of their loftiness, and with puppet heads that flapped their jaws. Then not to be forgotten, was King Philip who was padded as a fat goat, his son holding his lead.

The boys were roaring so hard with laughter they could not breathe. The noise of the amphitheatre was overwhelming as this packed, and overflowing audience, could not believe the sight on stage. It was lovely to laugh that hard, and to Nikanoras' delight his fellow comrades were enjoying it as much as he.

In the last act, more romantic parts were played, as the lovers, Aphrodite and Hephaestus flee the wrath of Hera.

And so it was finished and they were all indeed ready for some liquid refreshments. With the affectionate pair nuzzling and cooing ahead of them, Meleagros refrained from grabbing Nikanoras and joining them at the hip. Meleagros was a very fast learner, and he knew exactly what his lover's expectations were of him, and was amply rewarded.

Nikanoras hated to think he was training him, but whatever it was, the rewards worked. Meleagros was satisfied physically, and Nikanoras kept his pride. A better arrangement they could not have hoped for.

Blond haired Lysos led the way to the open forum where servants poured wine and men stripped for baths if they chose, socializing and catching up on the gossip. They found a space and sat comfortably on high stools as the servants hurried to cater to all the patrons who had just left the play.

Chasathenes, whose chin had a pronounced cleft, was still chuckling over act two, obviously reliving some of the lines in his head. "If only Philip were a fat old goat and harmless, the play would truly be amusing."

Thanking the servant for his goblet, Meleagros agreed completely. "They underestimate him, and it is foolish. He has moved north to Illyria and Thrace. If they think he will be satisfied there they may as well be as complacent as an actor between scenes."

"His aim is Athens and Sparta," Nikanoras said, "But he has to crush through us to get to them."

Lysos set down his goblet. "We should make peace with him. We cannot win against him."

Both Meleagros and Nikanoras glared at him. "How can you say that?" Nikanoras said in disgust.

Realizing his own blunder, fair Lysos stammered and tried to find a way out.

"No one has beaten the Sacred Band." Chasathenes growled at his lover. "I cannot wait until I am fighting him with my own two hands. He won't defeat us."

"Presently Thebes is more powerful than Sparta." Meleagros sneered into Lysos cower. "How dare you defy what is written from the gods themselves."

"Demosthenes continually warns us about Philip's will to rule all of us," Nikanoras leaned forward to them, whispering to get their attention. "That Athenian clown may posture as he does on stage, but, he knows well we fear the Macedonians, as well we should. Athens knows without us backing them, after our victory over the

Spartans, they are nothing. It is our army that holds out the hope of resisting Philip's power."

Meleagros had that look in his eye. A very sly smile that only Nikanoras perceived. He adored it when his lover spoke of their strength and future victory. A light would come to his eyes and little creases would form at the corners of his mouth and eyelids.

Sadly Lysos sat back to absorb his words, having been silenced by the majority. Shrugging, for he had nothing to add in his defense, he said, "How about a bath then?"

Nikanoras jerked his head up to see what he had missed as Lysos took hold of his lover's hand to lead the way. They were chirping like a pair of doves and it curdled Nikanoras' blood for some reason. But, it was his lot to be surrounded in male lovers. As he mused his fate, Meleagros, who was holding back with everything he had not to grab and drag him as he wanted to do, was sitting on his hands and biting his lip.

Noticing this finally, Nikanoras' frown cracked and he burst out laughing. One could not blame Meleagros for his efforts. He tried very hard to allow his lover his way, and for that Nikanoras was growing to adore him. "Yes, a hot soak sounds lovely." Nikanoras gulped the remainder of his wine, and reached for his lover's hand.

Hopping off the seat, Meleagros' grin couldn't be wider.

As they strolled behind the lovebirds, Nikanoras sighed. "What will we do, Meleagros, if Philip marches on us?"

"We will fight," Meleagros replied. "What choice have we, Nikki?" Their sides brushed gently as they strolled.

Imagining battling the most powerful army in the land, Nikanoras didn't think even a hot soak in a bath would soothe his troubled mind.

"Do not worry too much." Meleagros ducked his head as they entered a dim stone chamber through an arched doorway. "It is not in our hands, lover."

Nikanoras knew he was right. He had not had control over a thing since the day he was born. Why did he expect anything more now that he was older?

As servants rushed to assist them, they removed their clothing and were led to a steaming tiled pool. Lysos and Chasathenes were already seated in the water with goblets of wine in their fists. Hearing the blond giggling at something his lover had said, Nikanoras sat beside him to ask, "What, I wonder, do you two have to laugh about."

As Meleagros sat alongside Nikanoras, Lysos chuckled. "A shared secret between lovers, Nikanoras. Use your imagination."

And as he tried to do just that, Nikanoras turned around to see Meleagros rolling his eyes and shaking his head at his companion's naivety.

"What?" Nikanoras asked in confusion.

"Nothing. If I have to explain it, I will lose all faith in you." Meleagros sighed tiredly and sat back, closing his eyes to relax in the warmth.

As Nikanoras mulled over the comment, Lysos and Chasathenes appeared to be pitying Meleagros, for it was obvious their relationship was still lacking somehow.

****

Arriving at his father's home that evening, Nikanoras was greeted by Nazabine who bowed low and asked, "Do you needed, Master?"

Sleep was all that he desired, so he smiled and shook his head as he passed. It felt odd without his sister there. She would have been waiting, a smile of her lips, a kind word. Oh, how he missed her. Days he spent, plotting on how to see her again. Sometimes it seemed as if he were bleeding slowly, draining of his strength and life without her.

A strange sight Nikanoras thought he had seen as he passed the courtyard to his room. His mother was seated in her usual place on the bench and Arybos was with her, it appeared, holding her hand as he stood over her to chat. As Nazabine passed him in the hall, Nikanoras asked, "Is father at home?"

"He has just come in and is in the dining room, having wine with your erastes."

Was he? Nikanoras widened his eyes. Leaving his servant, Nikanoras peered into the dining room. His father was indeed seated with a goblet, gazing into the depths of the room. Another glass was placed at his opposite where a vacant chair sat in wait.

On his way once more to peek into the courtyard, Nikanoras was too late, for Arybos had left his mother's company and found him before he found Arybos.

"Lovely, Nikanoras. I have been praising your skills to your father."

As Arybos pressed Nikanoras back against the stone wall, his fingers caressing his face, Nikanoras met his eye with suspicion. "I should be appreciative of your compliments," Nikanoras said sarcastically. He wondered what exchange Arybos had with his mother while his father sat alone waiting for him. Perhaps he had been too mistrusting and it was no more than a greeting or a source of information about him.

"Yes, you should." Arybos purred seductively.

Nikanoras knew that look in his eye.

"Doesn't Father wait for you?" The last thing Nikanoras was in the mood for was pleasing Arybos.

Considering that fact and knowing it was true, Nikanoras could see Arybos' mind working on where to fit him in. Misery it was, that Nikanoras was not at liberty to resist or deny his erastes a thing. He was to accept his touch gracefully. How, when it revolted him, he had no idea. Was he the only one to feel this way about his mentor? He knew Meleagros did not despise Sostios.

"Go to your room. I shall meet you there momentarily." Arybos nudged him as he said this.

Groaning pathetically in his head about the thought of touching him, Nikanoras lowered his eyes and made his way to his chambers. Arybos' fingers got a touch of his bottom as he moved out of reach.

In whispered tones he could hear as Arybos explained to his father his excuse for meeting with his son in private. And what his father thought of it, Nikanoras could not guess. Only mute acceptance of the way it was to be.

Once more it irked Nikanoras as it seemed Arybos had some hold over his family. Of him none would speak an unkind word. And of what Arybos wanted from him, no one expressed a disapproving thought. His favors were payment to him for his education. But, did he desire his mother as well? Standing in the courtyard with her hand? Bestowing that special look? What secret did Arybos have over his father to keep him at bay and silent like a neutered mongrel? Did Arybos know something incriminating about him to keep him passive? Or, did others simply have the same arrangement?

I should remember to ask Meleagros about it. Surely I am not the only one.

Arybos' shadow coming toward him down the hall like a black spider flickering from the fire lit torches on the walls made his heart beat with anxiety. Nikanoras knew what to expect. Not creative, nor adventurous, Arybos wanted only one thing from him.

As he passed into his room, Arybos looked disappointed he was still clothed. "You waste my time, Nikanoras. You know better." It irritated and angered him. He was not a patient man and demanded respect and obedience.

Having no other choice than being resigned to his lot in life, Nikanoras bowed his head and set about disrobing for him. When he was naked Arybos had him kneel before him. Wondering when he was going to be too old for this service, he inhaled a deep breath and reluctantly, took him into his mouth.

"That's it, you lovely boy. You are as pretty as your mother."

Pausing, Nikanoras almost shouted, *'Do not talk of my mother!'* But instead, he tried to make this contact quick. He hated it. Simply hated it.

CHAPTER 5

As all out war loomed closer, they hit the training ground with a ferociousness only the large cats of the jungle could understand. In phalanxes fifty deep, they practiced marching and rushing the enemy, roaring in fury, their shields held high to deflect the arrows and cavalry attack, their swords severing anything before them. But Nikanoras wondered how this form of attack could penetrate that Macedonian army with the sarissa. How does one hew passed the fifteen foot spear? He asked this of Meleagros, and he smiled his most charming way and said, "From behind, my love."

Nikanoras tilted his head at that comment while Arybos was barking at him to pay attention. He could not get his head around it. From behind? How were they to pass behind the back of such a fighting machine with one of the fastest well equipped cavalry on land? Obviously some general in the Theban army had worked out their strategy, or so he had hoped.

After they were spent and had pleased their superiors and erastes with their performance, they were released for the night. Drenched in perspiration and dying of thirst, Nikanoras dragged himself behind Mycandor and Argos, yet two more who had managed to meet up and connect in this squadron of masculine couples. With Meleagros catching up to him from the rear, Nikanoras craved a bath and a meal like he had never eaten or bathed before.

"I yearn for the games again. This working of the ranks is getting tiresome." Argos moaned.

A chuckle slipped out of Nikanoras as he overheard.

Mycandor peered over his shoulder at him. "Yes, pretty, Nikki? What do you find so amusing?"

"As if the games can prepare us for our ultimate battle." He shook his head at the foolishness of the statement.

"You have lost all the fun in you," Argos said playfully. "Mellie, what have you done to your lover to make him so morose?"

"Mellie?" Nikanoras choked in laughter at the odd nickname.

With an effort to catch up, Meleagros finally fell in at his side. "That's Nikki for you. I do not take or leave him anything. He simply is."

"Do not talk about me as if I were not here." Nikanoras was in no mood for this. "Did he call you 'Mellie'?" He started to giggle again.

"It shows how lazy Argos is." Meleagros grunted in irritation. "Even too many syllables wears upon him."

"You call him 'Nikki,'" Argos defended himself.

"Augh." Nikanoras growled, "Enough petty nonsense. I need to go home."

"Home?" Meleagros gave him his wounded sparrow look. "I thought we-"

"Not tonight. I shall see you at exercise in the morning."

****

As he parted from them, the three stood still, staring. Argos nudged Meleagros for his attention. "Are you sure this is the lover you want to take with you into battle?"

If Nikanoras meant to torture him, he had succeeded. The time was drawing closer for them to leave for the war exercises. What chance did he have to find and nurture another? And besides, there was none other he adored.

"Leave him alone, Argos," Mycandor chided, "He has enough to deal with." With that spoken, Mycandor prodded his lover with him and left Meleagros standing by himself in the dark.

****

As Nikanoras opened the door to his home, Nazabine was there. "Do you need anything, master?"

"A bath, then a meal."

Nazabine nodded and hurried to attend both.

Before Nikanoras slipped and out of his clothing into the tub, he noticed his mother in her place in the courtyard, a fire burning to give her the light she needed to write a letter. Having no idea whom she corresponded to, he didn't think to pry. With an aching for Euridises in his heart, Nikanoras sat at her feet and leaned against her legs with a sigh.

"What is it, Nikanoras?"

There was some irritation in her voice. What had they expected of him? Was he never to be in need of reassuring? Was he to grow to be as cold-hearted as she?

"I miss sister."

First she exhaled in annoyance, then she set her writing tablet aside and nudged him to face her. With all the authority of his father, she began to lecture him, as his father would. "Nikanoras, you are almost sixteen years of age. Why do you persist in acting like a child? I think your attachment to your sister, and this house is the problem. You need to be away from here. We have babied you too much. I shall see to it you move out and are placed with the other boys who live at the school. Enough. Go."

With a wave of her elegant hand she had finished with him. So, it seemed, for life. Was this Sparta? Did he find himself in a place where maternal love is frowned upon suddenly? She meant to humiliate him, but in reality, it just saddened him. Slowly, through his exhaustion, he rose to his feet, towering over her, as he already came close to six feet in height. He shook his head. "Fine. If that is what you wish, you are well rid of me. But, Mother, what did I ever do to you other than ask you to love me?"

Before he found out if he was to get an answer to his impertinence, he left. The slave had his bath ready.

Soaking in its warmth, he came to the conclusion that there was only one person who had his interest at heart. And eventually, he would fight at his shoulder to save his life. Why was he so reluctant to open up and let him in?

Resentment. Nikanoras resented the things that he could not control. At times, he thought of running away to the hillside. But there he would be found by barbarian tribes, and murdered, or worse. This is his lot. He simply needed to accept it. Yet no amount of votives or sacrifice managed to make any difference. With all his heart, he didn't know what would. If only he had Euridises to talk to. Ask her counsel. But he knew what she would say. She had already spoken to him words of encouragement.

Love Meleagros, she said, be at peace and love him. Yes. He did indeed love Meleagros, and had no doubt Meleagros worshipped him. It needed to be enough. It had to be.

Unknown to him, that thief once again stole into his home. Nazabine bowed low, though Nikanoras knew his slave despised being ordered by him even more than from one of his own family. Curling his lip at the intruder, Nazabine allowed him entry, silently watching his direction once inside their domain.

Before he sought out Thessenike, Arybos lurked in the shadows of Saliukos' fresco-painted palace walls. Raising his bearded chin to the high archways and glass windows, he envisioned himself as master there.

As thoughts of that glory invaded his warped mind, he remembered a vow spoken once in gratitude. "For if ever anyone shall learn of this, I will be ruined, Arybos, loyal friend. Keep it secret till our death, and I will grant you my humblest gratitude."

At the time he eyed his friend, Saliukos, with contempt, Arybos knew that secret would turn himself from the penniless soldier into a glorious landowner. "Good, Saliukos, of course you can count on my discretion. What good will it do both of our pockets if you lose everything you own?"

Saliukos bowed his head. "Anything you wish, I will see to it you get."

"Of course you will. But I am not an unreasonable man. I will not ask you for your life."

Sniffing the air for her perfume, Arybos moved through the halls like a cobra. Before he made it to the open courtyard, where Thessenike always sat with her wax tablet, a splash was heard echoing from the baths. Detouring to make sure it was not his lovely woman who was naked and vulnerable, he stepped onto the tiled flooring to find Nikanoras.

He was just finishing, raising himself out of the pool when Arybos entered.

****

With the fire from the oil lamps glistening on his wine flushed skin, Nikanoras thought Arybos appeared to be like Cacus about to drag away some of Herakles sheep to eat. It angered Nikanoras that Arybos was always in his home.

Standing out of the water, dripping onto the tiles, Nikanoras was thankful to Nazabine who was there to towel him off. The thoughts in Nikanoras' head were treasonous as far as the political relationship that existed between he and this beast were concerned. He could do nothing about the system of pederasty, but he thought that his father could have chosen one of greater moral character than this. The more he dealt with Arybos, the uglier he became to him. If he were eighteen, he would challenge him. Shout at him that he was no longer welcome in this house. If necessary, he would kill him. But, at fifteen, he was still at the mercy of his parents' wishes and obligations. And Arybos knew it. Arybos' influence was growing, like that fat goat, Philip in Macedon. And though Nikanoras' body grew powerful and his skills as a soldier were impeccable, he was as helpless as a little girl to do anything against him. And, alas, this too, Arybos knew. Nikanoras imagined himself mature. A man. Would he come back home and avenge this hatred one day?

Arybos had been chosen by his father as his trainer, his teacher, his philosopher. And he, the unspoilt ephebe, was to accept this, or die.

As Arybos approached, that lustful gleam in his eye, black water rose in Nikanoras' throat. Would Arybos never tire of him? How many years would he have to be subjected to this? Surely he was close to being sent to the hills to war.

"Nikanoras," he purred, his soulless wet eyes reading his every line, like he had some mystery to solve.

Nazabine first darted a glance at Arybos' expression, obviously knew it well, and then bowed, leaving Nikanoras to his fate.

Though his tunic was waiting for him on the marble bench, Nikanoras knew it would be foolish to reach for it. As Arybos drew near, that sour smell of wine on his breath, he could tell Arybos had plenty after their training session. Overindulging was his favorite pastime.

"Is Father not here?" Trying to stall, Nikanoras was hoping his father would come in, distract Arybos, call him to his supper table.

"No, he is not." His right hand trembled as he reached out to touch him.

Lowering his head, avoiding that greedy smile and the way he licked his lips, Nikanoras swallowed down his anger. The choice was not his.

"On your hands and knees."

Nikanoras knelt down, dreading the act. When he felt the rustle of Arybos' garment and the pressure from behind, Nikanoras clenched his teeth in fury. The one thing that was tolerable if any, was that it was usually quick.

After Arybos had his pleasure, Nikanoras sunk back into the tub to recover, more mentally than physically, from the touch. Done with another vulgar session from the 'beast', Nikanoras scuffed wearily to his bed. In his ear he could hear his sweet sister telling him to accept his fate. In her version of his life he would rise through his torment and flourish, like a phoenix. When, he wondered, when?

Knowing he had been ejected from his home, Nikanoras slept little that night wondering what he needed to take with him. He planned it as if he would never return.

CHAPTER 6

Daybreak arrived cruelly.

As his mother watched him leave, she was humming happily, knowing she was cleaning house. Sister was gone, and now with him off to war training, she inched closer to her goal. Nikanoras was very glad he did not know her plan at the time, for it would have sickened him.

Packing his entire worldly possessions on the back of a horse, Nikanoras walked the long, narrow road to the school where he was to be housed with some of the other boys who were detested by their families. At least that was what he assumed.

He traveled out of his way to pass the home of Persepolos and his dear sister. He could not help but give it one more try. Leaving his horse in the courtyard, he approached the enormous wooden doors and craned his neck at the height. The general was as intimidating as his entryway. Broad, tall, weathered, and deeply etched.

Desperate to see Euridises again, Nikanoras thought of her just behind that wall of oak. His saving grace, his angel of mercy. Without a thought or a look back at the goddess Dawn as she made her way in the sky, he pounded that wall of wood with both fists, yelling out her name.

"Euridises! Please! I need you," he cried, his heart feeling as if it were choking him. "By the gods in heaven, come to me. Talk to me once more."

He knew. Stupid on occasion, naïve constantly, Nikanoras still knew. Though he roused the household, it would not be she who answered.

As he weakened at the effort, his cries turning inward, a black crow startled him as it flapped by. In terror, Nikanoras read it as an omen, and it was not good.

Resigned to pound once more, he raised both clenched fists to that door and again hammered it mercilessly.

As he expected, the great general himself answered his call.

Nikanoras backed up as the general loomed, armor covered, wide and bearded. Nikanoras cringed without intention at the intimidation he felt.

"The beggar returns to my door? Even after he was warned away?"

Wiping his tears from his face Nikanoras replied, "I am no beggar. How dare you speak that way to the son of Saliukos?"

"I have warned you for the last time."

Nikanoras tried to slip beyond him into the great columned hall. He yelled her name, as if by his voice alone he could pass through this barrier; over and over. Surely if Euridises knew he was there she would come.

First the general's large, callused hand shoved him back, then his sword shone bright in the new day's light.

"If you persist, I will cut you down!" he thundered.

His warning sent a shiver through Nikanoras at its sincerity. He had no doubt Persepolos wanted to. But, killing him would have been unwise, and the old would have to either invent a reason for his death, or hide Nikanoras' remains.

"Why can I not see her? What harm is there?" His words trembled like a beaten dog.

"This is your last warning." The blade was raised with violent intent.

With that curt threat ringing in his ears, Nikanoras walked away. The door was slammed shut behind him.

Unknown to him, Euridises had come, finally hearing the commotion and knowing he was there.

As her husband spun around, seeing her, his face red from fury, he pointed a stiff finger into her nose while still holding his sword. "Do not cross me. I am warning you. Stand clear of him."

With no option, she bowed her head. After Persepolos had stormed off, Euridises hurried to the window to get sight of her brother. All she found was his back just as it disappeared behind another marble columned building.

After Nikanoras had settled into a very plain room with only a single bed inside, he made his way to the training fields to attend his exercises. Upon his arrival he searched for Meleagros and avoided angry, hung-over Arybos.

On tiptoes, with his hand shielding the glare, Nikanoras waited, then, he waited some more. It was almost passed the hour for Meleagros to arrive on time. He searched for Lysos and Chasathenes and asked them, "Have you seen my lover?"

Both gave him a very strange glare and turned aside, not answering his question.

Nikanoras hurried to find another to ask. He came upon Argos and Mycandor. No sooner did he speak it, when the same reaction did he receive. Before they could turn away, he grabbed tall, spindly Mycandor in anger and made him face him.

"What is happening? Why are you behaving this way?"

With great reluctance Mycandor said, "Your 'lover', as you call him, has attempted to take his own life."

"What?" Like a rush of heavy stones falling down a cliff, the blood had drained from Nikanoras.

"Last night as you deserted him, you broke his heart." Mycandor sneered in disdain.

Attempting to avoid the glares of those around him, and knowing in a moment the erastes would begin their workout, he gripped Mycandor painfully. "Where is he?"

After he exchanged a glance with Argos whose nostrils were flaring in anger, in which no doubt Mycandor was seeking confirmation, Nikanoras shook him violently. "If you do not tell me now, I shall kill you!"

"The infirmary." Mycandor spat out the words, snorted in disgust and turned his back. The erastes were calling everyone to get in formation. Nikanoras turned and sprinted away, knowing the punishment for leaving the field would be brutal.

Hearing the shouts of Arybos and several others, including Polymodes and Sophates, Argos' and Mycandor's erastes, behind him, Nikanoras flew as fast as his two feet could carry him, until he could no longer be caught. Just as he thought his day could not get any worse, it had.

Before Arybos ran after Nikanoras to have his head, Sostios stayed him and said, "He seeks Meleagros, leave him. It is well he feels so strongly for him."

Distracted by the comment, Arybos turned back to Sostios, then he noticed the gaze of the others as they nodded in agreement. Arybos could not comment on his private thoughts, and knew he had time to mete out punishment later, on his own.

As he ran, gasping for air, Nikanoras burst through the door of the darkened hallway. Half out of his mind, he searched the warren-like lower floor, checking every cot. When he located Meleagros, lying still, he rushed him and took him into an embrace.

"What have you done? What have you done?" he wailed.

Appearing groggy, Meleagros opened his eyes. "Why do you care? Do you possess a guilty heart?"

"No! I possess a lover's heart. Oh, Meleagros, you silly fox. What have you done to yourself?"

At first Meleagros turned his face aside, as if the pain of Nikanoras being there was almost too much to tolerate. Then, gradually, he released his pride and collapsed against him.

Not realizing what Meleagros had meant to him, Nikanoras burst into tears and squeezed him as hard as he could to feel him close. "Do not underestimate my love for you. Though I am confused and alone in my thoughts, I will always love you and be devoted to you. Forgive me, lover, forgive me." Nikanoras clutched Meleagros to his chest tightly. He knew Meleagros was the only security he had. His life seemed to be crumbling from underneath his feet.

When Meleagros' caress pushed Nikanoras' long hair back from his face, they met his gazes.

Meleagros' tight muscles unwound and that mischievous light returned to his eyes. "Dear, Nikki..."

With the tears streaming down his face, Nikanoras knew, he did indeed have the bond they required of them to be included in the Sacred Band. Who else cared for him? What other human being in this violent and battle-ridden land thought of his happiness? Quite simply, no one. He was alone and love starved for the kind of nurturing only Meleagros seemed to share or was available to give.

Knowing Euridises would be proud, he once again imagined speaking with her to explain that he and Meleagros had indeed become like Achilles adoring his Patroclus.

****

As Nikanoras sat with his lover, Nikanoras was curious as to what his adorable Meleagros had done to himself.

Meleagros, a little embarrassed in the telling, described that night. "I decided to ingest as much wine as I could swallow. In a public place, crowded with men, I announced my intention to end my life. I raised my sword. But before I had even so much as nicked his skin, I was tackled and the sword was removed from my hand. After that, I was escorted here to the infirmary to sleep it off."

It was the thought that counted, and Nikanoras did not fault his lover for not really injuring himself. In fact, he was much relieved.

When they managed to get back to their training, the punishment they expected never came. All that had occurred upon their arrival was they were told to get in their place. Thinking it was an end to the subject Nikanoras foolishly put the incident aside and focused on his exercise.

Meleagros and he grew closer from that day forward.

Before Nikanoras bathed and made his way with Meleagros to eat, Arybos drew Nikanoras away from the rest.

Confused but not alarmed as he should have been, Nikanoras nodded to his lover that all was well. "I will meet you shortly," he said, thinking his erastes simply had something to discuss with him.

When Arybos led him to a chamber that had always been used as punishment, Nikanoras spun around in confusion. "I do not understand."

Closing them into the dim dank interior, Arybos took a leather strap from a hook that protruded from the stone. "How dare you embarrass me that way?"

"Embarrass you?" Shaking his head in disbelief, Nikanoras backed instinctively to the wall trying to think of the events of the day. Yes, he had left training to find Meleagros, but wasn't that what he should do?

"My commands to you, you ignore. You made a fool of me in front of the rest."

Still in denial, for he thought they were to nurture a bond for their lover that was like no other, Nikanoras was struggling to see why Arybos was not satisfied he had done the expected, right thing. In bewilderment he knew it had been the correct thing to do, as all his peers had said, not more than a few hours earlier. "But-"

"Stop defying me! Your father will not be pleased with your behavior. And I will see to it, he gets a full report on your willfulness."

"Arybos. Please," he begged. "What have I done?"

"Turn around. Stop questioning my authority. It does not suit you as my eromenos."

Though the sob was creeping up in his throat, Nikanoras held onto it, swallowing it back down. Facing that wall with its scraping of graffiti from those that had done time in it for punishment, he felt the first lick of the strap. Never in his life had he been whipped. On the contrary. He had been lavished upon, babied, and adored by his sister. It was what he was accustomed to. His father never raised a hand to him, and his mother's occasional slaps were tolerable.

As the pain echoed through his skin and raced like a razor across his body, he wondered why he deserved this agony?

If he could read Arybos' mind, he would see it. Frustration. Arybos was tired of waiting to claim the prize of his mother and his inheritance. And though he pretended to love him with the devotion of his mentor and teacher, he despised him like the plague. Nikanoras was the last obstacle to his goal. And he could not die in battle soon enough for him.

****

When Nikanoras did not show up at the baths, Meleagros searched for him. Wondering if his affections had yet taken another turn, his anxiety was getting the better of him. When Meleagros passed the deepest of shadows, he was stunned to find Nikanoras crouched into a ball in a corner of one of the columned arcades.

Rushing to his side, Meleagros cradled him in his arms, asking him repeatedly what had happened. When Nikanoras flinched from his embrace, Meleagros found the wheals on his lover's back. "Lover. Why? Why have you been punished like this?" Meleagros wailed, "It is my fault. I am to blame. I do not understand."

"Arybos detests me." Nikanoras breathed softly.

Leaning back to brush the damp hair from Nikanoras' face, Meleagros wiped his own tears with the backs of his hands quickly. "Sostios was proud of what you did. He told me he knew you were devoted to me. He said he was very pleased you reacted the way you did. All the boys were. It was what everyone wanted you to do. Oh, Nikki- What should I do? Should I tell Sostios of this deed?"

Nikanoras tried to straighten his back and not cringe in pain, finally meeting Meleagros' worried expression. "No. Do nothing. Arybos will only tell him what he wants to hear. This has nothing to do with you and everything to do with me."

"Again you talk in riddles." Meleagros helped him to stand.

"I cannot tell you anything more now. I am not sure of anything, and my words may come back to slay me."

"Your words go no farther than my ears." Meleagros turned Nikanoras around to see his back in better light. When he did he died inside at the brutality. Meleagros could not believe the amount of lashings he had endured. Choking down another sob, he held Nikanoras' elbow and escorted him down the shadowy arcade.

"I will get you tended. I will see to it you are cared for." Fresh tears coursing down his cheeks, Meleagros brought his lover to the infirmary.

The day, from daybreak to dusk, had been a living nightmare for Nikanoras. In all his fifteen years of life he had never thought people could be so cruel. Little did he know that this was but a tiny speck of what torment lie ahead.

August 341 BC

CHAPTER 7

In the art of war, strategy and tactics are more important than numbers as the army of Thebes had already proven against Sparta. But, as they marched in formation for the last two years, an exercise in preparation for the real battle, Nikanoras lacked faith as to the validity of the plan. Alone in his private room, Meleagros and he would sit on the floor with a wax tablet and stylus and draw out different scenarios of war games. They would take turns being King Philip, (grunting and spitting for fun) and plan their attack. Inevitably, again and again, that impenetrable phalanx of sarissa and horsemen led by Prince Alexander would encircle them and crush them. No matter how they played the game, or who was who, the end result was the same.

Who were they to approach their erastes and the military captains to point out the failings of the army? It simply was not done. At seventeen years of age, both Meleagros and he had begun to see flaws.

They beat the hoplites, so the populous thought anything was possible. Yet, the more rumors they heard about this brutish Macedonian king, the more concerned they were that their tactics were not as sound as they needed to be. They cannot count on their reputation and fierceness alone. If they thought the army of Macedon would quiver and shake against them, throw their spears into the air and spin in a dance of terror fleeing before them, they were sadly mistaken. They were aiming to take on warriors with a reputation as violent and determined as their own. He knew this. Meleagros knew this. Did anyone else?

On that broiling hot open field in summer, they gathered like a lightning storm to raise their shields and sabers and roar like caged lionesses as they ran into the fray. It looked good on a wax tablet, but how would it hold up to the true test of real warfare?

Not wanting to jinx the team and say a word about it, but, both he and Meleagros had their doubts.

'From behind' Meleagros had said. Yes, from behind. But, you must first break their line to get, 'behind'. That meant, opening a hole in their defense. How? Through the king on the right flank, five thousand horsemen strong? Or perhaps the left, with the Golden Boy and his Companions, as sworn to kill as the Sacred Band itself? Maybe they were expected to penetrate that line of sharp needles, hundreds thick? It was an insurmountable problem. They needed a plan that was sound. The old way of battle, simply running headlong to your death, didn't pan out on the playing field as it did before.

Pushing passed their weariness, and overcoming their skepticism, Nikanoras and his lover went through their tactical training with determination. Maybe, just maybe, the very thought of fighting the Sacred Band was enough to frighten their enemy. They were, indeed, undefeated. At least their predecessors were. The veterans were leaving it to them.

Nikanoras smiled at the conversation he and Meleagros were having as they beat back the wooden swords of the opposing side. "If only we could send the original Sacred Band to war against Philip. But, one cannot hope to send an army of fifty and sixty year olds into battle against twenty year olds."

"That would be known as the Sacred 'Elder' Band," Meleagros laughed at the thought, "And what fear could they hope to inspire? Not to sound too offensive, Nikki, for in their day they fought and were victorious again and again. No army wanted to face them. That was the time when Pelopidas was alive and drove this army himself." Meleagros wiped at his temple where a bead of sweat ran slowly. "It is useless to whine," he said in exhaustion and raised his aching arm to jab at the line once again.

"No, maybe not useless." Nikanoras smiled, but the grin died out quickly as he said his thoughts aloud, "A sad fate it had been for Pelopidas. Though he had led the Theban army to victory at Cynoscephalea, he was killed. More was the pity, for if he were here with us now, I have no doubt he would have altered the method of our attack."

Pausing, making sure he had Meleagros' attention for a moment as the fighting lulled, he continued, "As it stands, it is the same advance they had played twenty-five years before. Their logic, my gorgeous Meleagros? It had worked then, it will work now. We shall all see, won't we?" Nikanoras said bitterly and renewed his slashing and hewing.

With the clanging of their shiny new armor and the grunting under its unaccustomed weight, they pounded the dust and wielded their wooden weapons at play enemies.

When the light faded to a silver sheen and the heavy clouds moving in threatened to drench them, they ended their practice with an exhale of exhaustion and headed to find food. And wine.

Meleagros looked splendid in his armor. Some men were suited for it, being big and shapely elegant. Not like Argos and Chasathenes who seemed shrunken compared to their tall lovers.

Equally as tall as his partner, Nikanoras filled out the cuirass, arm guards, and greaves, and was powerful enough to keep the shield elevated for hours without dropping it down as so many did. The moment the shield was lowered, as punishment, their instructors would pelt them with rocks.

In reality, it would be arrows. Lesson learned. And with Arybos taking aim at him, he knew better than to give him an opportunity to whip a stone at his face.

With his body posture betraying his weariness, Meleagros' helmet was tipped forward since he was too tired to make the effort to pull it off.

Nikanoras had his under his right arm. His long hair was sticking to his neck and cheeks from his sweat, and with his other hand carrying his shield he just didn't have a third to push it from his face. So shaking his head and blowing like a mare, he tried to get it out of his eyes.

When Meleagros heard the odd noises, he stopped to see what his lover was up to.

As he matured, Nikanoras thought Meleagros' beauty grew astonishing. He was seventeen and absolutely perfect. With those darkly lashed grey-blue irises peering out of their metal mask, Nikanoras could tell he was eyeing him with curiosity.

"Are you mad?" Meleagros asked.

"Yes." Punchy from exhaustion, Nikanoras giggled in return.

"Why are you making all those ridiculous sounds?"

To explain why, he shook his head and blew out, trying to get the hair back from his face, then raised up two occupied hands.

"Nikki, you are a sight." He laughed softly, too tired to give it much more, and checked first to see how dirty his hand was before pushing back all that dark hair from Nikanoras' forehead and cheeks.

A few hundred were still marching around them, all eager to get out of their metal gear and eat. Nikanoras had closed his eyes and tilted his chin up to assist Meleagros in this very important task when Meleagros cupped the back of his head and pecked his lips.

Blinking wide, Nikanoras laughed at him as everyone who witnessed it, shouted, whistled, or made crude remarks as they passed. When a reckless hand found his bottom for a squeeze, Nikanoras jumped and twisted around to see who it had been.

Both Meleagros and he leaned around the throng, only to find too many impish glances to guess.

Before Nikanoras shouted something obscene into the crowd in response, Meleagros held him back and shook his head.

Nikanoras exhaled tiredly in agreement and they carried on, making their way like iron cattle, to their feeding ground.

First order of business was to head back to Nikanoras' room, which had become their shared room. Meleagros had moved in over a year ago. It was a tight space for two, but neither seemed to mind. It was company, it was conversation, and it was affection. He assisted Meleagros, and he, returning the favor, helped get all that weight off their bodies.

Naked and famished, Nikanoras searched for a clean tunic to

wear. Not having servants at their feet was truly inconvenient. As he slipped the cleanest one he could find over his head, Meleagros was standing very still, his skin gleaming in the dim moonlight that had begun to peek through the clouds and into their only window.

Though he never attempted to play the dominant sexual partner again, Meleagros did have his ways of making sure his lover knew when he was hungry. Like this time; leaning naked against the door, his hands behind his back, his expression as desirable as the lovely Eros, and his length hard and rising from his body.

As Nikanoras stood there, drinking that image in, he wondered of the divine gods and if they had given his lover their powers of seduction, for he was a master of the art. Though Meleagros did nothing, absolutely nothing to reach out to Nikanoras, urge him, or touch him aggressively, for he had learned that lesson years before, he still was able to get everything he wanted from Nikanoras at any time he desired.

Nikanoras was, in reality, his slave, though they pretended he was in charge. Not unlike a true marriage he had been told by his companions in jest.

In the stillness of that room, in need of fire to combat the growing darkness, Nikanoras stared at one whom he was certain was simply the most beautiful male he had ever witnessed. The charm had worked and he was entrapped by it.

Before he removed his tunic, Nikanoras approached Meleagros very slowly, as if he needed to savor what he was about to partake in. And the good boy he was, Meleagros stayed still and waited while his lover made all the moves. Nikanoras had to love him for that.

When Nikanoras was near enough to feel his exhale, he very delicately, reached to cup that exquisite face. In the dimness, in the shadow, with his long silky hair and smooth jaw, Meleagros was his lovely woman. The one he had dreamed of owning, forever.

Yet as they touched, and the loving became rougher, Meleagros was the powerful warrior Nikanoras adored.

Their lips met and Nikanoras could taste the sweat and grit from their training. He sucked at Meleagros' mouth and tongue, going mad for him.

Meleagros removed the tunic from Nikanoras, whipping it back to the floor and they resumed the passionate kissing.

Meleagros' muscles were like steel as Nikanoras ran his hands over him. Every ripple of his lover's form made Nikanoras react with fire. They stumbled across the room to the bed, Meleagros under Nikanoras, falling back and opening his legs. Nikanoras' exhaustion had left as the desire between them rose. With a touch of olive oil, Nikanoras thrust his length inside Meleagros, claiming him once again.

With so handsome a partner, all Nikanoras had to do was watch the act and his body gave up the pleasure. As he pressed as close to Meleagros as he could while deep inside him, he caught the glimmer of lust in his man's light eyes. Nikanoras pulled out, never hesitating to return the pleasure. He engulfed Meleagros' length into his mouth and the moment he sucked his lover gave him his seed. Hearing Meleagros' deep throaty growl was pure honey to Nikanoras. As he caught his breath and stared at his sated man, he smiled. The physical love made their bond like armor, strong and impenetrable.

****

Since they were in advanced training, their erastes were needed less for their battle practice and solely for their academics. The relief this gave Nikanoras to be away from Arybos for longer lengths of time was as if someone had lifted all the weight of his armor from his shoulders and set him free. Not that Arybos did not still get his share of Nikanoras for their studies continued every morning before daybreak.

Yet another benefit of this schedule was that Arybos was not at hand when Nikanoras finished for the evening. Quickly Meleagros and he would vanish so the beast could not find him.

Little did Nikanoras know, Arybos was living at his home in his absence. Missing him Arybos was not, for the continuous courting of Thessenike kept him too occupied to care.

Much to Nikanoras' delight, even the physical contact with Arybos abated. It was unseemly for the relationship of erastes and eromenos to continue after the eromenos arrives at manhood. At seventeen years of age, this change was coming to Nikanoras, making him into a very large strong male. Arybos was having a difficult time intimidating him. Though his power over him had not lessened in other ways, Arybos had to conform to the mores of society. And that meant, letting Nikanoras get on with his life and loves.

Nikanoras made sure their meetings were always in occupied, crowded places. Arybos was not given the opportunity to ask, or even imply he wanted Nikanoras to satisfy him sexually. Nikanoras made a point of never seeing him alone. Keeping Meleagros with him constantly deterred Arybos from the chance to force Nikanoras into submission.

Nikanoras was so grateful those days had gone, he cried.

And his lover knew as well what he endured. Though Meleagros risked his own neck, he glared at Arybos whenever he showed himself other than as tutor. His own erastes, Sostios, had long ago given up that part of their relationship. As was expected, Sostios did only what was necessary, and never took advantage of a young eromenos. This was more the norm.

Nikanoras was the unlucky one, but, he didn't need to be reminded of this. Whenever that bearded wicked smirk showed up, Nikanoras knew.

The baths were overcrowded with bodies. If they had the strength they would have made for the one farther out of town. After their training, the nearest one was jammed with young males all yearning to cleanse the dust from themselves.

Wine was pouring like the water into the mouths of the newly bred Sacred Band, and laugh and exchange gossip they did, as up north, Philip and his dogs of war, beat back Thrace as Thessaly capitulated to his every demand.

After Nikanoras and Meleagros had cleaned their skin and sated their thirst, they walked together to the temple of Apollo to leave a gift and ask for favors. With some fresh fruit in a metal bowl, Meleagros and he walked in the direction of the hills to honor the god.

Hearing footfalls behind them, they spun around to find one of his father's house slaves. Nazabine was panting and catching his breath, but very glad to have located Nikanoras.

"What is it, Nazabine?" A chill ran through Nikanoras at his urgency.

"Your father, he begs you to come to him. He has some news he needs to give in person."

"Is he ill?"

"No...please, come now." With his outstretched hand Nazabine urged him on.

Meleagros gave a nod to his lover and they both followed Nazabine back to Nikanoras' palace.

Though he did still think of it as his home, Nikanoras had not been there since his mother had expelled him from it, more than two years ago. Trying not to run, keeping their pace dignified, he used the time to go over and over different scenarios in his head as to why he was being summoned this way. None he came up with made any sense.

At the door he hesitated, loathe to even make eye contact with his mother. "Where is Father?" he asked his servant before he stepped one foot inside.

"Come. In the dining room." Again Nazabine beckoned, bowing and showing him the way.

As long as he is not in the courtyard.

Nikanoras knew very well that was where his mother would be. Taking Meleagros' hand for courage as he set the bowl of fruit aside for the time, they wove the corridors to a well lit room with colorful murals on the walls and marble tiles on the floors.

He hadn't the time to ask what Meleagros thought of his father's palace. It was similar to his own, so he assumed his lover was not overwhelmed.

Looking bent over and weary, Saliukos was seated in the dining hall facing the table, a finished glass of wine before him, the pitcher near, within reach.

To Nikanoras' disgust, standing behind his father's right shoulder was the snake, Arybos. The very sight of the unsavory man chilled him to the bone. Though he had no idea Arybos had occupied this palace every night since he had vacated, it still haunted him as to why he appeared to have taken over his father's household.

Seeing that wicked creature himself, Meleagros' lip curled in a snarl of disdain.

Nikanoras felt Meleagros squeezing his hand tightly, knowing he wanted to remind Nikanoras he was there for him. It was the first time Meleagros had met Nikanoras' father.

Nikanoras wondered if Meleagros was surprised by how old and weak he appeared.

When they spoke of him, Nikanoras had given Meleagros the impression of a robust, powerful man.

"What treachery has made the fine statesman Saliukos into a beaten worm?" he asked.

Nikanoras said, "You have only to look at the vermin behind the poor man for your answer."

After showing his lover a seat, Nikanoras sat next to him, across from his father. Nazabine poured each of them a cup of wine, then left on silent feet.

It had been so long since he had laid eyes on his father, Nikanoras simply studied his appearance. To his horror he found it extremely worn and growing old before his time. Though he had only just turned forty, he seemed spent beyond his years. Politics, war, and his unknown hidden past had certainly taken their toll on him.

In the odd silence, the reassuring touch from Meleagros on his knee was comforting. No one spoke. Nikanoras was wondering why his father was taking so long to speak his mind. Arybos had that smug grin on his lips. It was as though he knew what would take place tonight would please him, yet to the rest it would be agony.

Nikanoras waited for a reaction from Saliukos, especially since his father had never met his lover. Even in this distressing moment, Nikanoras was quite sure the look and nature of Meleagros would please him. After all, this was what he had planned for him. A male partner. He *better* be well pleased.

After one more sip of his fresh wine, Saliukos stood, his purple robe swaying gently as he walked. His beard he kept cropped short and his hair as well. As was the style of the young men in the image of the Prince of Macedon, Nikanoras had always preferred his face clean shaven and his hair very long, as well as Meleagros. Tempted as he was to ask his father what was the matter, he did not. He simply waited as a gentleman and a warrior should. It was not his move, it was his father's.

With the firelight flickering across his deeply lined brow, after checking to see what sinister expression was behind him on Arybos' face, he finally met his son's gaze.

"Your sister...." he began.

Inhaling a petrified breath, Nikanoras' skin prickled with a warning.

"She has died in childbirth."

Feeling his lover's stare trying to penetrate his thoughts, his father's readying for his reaction, and Arybos about to shout out in glee at his anguish, Nikanoras sat numb. Euridises dead?

Although she had been torn from him years before, he'd hoped she was content and he knew she was very much alive. Thoughts of her were as constant as the waters rushing passed the Cephissus River, and though he understood she could not wander the streets freely, he still had hopes of glimpsing her at the marketplaces or in the temple of the gods.

His sister, his nursemaid, his lovely woman, was taken from him forever.

As his father waited patiently, his steady gaze on his son, Saliukos tried to give him time to react. When Nikanoras did not, he continued, "She will be given a proper funeral. It will be soon. When the date is decided, I shall send word for you so you may attend." Then he once again checked with his son's mentor for his approving nod.

It sickened Nikanoras this approval was needed. What had become of his father? The proud statesman cowering to the will of his subordinate?

Clearing his throat first, Nikanoras said, "Thank you, Father," with as little emotion as he could. It was killing him. Meleagros knew he was about to explode. He just didn't know when.

"What is the name of your companion?" Saliukos asked softly, seeing his son was taking the news like a man.

"This is Meleagros, son of Xenophos," Nikanoras announced with pride.

"Ah, yes, I know the statesman Xenophos," he said with a sigh. "A strong and honorable man."

Like a true noble, Meleagros bowed his head, accepting the praise, though Nikanoras knew Meleagros did not care in the least what anyone thought of the his father.

They paused. Nothing more seemed to be about to be said. As Nikanoras rose up to take his leave, his mother entered the room. It was unusual. This was a man's dining hall and she never ate with her husband.

Nikanoras' gaze raced over to Arybos to see his reaction. The sensuous smile was so obvious it was as if his eyes were just opened. His father did not even acknowledge her presence.

As propriety dictated, Meleagros stood and bowed his head to her in respect. He was always the perfect gentleman.

"How are you faring in the housing?" she asked.

Not wanting her to know he was miserable and all his garments needed tending, he said, "Well." Again his eyes darted to Arybos. Why did she ask him when she had her spy?

His mother was too sharp in intellect and knew when he was lying. "I'll give you one of the slaves. One can only imagine the filth you are living with."

About to protest in reflex, Meleagros elbowed him in the ribs, thinking of the help and clean clothing.

After he flinched and recovered, Nikanoras said, "Thank you, Mother."

She scrutinized the appearance of Meleagros.

In reflex, Nikanoras took a step back from him, wanting to see him as she did. They had nothing to complain about. He was lovely and elegant.

Again it was silent. The strangeness of the meeting was not lost on him. His father, as weak as a beaten starving mutt, his mother, smug in her power, and Arybos, the silent victor over what was soon to be his spoils. It sickened him.

Though he was beginning to see the plan in its entirety, Nikanoras was still at a loss to do a thing to prevent the inevitable. What was he to do? Convince his frail father that he was being consumed by a leech? That his wife was in on the blood-sucking plan? How absurd it would be coming from his mouth.

With a heavy sigh, Nikanoras moved away from the table and was about to leave when, keeping his back to the other two, Saliukos stopped him and handed him a purse filled with coins. Guilt must have arrived. Their daughter was dead and their son they had sent away to die in war. Suddenly Nikanoras wondered if he was being paid for his father's stricken heart.

But, it was another reason, one he did not know at the time; his father was attempting to give him some of what was his, before it was no longer in his hands.

At this unexpected gift, Arybos bristled, wondering how much wealth was being passed into the ungrateful delinquent's hand.

Blind to the mental exchange, the anger between Arybos and his father, Nikanoras nodded in thanks and made his way out.

Saliukos struggled to communicate to his son while surrounded by enemies; his mother, like a Fury on his left, and Arybos hovering like a vulture on his right. Saliukos knew his time was growing short. In his thoughts he was wondering how to reveal to his son all the old mysteries. In horror, he feared telling him his past so that he too would be appalled, disgusted, and a traitor to his honor. Like a coward, he said nothing as Nikanoras left.

"That was very odd, Nikki," Meleagros whispered as they put some distance behind them.

Tightening his lip before he responded, Nikanoras didn't answer immediately, too many interfering thoughts were competing in his mind.

Unluckily for Nazabine, he had been elected to follow them and tidy up their lodgings and clean their garments. Used to service, he took it calmly and once they had settled in, he picked everything up off the floor and took it with him to wash.

Sitting on their bed together, one single oil lamp lit, Meleagros stared at his lover in anticipation. He knew it would eventually hit him.

In the sterile silence of that simple room, Nikanoras burst open like the flood of Poseidon and cried like a baby. The one who had loved him and been loved with complete devotion by him, had vanished. How many roamed this land that still held love in their hearts for him? So few it was painful.

Though he tried to comfort him, Meleagros could not. Nikanoras' beloved Euridises had passed like a psyche into the realm of Hades.

Good-bye, sweet sister, good-bye. And the omen of the black crow Nikanoras had seen the day he tried to visit her, had finally come to pass.

CHAPTER 8

On the day of Nikanoras' sister's funeral their captains decided to parade them through the streets in honor of the feast of Dionysus.

Unable to prevent it, Nikanoras was forced to dress in his armor, shining clean with a little help from Nazabine, and march in rank to show the town of Thebes they need not fear Macedon and her growing might, that the Sacred Band would protect them. Three hundred of them newly trained, hungry for battle, and proud as gamecock, positioned central to the procession of military, behind the archers and basic phalanx, and before the small cavalry. Their faithful citizens lined the streets to cheer and throw flowers at them, resting assured they would protect them from harm.

While Meleagros marched beside him, Nikanoras could feel his lover's tension and regret knowing Nikanoras was missing a farewell that meant the world to him. What choice did he have? His back had been whipped enough by Arybos.

Though Arybos promised his father he could attend, it was yet another lie. Feigning he did not know of the parade and was powerless to do anything to excuse him, Arybos deliberately brought pain to Nikanoras' heart and left that gaping wound free of the closure he needed so desperately.

Nikanoras knew he would get to mourn her and grieve in his own time but, missing her funeral was unacceptable.

Before the parade, as they dressed, Meleagros kept his eye on him. While Nazabine crouched to fasten Nikanoras' greaves, Meleagros whispered, "It is a test, my sweet Nikki."

Slowly moving his attention from Nazabine's task to his companion's comment, Nikanoras blinked his moistened lashes to try and understand.

Meleagros said, "What we go through, our trials and tribulations, Nikki, it is all a way for the gods to test our endurance, our inner strength."

After a moment, allowing the slave to finish, Nikanoras said hoarsely, "Then I have failed miserably."

Bowing, standing aside to express he was through, Nazabine kept his head lowered, trying not to interfere. It was no secret Nikanoras had been crying every night since he had come from his father's house.

Meleagros approached Nikanoras quickly to comfort him. "No. You have not failed. You will come through this sadness, Nikki. I will make certain of it."

Staring into those light eyes, feeling Meleagros' caress on his cheek, Nikanoras pleaded with himself to find some hidden resources. This man, and every other one in his band, counted on him.

Once at the Electran Gates, they broke rank to ready for the games. Before removing his helmet, which included its fancy white horse hair crest for the occasion, Nikanoras' group headed behind the stone walls of the open-air arena to strip for the festivities.

As they filed passed, a man caught Nikanoras' eye. His mood volatile, his preoccupation dangerous, Nikanoras could not keep focused on the event, nor the coming celebration. The last thing he needed was to celebrate. Waiting, allowing his brain to catch up with his other senses, Nikanoras realized who it was that was glaring at him with intense hatred. And it took nothing for Nikanoras to react and return that volcanic rage.

Crashing through the mob of soldiers, Nikanoras wrapped his hands around this man's throat, choking him to death.

In the chaos that followed, several men were behind Nikanoras pulling him back, Meleagros was one. To the shock of everyone around, Nikanoras had singled out his sister's widower, General Persepolos.

"You bastard!" Out of his mind with grief, Nikanoras spat out the words, feeling like a wild animal. "How dare you come here to celebrate! What of my sister. What of Euridises!"

Meleagros pawed at Nikanoras to shut up, trying to clamp down his flailing arms and cover his mouth at the same time. "Nikki! Stop! You shall get yourself killed!"

Blind to everyone and everything around him but this one enemy, Nikanoras struggled against the force that held him back, leaning, straining to be allowed to rip this man to shreds. "She is dead! My beloved- my very soul. And instead of mourning her, where are you? It is you that deserves to die. Not my poor innocent sister!"

The anger was merging to tears of anguish quickly. Unable to wipe his eyes or free his hands, the water rushed down his red face, blurring his vision.

Holding his breath, petrified of his lover's fate, Meleagros studied the punishing eyes of this powerful general in horror. He knew it was insane of Nikanoras to accuse the general of her death, though Nikanoras did. Yes, it was his seed that had impregnated Euridises, but, as he explained to Nikanoras several nights in a row, the man had no way of knowing she would die in the process of making him an heir. Yet, in the dark of night, while they could not sleep, Nikanoras' grief was unleashed as anger. And it was Persepolos who had made sure he kept them apart for the last three years of her life.

When that supreme ruler of the army caught his breath and straightened out his clothing, he glared at Nikanoras as if he were about to pronounce his sentence of death.

Slowly Nikanoras' own commanders realized Nikanoras was at the center of a commotion. He was torn from his friends and lover, and held as a captive while they decided how to deal with him.

Meleagros was about to wail in agony at seeing Nikanoras held by two captains. Meleagros almost collapsed to his knees in terror at losing his lover.

Lysos and Chasathenes held him up, unable to whisper comfort to him, for they knew the consequences of Nikanoras' actions would be swift and brutal.

Standing among the crowd, having never expected such a wonderful turn of events, Arybos thought his wishes had been answered. He no longer had to wait for the fray of battle for Nikanoras' demise. Now he could be put to death quickly.

As a deep murmur of male voices discussed the problem, Meleagros went wild clawing his way to Nikanoras. "No! I beg of you," he pleaded, "Have mercy on my lover! It is just that he is out of his head with sorrow over his sister's loss. Please!" Tears streamed down Meleagros' face. "You must spare him. He is a loyal good man. You have all misunderstood his motives. It is love. Love for his sister. Do not harm him. I am begging, pleading with my very life. By the gods, do not harm one hair on his head!"

Through his dull senses, Nikanoras heard his lover crying at the possibility of losing him. Everything else around him had gone dim. In some part of his mind, it didn't matter. Even if he was put to death, it simply mattered not.

After a very long pause where no solution to the problem was readily found, all eyes turned to the general. His chest was heaving as the son of Saliukos awaited his fate. Left to him he was certain it would be a painful death.

Lowering his head to accept his fate, it was fortunate Nikanoras never thought to find Arybos in the crowd, for his expression would have stunned him. Hidden deep beneath his facade of care, lay a toxic snake with its fangs bared.

As Persepolos considered, indeed, the way he wanted the young man to die, he suddenly noticed that every eye in that overwhelming crowd of men was on him. Was he to dole out death to one of the Sacred Band? Now? When every day brought Philip of Macedon closer to their door like a wolf who stalks helpless sheep? The explanation had sufficed for so many. Despondency over the loss of his sibling. Surely the boy couldn't be punished for that.

And that handsome male, his lover- the weeping he was doing, the pampering of the rest of the companions was heart-rending. This was not a common soldier. This was one of the specials, the elite. No, it was not as easy a solution as it appeared. He had to think of the politics of the decision as well. He wanted to remain in good standing with the military, the captains, and most of all, the populous who stood on tiptoes and kept silent as the scene played out.

As those murmurs made it to his very keen administrative ears, he next found the glare of Nikanoras' regime. All two hundred and ninety-nine of his comrades were there, waiting. Holding their breath. The morale of the entire band was in his hands.

Against every fiber of his being, the general hollered, "Release him!" and dismissed the incident with a wave.

Though Nikanoras knew in his heart his motivation was purely political, he nearly passed out from the relief.

Shocked at this show of weakness, Arybos gaped in horror at what he would have hedged as a sure bet.

His tears of sorrow exchanged for joy, Meleagros did not care the reasons. As soon as the captain-guard had set free Nikanoras' arms, he raced to drag him away before the general changed his mind.

Behind them the hum of approval followed. Many shook the general's hand and told him he had done well; the boy was so young and needed the time to get through his ordeal. To Arybos they pat his back and consoled him; not to fear, his student was safe and sound.

But, as Nikanoras was escorted away, two men gnashed their teeth at his very existence. And that naïve innocence that Arybos had named so accurately in Nikanoras, did him no service.

That day he had succeeded in making another powerful enemy. Not that there was any love lost between them before, but,

Nikanoras had been unimportant to him. Not any longer. Now he had embarrassed him in public.

As he and Meleagros continued to the changing room, Nikanoras said softly, "I am quite sure the general will do anything in his power to see I am killed in battle, if not before." Removing his helmet and tucking it under his arm, he sighed. "It is just a delay in my demise, not a cure for it."

"Do not speak such omens." Meleagros shoved him into the changing rooms and started unlacing his chest guard. "It is bad enough I have to protect you from the enemy. Do not make my job an impossible one."

Without acknowledging he had been given a second chance at being alive, Nikanoras yelled, "He isn't even at her funeral! What does he do to mourn her loss? He heads to the games. To drink. To bet."

"Shut up, Nikki." Meleagros looked around in paranoia, but only his own comrades were at hand. "Maybe this is the way he can get his mind off of her." Meleagros knelt to unfasten his lover's greaves.

Fair-haired Lysos was standing near, his partner, Chasathenes was tending him as Meleagros was to Nikanoras. "He is right, Nikki, this may be his way of coping."

"Do not tempt the gods a second time," Mycandor said over the noise. "We need you on the battlefield, my lovely. Not nailed to a cross."

Nikanoras felt Meleagros shudder at that very real possibility. "Please be sensible," his lover begged, "I will die without you. Don't act like a fool."

Finally free of his armor Nikanoras began working on Meleagros'. "When have you known me to be sensible?" he grumbled.

"Never." Muscular, squat Argos put in his two drachma's worth, then burst out laughing at his own wit.

Nikanoras warned him, "You had better not be my adversary in pankration for I am in no mood to be kind."

A silly moment of whistles and hisses followed his threat. After that, everyone laughed, mostly to relieve the tension.

When Nikanoras' anger subsided, he finally did come to his senses and realized how close he had come to dying for his rage. It was not how he would choose to go. It was his plan to die with the Sacred Band and his lover, or to live with him. Nothing else would suffice.

The stomping and cheering of the arena crowd had begun. Standing proud as they were coated with oil, they paired up for their matches. His commanders knew his present state of mind and that he may very well kill someone if he were to be put to combat. Against Arybos' suggestion, for he wanted to see him fight, and most definitely get a beating, Arybos shoved Nikanoras toward the runners.

Meleagros was waiting in his place to spar with the other plankratiasts. The group could see he was ready to knock someone's head off as well, but he did not show it to the ranking officers, lest he be deprived of a good fight.

As they lined up for their stadion race, a short but grueling sprint, Nikanoras stood tall, touched his breast, and then raised his fist to the heavens. "For you, my dearest Euridises, I run this in your honor."

At the ready, they crouched into their starting positions, waiting for the shout to go.

When that one word passed the starter's lips, Nikanoras shot off like an arrow toward the finish line. With his comrades pumping their arms and shouting encouragement, he ground his jaw and pounded the dirt wildly, determined to do his sister proud. With his great stride, he managed to dive passed the rest and win first place in this quarter mile sprint.

As he bent over his knees to attempt to gain air, Mycandor, who had run it with him, patted his back and congratulated him. "But, you need recover quickly. Your lover is about to start his fight. You should not miss this."

Nodding in agreement, Nikanoras managed to straighten his back and walk with him, as several others who had raced reached to touch his hand in praise.

With his heart rate and respiration resuming their normal pace, he made his way over to the grassy patch Meleagros was standing on. Someone had already wrapped his knuckles with leather, and the look on his face as he glared at his opponent sent a shiver down Nikanoras' back. "Oh, my sweet Herakles..." he breathed in awe.

To spar such a formidable man, the captains had found one of the men of the regular phalanx, not of their own band. Glad Nikanoras was to see he would pulverize a stranger. For Nikanoras knew his lover. Not only was he beautiful, he was very powerful.

The young male he was set to battle tried to appear just as strong, but he was noticeably thinner. These bouts are set by age, not size. Nikanoras learned he should never be cocky, however, for some of these wiry males are as quick as a cobra and very tough to beat.

As the two fighters came ready, the runners were urged to stand back so the arena crowd had a better view of the contest. At first they obeyed, but they all edged up once the fighting began.

With Meleagros arms poised in a battle position, his long brown hair running down his back and shoulders, and his solid muscular body as tense as a panther about to strike, Nikanoras had to admit he was not only proud he was his, but going a little mad for him.

As he dodged the first punch thrown by this boy, Meleagros attacked and nailed him in the face, not once, but twice. Though it dazed the boy slightly, he was still able to kick his lover in the side, doubling him up. Cringing at the bruising he would endure, win or lose, Nikanoras fought back the urge to desire this boy's blood for the pain he was causing his partner.

As they circled again, ducking and diving each other's punches, Meleagros managed a good shot to the boy's left eyebrow, splitting the skin. Though he was fighting off the red drops that drained in, the blood blinded the boy's right eye.

It was Meleagros' chance to move in for the kill. And he literally did. He unleashed a pounding that left blood spatters from the coating his right leather strip had absorbed from that seeping eyebrow, all over the boy's chest and stomach. Even as the boy crouched to protect his mid-section, Meleagros opened up his fury even further, by beating the boy down to the grass until he was called off the bout. It took three men to drag him back.

It was a state Nikanoras had never seen him in. The trained killing machine was inside him. No doubt did he have that with this man beside him, he would be invincible in war.

Loving the blood-sport, the noise from the crowd was deafening. Meleagros' performance was merely backing up the truth of what they had heard about the Sacred Band. Today they had seen it for themselves. They were their dream come true. Warriors who would fight to the death. Powerfully built, elegantly held, and absolutely beautiful.

When Meleagros finally calmed down enough to raise his head to the mob, both his bloody hands shot over his head in a victory sign. The screaming from the amphitheatre was deafening.

Under his breath, Nikanoras said, "Oh, my lover...there has never been another like you."

After absorbing the adulation and cheers from the stands, Meleagros fell in at his lover's side as they walked to the back of the arena. Unwinding his leather straps for him, as Meleagros still struggled to breathe normally, Nikanoras purred, "You were amazing."

That wonderful impish glint came to his light eyes. "For Euridises."

"Yes, for Euridises." Nikanoras returned his smile twofold.

Without water at hand, Nikanoras doused Meleagros with clean olive oil and took a strigil to him to scrape the blood of his rival off of him. As Meleagros stood calmly for the task, Nikanoras leaned to his ear to whisper, "I adore you." The fact was, Nikanoras could not hide his attraction for Meleagros. His naked body was showing his lover how excited he made him.

As if Nikanoras had awarded him that crown of gold leaves for his victory, he grinned in complete pleasure. "As I adore you, Nikki." Meleagros gave Nikanoras' cock a stroke.

"I am proud you will be fighting at my side." Just as Nikanoras leaned in for a kiss, the pack of men who were coming in to clean up made groaning sounds at their declaration of love for each other.

Nikanoras and Meleagros knew it was good-natured teasing, for each one of them had a lover they too, took pride in owning.

Cleaned up, back in their armor for the rest of the festivities, which included a sacrifice and a feast, the men moved to another columned arcade. There Nikanoras and Meleagros met with another surprise.

Awaiting them as they exited the stadium, two nobles were searching the throng, pointing at Meleagros. Nikanoras noticed their waves and big smiles.

It was Nikanoras' finally first opportunity to meet his lover's father and sibling. Knowing Meleagros was not in good standing with either, Meleagros appeared stunned to see them both there attending the games.

"At your victory," Xenophos said, "I was given much praise by my peers. It was a compliment I could not ignore."

Nikanoras thought Xenophos appeared very modest, and perhaps had accepted the adulation in stride.

"I had no idea you had grown into a very powerful young man. At nineteen your brother Ephisomines cannot boast so well."

Nikanoras inspected the man who Xenophos claimed to be Meleagros' brother. He was the complete opposite of a mighty warrior. Narrow and thin as a rail, his features reminded one of a bird of prey. A beak of a nose, and a pointed jaw, he appeared to be about to sprout wings and flap away, mouse meat hanging from his lips.

The air of condescension coming from so ugly a person was as if he stunk of an odor so offensive it was well to keep your distance.

"Father." Meleagros knew not to ignore him, for he was his benefactor as well as his kin. "I had no idea you were here."

It was obvious to Nikanoras that this meeting was a strain on his lover though Meleagros hid his true feelings well. To say Nikanoras was shocked silent when Ephisomines opened his mouth to speak with so much femininity, he almost gave away his gape in horror. The effeminate lisp and gestures were so outrageous he had no idea why this boy was tolerated in high society.

It occurred to him Meleagros' father had taken pity on him, educating him and given him advantages he would never have imagined left on his own. Loving men was acceptable in Thebes even encouraged, as it was throughout the Greek world, but this type of emasculation was frowned upon at best. Never had Meleagros even hinted the behavior of his brother to him. Nikanoras understood entirely that this was as a source of embarrassment for him. Though to Meleagros' father, blind to the obvious, Ephisomines was the pampered brat of the family. Luckily for him he had brains, for nothing else was given to him by the gods.

"Well done, Meleagros." With a foppish gesture, Ephisomines handed out some rare praise to his lovely brother. "I had no idea you had it in you. You were so spoilt by our nursemaid."

Trying to keep his humor, Meleagros replied, "This one. He talks as if I were the spoiled favorite."

Their father, not waiting until the conversation turned sour, found Nikanoras standing there in awe at this whole family experience, and changed the topic to his existence. "You do well to remember your manners and introduce your comrade."

Coming aware of his presence in this awkwardness, Meleagros stammered at the oversight and gestured to him, revealing his name. "Father, brother, this is my partner, Nikanoras son of Saliukos."

When Ephisomines eyes did a sensual sweep of his entirety, Nikanoras shivered. Having no choice but to reach out a hand of greeting, lest he insult them, the grip was so lecherously grasping, Ephisomines did not hide his attraction for him very well.

Licking his lips hungrily as if Nikanoras were a meal about to be savored, he said to his brother, "Do not tell me you are lucky enough to be paired off with this one. Oh, Father, if I knew they handed out one of these to each soldier, I would not have you send me to university."

"Behave yourself, Ephisomines." Red faced, Xenophos did not appear completely tolerant of his son's extravagances.

Meleagros grinning like the victor with the true prize he said, "Yes, one to each. Pity, poor brother, you stepped out of your place in line." Addressing his father once more, he added, "It is good to see you, Father, give Mother my regards. Come, lover."

With his stare riveted to Ephisomines in fascination, Nikanoras was dragged away. Daring to peer back, Nikanoras got a wink and a smile, as if asking him for some secret rendezvous.

Before Nikanoras could say what he thought about it to Meleagros, Meleagros was shaking his head to prevent him. "Do not state the obvious."

Seeing the mischievous twinkle in his lover's pretty eyes, Nikanoras laughed.

Meleagros said, "I have to admit, I am very lucky indeed."

"You are. Not only do you have the looks in the family, you have me!" Nikanoras teased.

•

Passing along the cut marble arched arcades, they caught scent of meat roasting. In the firelight of evening, the shimmering reflections of orange and yellow flickered on every metal armor plate and helm.

Nikanoras filled his bowl with an aromatic stew. He had no idea he was so hungry until the sight of the food reminded him.

Already stuffing bread into his mouth as he moved in the line behind him, Meleagros spoke as he chewed, "We do well to remember this meal. I fear once we are away at training in the hills this type of fare will be but a memory."

"No doubt." Nikanoras peered back at him to smile. When he found him gobbling more food as he stood than went in his bowl, he said, "Oh, you are a sight. You would think they haven't fed us for a week."

Arybos spun around quickly. "It seems our Nikanoras has recovered well from his earlier ordeal."

Sostios sipped his wine from his goblet. "He is a resilient boy. I would not worry too much for him, Arybos."

Distracted, tossing daggers into Nikanoras' back, Arybos finally heard the consoling words. Using his best faux grin over his black heart, he replied, "Oh, I know he is. The very picture of the perfect student."

Sostios asked, "Is his father, Saliukos not present this evening?"

"No. I fear he is weakening of late. Who knows what disease may be eating its way in him. He appears to me much older than a man of my age."

Raising his eyebrows at the information, Sostios said, "I haven't seen him for a long while. Perhaps I should drop in on him—"

"No!" Arybos said, then shook his head to soften the effect, "No, dear friend. He wishes to be left undisturbed."

Sostios searched for Nikanoras in the crowd again. He found him sipping wine and surrounded by his peers. He felt pity for the poor boy. It seemed nothing but grief found him.

CHAPTER 9

Not nearly as hung over as his lover from a night of drinking far too much wine, Nikanoras set out the next morning on his own with his loaded purse of coins to the marketplace to buy some fresh fruit.

Since he was nursing a bad head, Meleagros was back in their room, sleeping in for once, as their commanding officers were setting up a night fight scenario to torment them with.

With Nazabine by his side, they walked the hot uneven stone streets to the center of town. In the shadow of the Mycenaean Palace, several dozen stands were set up with everything one could desire. Thinking of their hunger to come late at night from the exercises they would endure, he filled Nazabine's basket with fresh grapes, figs, apples, and some wheat cakes. Next, a tall jug of wine for Meleagros just because he adored him, as well as new tunic of pure white.

He was more than a little stunned at the tidy sum his father had bestowed upon him. Perhaps Nikanoras had done something right by him for a change. He didn't spend it all in one place, lest it be a year before the next handout. He'd half a mind to seek him out to thank him, but, he did not want to go home with the possibility of seeing his mother.

Looking to the towering courthouse, Nikanoras thought about walking the halls in search of him. But, it was nothing more than a passing fancy. Saliukos would never expect him to do so, and on the contrary, might find it offensive. And though the thought was pleasing to Nikanoras to show his appreciation for the fine gift, he knew it was neither necessary nor appropriate.

Not content to leave once he had everything he needed, Nikanoras wanted to see what other wares where brought in from the far reaches of the Greek world and from Persia as well.

The scent of exotic spices filled the air, as the sellers of these wonderful items hawked and praised their produce.

Lifting up an unusual fruit, he sniffed its scent curiously. When something caught his eye, Nikanoras inhaled sharply and resisted the urge to actually duck out of sight. He set the fruit back down and followed behind this 'apparition', forgetting Nazabine who was busy picking out fresh cheeses and bread.

He hid himself behind a marble covered Doric column of the shopping arcade and focused on something he could not believe he was witnessing.

His mother was outdoors! in her bright flowing gown, a gold chain around her neck. And at her side was the wicked, conspiring, conniving snake, Arybos, laughing gaily. Hooked arm in arm! In public! Scandalous! Perfectly scandalous!

Jumping out of his skin when Nazabine grabbed him by his shoulder from behind, Nikanoras caught his breath and turned to see why his servant had shaken him. Nikanoras gaped in fear at the approaching mad bull in the heat of the burning sun; his sister's widower, General Persepolos.

Numb from all he had witnessed, the last thing he needed was to square off once again with a man who was out for his blood, especially when he was unarmed with only a tunic and sandals to cover his nakedness.

He raced from column to column as Nazabine set up a marvelous distraction of dumping the basket contents in the general's path and then almost tripping him when he went to step over it.

Nikanoras was so grateful he owed him his kiss of gratitude. Losing himself in the mob of shoppers once again, certain he would be swallowed up in the throng, Nikanoras hid behind a tall display of fruits and vegetables.

One of the slaves behind the stand shouted at him, "Buy something!"

As he was about to disappear, for he had no idea where Persepolos was, he smiled at her politely. It was then he froze. This woman appeared to be his sister, Euridises, but younger, and most certainly dressed as a slave. Her long brown hair was a bit unkempt, her bright dark eyes were weary, but her features were unmistakable.

"Come closer." He waved for her to come out from behind the cart.

As she checked to see if she was allowed, Nikanoras felt Nazabine's hand on his arm. He whispered to him, "Does she not appear to be like my sister?"

Before he received a response from him, the woman was in front of Nikanoras tilting her head in curiosity at his interest.

"What is your name?" He was panting from the excitement.

"It is Kyna." She lowered her lashes in respect.

He had no idea how long he stood there, gawking at her. The resemblance was driving him mad. Behind him Nazabine grew impatient, expecting the general at their backs at any moment.

"Where is your master?" Nikanoras asked her.

With a gesture of her head she indicated a portly older male who was staring at him, waiting for the request to bed her and how much money he would earn from it.

"Stay here," he told her, then gripped his slave and brought him aside. "Go back to my quarters. Tell Meleagros when he awakens that I shall be back soon. Do not tell him why I am not with you."

"But..." Before Nazabine could stop him, Nikanoras hurried to Kyna and began negotiating for a few hours with her.

His eyes darting in panic around him, Nazabine stood by, watching in anxiety. There was something he knew that he was in dire need to reveal to Nikanoras. Though he tried to catch his attention again, he could not, and simply watched as Nikanoras paid the man and held onto Kyna, rushing her away.

The excitement in Nikanoras was mounting. With his hand firmly around her elbow, he led her away from the bustle of the center of town and brought her to the hills where the shady trees swayed and the cool breezes blew. Out of the sight of the rest of the world, he sat her down and could not stop staring at her. "Kyna, Kyna…"

She was very shy to his gaze and her smile was sweet and innocent.

"Tell me about yourself. From where did you come? Who are your parents?"

This surprised her. "Why do you ask this?"

"You…you look-" He stopped himself. He was talking nonsense. He was to do what he had paid for and then return her as promised. "You are so beautiful." With his index finger he caressed the softness of her cheek. He was just turned seventeen this summer and he would guess she was only a few years older than he.

She knew very well why he had bought her time. When her eyes closed her long lashes glistened in the slivers of sun that flickered through the tall canopy of trees.

Quickly, he raised the tunic over his head and spread it out on the grass. Naked and most certainly already hers, he opened his arms to her. "Come to me."

As if he were cradling a butterfly, he held her tenderly and pressed his lips to hers

****

When Nazabine returned with the basket of goods, Meleagros woke. Sitting up and rubbing his face tiredly, he yawned and asked, "Where is Nikanoras?"

The expression fell from Nazabine's face as he set the things in his basket down.

At his delay in answering, Meleagros rose to his feet and was about to get angry.

Nazabine knelt down obediently and said, "He has found a woman who resembles his sister."

"Euridises?" Meleagros asked.

"Yes. He is with her now."

Meleagros didn't know what to do or think. "Where?"

"I do not know, but…"

Approaching the slave menacingly, Meleagros was in no mood for games. "But, what?"

When Nazabine met his eyes, Meleagros' fury frightened him. "Please, you must be the one to tell him."

"Tell him what?" Meleagros roared impatiently, very upset at the news that his lover was bedding a whore.

"This woman. She was found in the hills when she was an infant. She was brought up and sold as a slave. Do you see?"

Growing more volatile with the information he had received and the game this slave was playing, Meleagros was about to get violent. "No. I do not see."

"Saliukos, his father, had two daughters exposed on the hillside."

It took a moment, and then the realization hit Meleagros' in the face. "And yet you know not where he is?"

"If I were to guess, it is by the temple of Apollo, in the shade of the tall trees. And beware. General Persepolos is also about."

After a kiss to her lips, Nikanoras felt Kyna gasped in fear. She hid behind him and Nikanoras expected to see the general.

It was worse. It was Meleagros in his armor, sword exposed, storming up the hillside. Even through his helmet Nikanoras could read the anger in his gaze. Placing Kyna behind him, Nikanoras slipped his tunic on and awaited his approach.

"Before you begin," Nikanoras said, holding up his hand, "Remember how much I love you. I just wanted the experience of sleeping with a woman before we are on campaign."

"Do you know who she is?" Meleagros roared, clenching his hilt like he would most certainly use the weapon.

This confused Nikanoras. He expected accusations, jealousy, but, not who was she? It was obvious. She was a slave.

Seeing his lover was slow to understand, Meleagros shoved him back so he could get a good look at her. Instantly he recognized the family resemblance. "Nikki, what have you done?"

"What have I done? Nothing but a kiss." Nikanoras put his tunic over his head. "Do not be jealous, lover. Sheath your sword."

When he held it in both hands as if to take a powerful cut through Kyna, Nikanoras gasped in horror and tried to shield her. He was unarmed and totally baffled by what his lover was planning on doing.

Kyna backed up instinctively.

"Leave her." Nikanoras was wondering if Meleagros truly intended on slaying her or this was some type of show on his behalf.

Making an advance on her, Meleagros growled, raising his blade as if he meant to strike her in half.

Having no doubt any longer of his intentions, Nikanoras dove for him to stave off his blow as Kyna cried out in fear and took off running down the hill.

"Are you mad?" Nikanoras struggled to make him search his eyes to come to his senses.

A breath rushed out of Meleagros' chest in anger as he lowered his sword. He gripped Nikanoras' tunic under his throat and pulled him closer. "Did you not think? Did you not wonder why she seems like your beloved Euridises?"

Nikanoras shook his head, stammering some incoherent sounds. Then in a cliché gesture, he opened his palms in question.

"She *is* your sister. Use your head, you bastard. Your father had two of your female siblings exposed in the hills. You know how common it is for them to be taken and sold as slaves?"

"My...My..." None of this was sinking in, or if it was, its reality was killing him.

With that one powerful hand he had used to grip him, Meleagros shoved him back. "We need to head to practice." No doubt disappointed, Nikanoras could hear his grumbling as he started moving down the sloped path, sheathing his sword.

Nothing could explain the ill feeling Nikanoras had in his limbs at that moment. Though he was not aware of his surroundings, and certainly not thinking straight, he followed behind that tall soldier from the Sacred Band until he led him to where his slave was waiting. As quickly as he could, Nazabine dressed Nikanoras for battle.

Nikanoras knew Meleagros was infuriated with him. He had betrayed his lover.

How would Nikanoras explain to him that belonging to this corps d'elite was his father's notion, not his? What he wanted out of life consisted of a woman and sons. Not a loathsome erastes and a pretty male lover.

As Meleagros waited, head bowed, eyes closed, leaning against a wall for support, all the metal on his tall frame glimmering like shining evening stars, Nikanoras knew he had wounded his heart so deeply, Meleagros was questioning everything about their partnership and commitment.

Once dressed as his mirror image, in all his gear, Nikanoras moved to confront him. Before Meleagros could turn aside in disgust, Nikanoras gripped him and pushed him back against the wall violently. "Done. No more. It is out of my system."

"Why do you lie? Go fuck your whores, I do not care." He growled.

"I do not lie. No one means to me what you do."

"One did," he said through clenched teeth.

"And she is dead."

"No, you have found her replacement!" he screamed, the bitterness was like a festering wound he could not contain.

"And tomorrow we march for the advanced training. So?"

"Why don't you go buy her? Maybe she will wait." Toxic venom sarcasm; Nikanoras had expected no less.

"Stop this. Please. It is you that I love. You that I am devoted to, and you, my lovely Meleagros, I go to fight or die with. Not the slave girl." Somehow Nikanoras was to convince him of this, and himself as well.

A long painful breath came out of Meleagros' broad chest. When he finally met his lover's eyes, leaning, chest plate to chest plate, Nikanoras kissed his pout. "Do you love me?" he asked.

"You know I do."

"Then, that is all that we require," Nikanoras smiled.

As his light eyes found Nikanoras' in the dimness of dusk, a glimmer of fire flashed through them. "Not all."

Reading that expression like the scribble on a wax tablet, Nikanoras whispered, "I love you, Meleagros. With all of my heart."

Meleagros' features finally softened at his confession.

"Come, I am in no mood for a whipping. And Arybos needs little in way of an excuse to hold a strap in his hand." Nikanoras grabbed Meleagros' fingers and they raced to the night battle.

"But a whipping is just what you deserve." Meleagros' eyes still betrayed some pain.

"Yes. True. All right. I will take my punishment," he said, hoping to get more than a sly smile.

When he did not, Nikanoras knew he had more making up to do, for they could not go into battle with this misgiving in their hearts. "Oh, in all the confusion, I forgot to mention. I spotted Arybos at the markets escorting my mother. What do you make of that?"

When he received an expression of shock, Nikanoras knew Meleagros thoughts were the same as his own. It was almost too scandalous to discuss.

CHAPTER 10

Dawn broke, and they thanked the gods they had survived the night. Released from their torture, Meleagros and he dragged themselves back to the safety of their shadowy room. As piece by piece Nazabine removed their armor, it was only then they could see firsthand the extent of the wounds they had endured.

The mock scenes were anything but. In the disorienting flicker of torch and roaring firelight, they battled against black-garbed foe, their wooden swords breaking moments after they lashed out at their shields leaving them to fight hand to hand. As he grappled with men masked, but for their eyes for pure intimidation, Nikanoras wondered if they meant to kill them. It seemed if the men of the band were to give up, someone would be there to shove in the knife.

When Nikanoras was so weary he thought he could not throw yet another punch, Meleagros was there to intervene with so much power and stamina he could only marvel at his lover's strength.

Earlier, in the blackness of battle, Nikanoras tried to catch his breath, "I have no weapons. The first slash I made splintered my sword."

"You are too powerful for your own good." Meleagros smiled, his face covered in soot and sweat. "Check him out." Meleagros nodded to the man they had just pretended to murder.

While Meleagros watched his back, Nikanoras crawled on his belly toward the fallen man. "Do nothing sly," Nikanoras warned him, "We have already killed you."

93

As the whites of the man's eyes shown in the dimness through the mask, they followed Nikanoras' progress as he approached. Lying still, pretending to be cut down, the mock enemy held his breath as he waited.

Checking the area first, Nikanoras then knelt up and shoved back the man's dark robe. Indeed the man had an intact wooden weapon still in his fist. When Nikanoras went for it, it was gripped tightly.

"Hey!" Nikanoras shouted, "Dead men don't hold on tightly to weapons. Give it up."

Meleagros crouched down and approached them, keeping alert to the movements around him. "Trouble with the corpse, Nikki?" He giggled.

"He's cheating. I cut his throat, and now he won't give up his dagger." They began wrestling for it. Suddenly the 'corpse' had come back to life.

"Don't make me kill you again." Nikanoras whined, "I am tired. You need play dead."

In no mood for the irritation of a cheating combatant, Meleagros grabbed his hair through the cloth hood and yanked back the man's head. Then he held his wooden sword over his throat. "I shall not be kind to your remains," he warned.

Those dark eyes flashed to Meleagros' furious glare. The weapon was released into Nikanoras' hand instantly.

"Cheater," Nikanoras muttered as he claimed the weapon.

"No time for lament, lover, look behind you." Rising up to his feet, Meleagros slashed out at the oncoming shield and wooden pointless spear.

Still on his hands and knees, Nikanoras rolled into the shins of the fiend and toppled him over as Meleagros simulated stabbing him in the chest.

"Now lay still or we shall get nasty." Nikanoras growled.

"More on their way." Meleagros pointed with his sword.

Inhaling for strength, Nikanoras tried to find his second wind and roared as he attacked the shadowy figures that were advancing in a non-stop queue.

Hewing, slashing wildly, his new wooden weapon shattered like the first, into a stunted broken stick.

Once they had vanquished the enemy together, onward they crept to the next skirmish feeling the ground for any weapon left intact. On their knees, brushing elbows keeping them tight, they ambushed more black-masked soldiers, knowing only when they simulated a truly fatal wound would they lay still. They found attacking from behind and slicing throats effective in the deepening night.

Only once did Nikanoras have enough time to stand tall and look around him. It was easy to become absorbed in the clashing of one on one, to never to have time to lift his head and appraise their environment. Nikanoras knew this was the opposite of what they teach. The fighting group is to be completely aware of their surroundings, as if they could spin like tops in the midst of the fray. But there was sense in this as in everything they taught. How else was he to know what his commanding officer was doing or where the direction of action will lead?

But in this mock battle, learning was pain. By battering them repeatedly, their teachers hoped to toughen their bodies as well as their hearts, and bring their endurance levels up to par with Macedon. It was said their soldiers could fight non-stop for a full thirty minutes before suffering exhaustion. They had their work cut out for them to compete as well.

As the filthy armor dropped to the packed clay floor, Nikanoras cringed and didn't want to see the damage done to him. This horrific bruising, all with wooden blades and pointless arrows. Though a bath and a jug of wine was what he had thought he would crave the most, all he could do was drop into bed, his lover already dead to the world beside him. Iolaus with his Herakles, fighting by his side as his beloved, and they had come out of that simulated warfare, alive.

****

By noon sun they began to rouse them. It was then he could see how filthy they were and Nikanoras' stomach was so empty it was crying out in pain. Feeling as if he had been beaten with a club,

Nikanoras groaned as he made his slow path to the wine jug. With limbs almost too aching to pour, he gasped and his joints creaked as he tipped the contents into a cup.

At a giggle behind his back, Nikanoras knew his lover was awake. "Go back to sleep," said Nikanoras, not even turning to look at him.

"Give us some wine," came the throaty whisper of Meleagros.

Refilling it again, Nikanoras tried to stand straight though his back was in agony. "Here." He handed it to his lover, able to study his face. From where his helmet stopped, across his nose and cheekbones down, Meleagros was covered in the dusty filth of the field. It darkened his shadow considerably. Having very black hair and mocha skin, Meleagros had begun shaving a beard. Nikanoras shaved as well, though he doubted if much was growing.

"Look at you." Shaking his head, Nikanoras tried to laugh, but his ribs hurt too much for anything more than a restrained chuckle.

After gulping the cup of wine, Meleagros climbed out of the bed to have a better look at himself in the proper light of day. "By the gods..." he moaned, as every limb had a deep blushing bruise, which was the promise of black and blue to come.

After admiring Meleagros' colorful body, Nikanoras clenched his jaw and prepared to look at his own. Raising his arms first, his hands and knuckles were bloodied, the skin peeled from their knobs. Across his forearms were red wheals from the whipping effect of the wooden swords. He suffered some chaffing from the chest armor, but his torso seemed intact. His thighs and calves, however, were a lovely match for his arms.

"Poor baby." Meleagros teased, making his lower lip protrude.

"Did you think this is fun? If we were in a live battle, think of the gaping wounds."

"In live battle, one would truly fall when attacked. What nonsense as they kept rising again and again." The frustration was evident in Meleagros' voice. "I vanquished several through the chest and stomach, and did they fall?" Both his hands he had thrown up in disgust. "Not only did they not play dead. They ganged up on me and attacked me three on one."

"Where was I?" It mystified Nikanoras that he could have been absent for such a battle.

"Fighting your own 'dead'."

Their attention was distracted as Nazabine came into their quarters with a large platter of food. Bowing his head he asked, "I was hoping you were awake. Would you like to bathe first?"

Meleagros almost toppled Nikanoras over as he advanced on the food. Wisely, the slave set it down as the feeding frenzy began.

Watching his lover stuff warm bread and cheese into his mouth, Nikanoras almost forgot his own starvation, and knelt down next to him, lest he devour all.

Washed and their wounds tended as best as they could be, they packed their kits for their march. Only moments before they were about to leave and join the rest of their squadron, Nikanoras was surprised to see his father standing at his door.

Judging by the look of him, his pale pallor, Nikanoras assumed Saliukos would never set eyes on him again in this lifetime.

"Father?" He wondered if he had found out about his mother and Arybos walking hand in hand at the market, or maybe it was up to him to tell? Or to not?

At that word, Meleagros spun around to look.

"I just wanted to see you off."

In his white robe edged with scarlet, his trimmed beard and heavily furrowed brow, Saliukos could have been an ambassador or ranking even higher.

One thing Nikanoras envied about that man was his aura. Power begot power, like riches begot riches. Though he did not become corrupt as others had, his father was most certainly frightening in his sheer presence.

Unknown to Nikanoras, it was his father's turbulent youth that was the source of all his current problems with Arybos. As a boy of thirteen, he was bribed into becoming a spy for the Spartan King. Two years later he broke his ties with them and ran from them. Learning things in that wild land he could use against them, he was then the double agent, who gave Thebes vital information on ways to defeat the Spartans in battle and was rewarded with riches and land. Only one soul knew of his father's lapse of loyalty, one that was never repeated, and that man was Arybos.

Here Nikanoras was, a soldier training to be the mightiest of warriors, trembling in fear at the mere sight of his father in his fine robes.

"Yes, thank you, Father." What was he to do? Kneel at his feet and kiss his hand like he had been crowned king? This whole display confused Nikanoras and felt out of character for his father. Though he yearned for it with all his heart, he and his father were never as close as he wished they could be.

And now that chance was slipping further away as Nikanoras left to the mountain training grounds.

With both of them at a loss, something Nikanoras regretted to the day he died, for it was to be their last meeting, Saliukos handed him another purse filled with coins.

"May the strength of the gods be with you." This was not what Saliukos had hoped for. Not a son to march to meet Macedon. With all his heart he wanted Nikanoras to marry, to live in the palace and use his mind, not his body to defend Thebes. It had all been a terrible mistake. And as he stood there, looking at his handsome, athletic son, in his gleaming armor, it was the first time he truly knew this young, innocent boy was going to suffer the consequences of his own mistakes.

As Nikanoras took the heavy leather bag, he met his father's gaze boldly. "Say good-bye to my mother." It was on the tip of his tongue, telling him of Arybos in the markets. His father should know. Someone should alert him. Why was it it could not be him?

That man nodded and vanished. If he had not the wealth of his father's pockets in his hands, Nikanoras would have thought he had a fleeting vision.

An odd sensation washed over Nikanoras as if his father knew he was going to march to his death. Yet, there was something else on his father's mind. Something he yearned to tell him. Was it about Arybos' obvious affection for his mother? What would his father have said, given the freedom of heart and will?

Meleagros stood at his side. At the sense of his warmth and the touch of his hand, Nikanoras blinked and was brought back to the present.

"You mean most to him, Nikki. Do not think he has gotten well rid."

Shaking off the flood of disciplinary memories that followed, Nikanoras traded that depressing sight for the loving lovely face of his comrade in arms. "No. I do not place that burden on either of us. He did what he thought was best. But, Meleagros, he seems so laden with pain. The more I know, the less I wish I did. Remember me telling you of Arybos in the marketplace?"

Giving him his reassuring smile, Meleagros said, "You can do nothing. You must steer clear of this. If you intervene in the affairs of your mentor and father, you will be the worst for it. Believe me, Nikki. And you know I am right. Your father did what he thought was best for you. Yes?"

Neither of them were convinced of the truth in that line, but who were they to question his motives? It was too late for any turning back. And at this moment in time, staring at his lover's loyal gaze, Nikanoras truly began to believe he did not regret a thing.

****

With a heavy heart his father walked back to his palace. Looking back, he tried to believe he had not had such a bad life. At forty years of age, he had accomplished much in the senate. But slowly, things were slipping from his grasp. His wife was being lured from him, his daughter taken to the heavens, and now his son, sent to the bloodiest of battles because of his membership with the fiercest fighters. No heir will be left to claim the inheritance of palace and gold. All he had aspired to had gone slipping through his hand, simply because of a child's mistake in judgment.

And as he scuffed his sandal leather through the well worn marble of his doorway, he heard the whisper of venomous gossip coming from his own halls. A stranger he had become to his own home as the two lovers conspired to his demise as his son was sent away. And he was powerless to do a thing about it.

CHAPTER 11

So smug were he and Meleagros to think the worst of their training behind them for they had not yet marched. This was not the little prancing around to and from practice battlefields. This meant shouldering their packs, their food rations, their weapons, shields, water, tents, already clothed in their military armor, and no slave. Nazabine had been sent back home. So sorely would the two of them miss him, they cried more for that loss than their own mothers.

Their next feigned battle was to be fought in the rugged hills of Cithaeron. Ironically as they played war games, Philip and his host army were engaged in real conflict with the Thracians far north of where they were, only later to envelope their neighbors the Phocians, bringing it close enough to their back door. News of his advance trickled down to them over the evening watch fires. In hope Nikanoras kept waiting to hear he had been routed and dismantled. On the contrary, he was taking all he battled as his own, and a mercenary army, like none known before him, was growing like mold on stale bread.

But, convinced they were placed on this land to vanquish him, they showed no outward fear or hesitation. Nikanoras knew there were more than a few of the men around him who were wholly convinced they were Philip's doom. His own verdict was not yet in.

With this unaccustomed weight on his back, he kept his face a mask and cringed at the smaller males in the ranks. Lysos and Argos seemed to bend under the burden, but, though they had not the great height, they were like mules with legs as strong as tree stumps. Toughness and discipline. That is what the elite war machine must possess.

Echoes of Meleagros' words came back to him for some unknown reason. "From behind," he had said as to how they were to be effective against that Macedonian wall of spines. Nikanoras still had not seen tactics that enabled them to come from behind when in battle with the massive phalanx all armed with fifteen foot sarissa. When were they to be taught that?

Was it depending on the archers to open the way? Or the cavalry? Who would divide this wall of spears so they may grapple hand to hand? He was hoping this lesson was still to come.

Twenty miles and a few broken sandals later, they were in the Cithaeron mountain range that rose between their home and the sea. Circumventing the water gap that fed the river Ismenos, to the spike of land that broke into rocky islets, dusk was upon them as they stopped to set up camp. It was the farthest Nikanoras had ever been from his home; that lovely garden laden plateau awash with streams and wild flowers. No one would be so foolish as to wander too distant in foreign lands. Not without an army at your back. It was hostile, no matter the direction. To the southeast, treacherous Athens, south, the violent Spartans and Corinthians. Don't even mention north and the threat of Macedon. One could bypass Pella and take a ship across the great Mediterranean Sea, only to come head on to Troy or Miletus. No, it was not a friendly time in history Nikanoras mused sadly.

A fleeting vision of peace and tranquility between neighbors passed through his mind, but it was unrealistic to think any other land would be content to make love not war. Violence was the core of a man's existence. War was like eating. It was essential and constant.

Since surrender was not in the late Pelopidas' vocabulary, and consequently, not in the newest recruits either, they were destined for a battle to end all battles. Or if not end it, decide fate either way.

Lifting the weight off his lover, Nikanoras smiled as Meleagros groaned and appeared to float above the dirt a few cubits.

"Good. Return the favor." Nikanoras spun around to give him his back. Having no idea how horrible the pain was until it was removed, Nikanoras echoed his own moans without meaning to.

Their fellow comrades unburdened as well as they formed a semi-circle and thought nothing more than food and rest.

"I have never been more exhausted." Mycandor rubbed his weary face.

"Nor hungry," his lover Argos added.

"Help me with the tent." Nikanoras nudged Meleagros before he contemplated sitting down. He knew if his lover made it horizontal, he would not be brought back up.

With the predictable grumble of annoyance, Meleagros reached out his hand for the pegs. Just as they set it, the commanders were roaming, making sure they were doing anything but resting comfortably.

They roared and barked orders at them, like the men were sheep to be ushered to sacrificial slaughter. They cadets had much more to do before they could bed down or sip watered down wine. The only good news was that their mentors were left behind. Though Nikanoras would have liked to see soft, pale Arybos venture a hike such as this and get him away from his mother, he was glad he did not have to be governed by his rule or intimidated into touching him.

In the mountain forests the air cooled quickly with the constant wind that blew across the water. The sweat soon dried from their bodies. As storm clouds rumbled above the tips of the hills, they wrapped their woolen capes around them and waited in the food lines for bread and broth.

Given little, but enough to take off the edge, they were finally granted leave to rest and ready themselves for an early start and yet, more marching.

With a crackling fire to gaze lazily at, Nikanoras rested against Meleagros' lap as Meleagros toyed with Nikanoras' long hair.

Chasathenes and Lysos, as well as Mycandor and Argos were seated with them, appearing too numb to think or speak. With the crunching of leather on stone, Chasathenes caught sight of someone he knew. Raising his hand in greeting, all six sets of eyes met the elderly ones coming to join their company.

Chasathenes introduced a friend of his dead general father. Chasathenes gestured to a heavy set, weather worn male, who seemed to have tree bark for skin, and wet pebbles for eyes.

Antakinas made his way to his seat with aching stiff limbs. Judging him to be in his sixties, one had to admire him for making the march along with such a young squad. They were mere babies compared to such ancient wisdom.

His deep gravelly voice appeared to seep out of him with a great effort. But, his smile was warm as was his gaze. After the murmur of their names and fathers filled the air, like a roll call of aristocracy over the heat waves of the burning wood, Antakinas wove for them a tale of his own experience battling in the Sacred Band.

"Forty-one years ago I was a young man in my twenties. Pelopidas sent us to the battle with Sparta in Leuctra. He had taken over the charge of our troop from Gorgidas, who had a different strategy for the band. Thought Gorgidas, we should be scattered like sand between the ranks of the infantry. But, mixed with the lower ranks, how could we show off our highly skilled techniques? Pelopidas reunited our men to form a very powerful singular unit. As you shall see, the six of you shoulder to shoulder will be even more invincible than single pairs. Now envision all three hundred with that in mind." He shifted his position on the hard ground and continued.

"Though Sparta appeared to be the most powerful army on land, the administrators kept their fears to themselves. With Pelopidas and Epaminondas calling us unbeatable, we faced the might of the biggest threat to Thebes yet born."

Listening to him, like it was some sort of folk tale, Nikanoras' eyes grew weary as he sank back onto Meleagros' lap. Though he knew Meleagros was enrapt, his petting was putting Nikanoras to sleep.

"With our entire army preparing for battle, we were told the Spartans, quite simply, *could* be beaten. And we were the hope to do it." Antakinas' dark eyes circled the silent young ones around him. They had all heard tales from that battle, but none knew a personal survivor. Most men had died of old age or disease. Chasathenes' father had perished in the battle Antakinas was describing. They all knew it and wondered how the retelling of the tale would affect him.

"You are being trained now with the army set in rows fifty deep, not twelve deep like in the past when we met on the road of Leuctra. The Spartans thought they could surround us. Thinking they were a match for our cavalry, the horses crashed into their lines pressing the Spartan's ranks back into its own lines."

As the story progressed, Nikanoras could sense Meleagros' stress level rising. His petting had ceased and his muscles hardened.

Clearing his throat and sipping some watered-down wine, Antakinas kept going as if they were waiting for the outcome of the tale, though each of them knew it. "Confusion reigned. The moment the line was in shambles, the Sacred Band was given the order to attack." Stopping for an appropriate pause, this story-teller even had Nikanoras' sleepy attention at the moment.

"Completely stunned by our strength and savagery, the Spartans could do little to stop our advance. And the defining moment came when we lay eyes on the Spartan King. Cleombrotus had set up his command close to where the cavalry had burst through. At the sight of that hated rival, we were unstoppable."

Sitting up to get a better view of the old man's face, Nikanoras knew the man was reliving that very day.

"Even though the King was guarded by three hundred personal bodyguards, we massacred every one. With their death, followed by the death of the King himself, and with the heavy casualties befallen the Spartan army, they called for a truce. The battle was won. The dead were buried."

As he imagined the scene so brutally, Nikanoras knew these little play-acting battles were nothing to the real event. It is another thing entirely to be actually slaying men, watching your own men fall to bloody ruin, and getting sliced by a razor sharp blade.

When Nikanoras looked back to see his lover's expression, there was an unearthly gleam to Meleagros' smile. In the firelight he seemed a god come to earth. His shining eyes reflecting the burning shards. Nikanoras could tell the fever of battle was boiling in his veins.

That night as they lie on their mat, curled for warmth, he thought of the older legion at the battle of Leuctra. The cavalry had broken the Spartan line. But, Spartans do not carry fifteen foot sarissa. Someone needed to tell him how these tactics were to work before he too would have the gleam of victory in his eye.

As he lay still beside Meleagros in their tent, Nikanoras went over again what Antakinas had whispered to him after the speech as he beckoned to him before he left.

Antakinas and he walked a few paces from his group and halted. A prickle of warning washed over Nikanoras.

"You are Nikanoras son of Saliukos." The old man seemed to want to be certain before he spoke.

"Yes, sir." Nikanoras nodded, reassuring.

"Two things I must tell you."

"Sir?" What on earth could this man know about him? He was intrigued.

After another glance around for privacy, Antakinas said in a very deep soft voice, "Beware General Persepolos, for he has close ties with your commanders."

As his throat closed tighter, Nikanoras managed to squeak out, "What should I do?"

"Be ever vigilant. Watch those around you in the skirmishes, and in particular, in real battle."

"Of my own men?" He gasped.

Hushing him, Antakinas peered around, then said, "Not of the Sacred Band itself. But of others in the rank. Mercenaries. He has your death in his mind. The man is filled with ego and pride and will not forget your public insult easily."

Nikanoras asked hesitantly, "What is the second thing?"

"Beware Arybos."

And of this he would say no more.

Nikanoras moved closer to Meleagros on the floor of their tent. He rested his length against him, trying to feel peace, but it was not coming.

"My love?"

"I am sorry to wake you." Nikanoras kissed his hot skin.
"Do not worry, Nikki. It is in the hands of the gods."
Nikanoras sighed loudly, closing his eyes.

CHAPTER 12

Later that night, Nikanoras awoke to find Meleagros with his eyes wide open staring at the ceiling of the tent. With the dim moonlight seeping passed the tent fabric, he made out his profile and shoulders exposed from the wool blanket.

"Why do you not sleep? Tomorrow will be a torturous day."

"Maybe that is why." Meleagros' voice was raw with exhaustion.

Leaning up on his elbow to get the best view of his expressions, Nikanoras petted back the soft hair from his forehead and let out a sigh. "Speak to me."

For a moment it seemed pain flashed across him, for he closed his eyes and tilted his face away from Nikanoras' gaze. Reaching out for him in the dimness, Nikanoras wondered if he was frightened by the tale he had heard at the evening fire. He hadn't told him of Antakinas' warnings for him. Meleagros seemed to have enough on his mind.

Reluctantly Meleagros faced him. After Nikanoras heard his answer, he wished he had not asked.

"I look upon Lysos and I see his devotion to Chasathenes. Again Mycandor to his Argos...but—"

"You still doubt my devotion?" Nikanoras lowered his voice as he heard it echo in the silence. "This is still about the slave girl."

Meleagros turned his back to him, punching the matting in frustration.

"You battle with a memory, Meleagros. It is futile. You are my true love."

In a rage he spun back to meet his eyes. The shock of his anger almost caused Nikanoras to turn aside. "A memory? She is a goddess to

108

you. Her death only made her greater in your eyes."

"Stop this." The urge to cover his ears was growing.

Sitting up in the shadowy darkness, Meleagros gripped his shoulders and shook him. "We will mean life and death to each other, Nikki. What does your heart tell you? Where do you want to be? Here with me, or back in your father's palace?"

Meleagros knew his lover too well. Though others understood naught, Meleagros was very aware he went into this battle with trepidation and suspicion. Hearing his complaints about tactics, hating his father for committing him to the Sacred Band instead of university, and finally, loving a slave girl because she was the image of the one he adored most in life. Was it any wonder he asked these questions of him? And to make his life more a misery, the others of the band had echoed his concern.

Meleagros recalled a conversation he had with the other men.

"Are you certain he is committed to you," Lysos asked, pulling Meleagros aside during a break in training.

"What does he confide in the night?" Chasathenes whispered, "Does he assure you he is to be trusted as your companion?"

"Do you make love?" Argos interjected his question loudly, humiliating Meleagros even further.

"Argos." Mycandor nudged him. "That is so personal a subject. Do not force Meleagros to answer when the truth is painful."

Glaring at them in anger, Meleagros snarled, "Of course we make love. Stop all this interrogation. He is committed to me. Why do you all badger me? Let me be." Throwing up his hands in frustration, Meleagros stormed away from their exchanged expressions of worry, only to repeat the same questions to himself over and over until he was insecure and miserable.

Two choices had Nikanoras: the truth, or to lie.

This man, this remarkable man whose looks rivaled Adonis and whose strength topped Herakles, had once tried to kill himself when he had shown his indifference. In truth, Meleagros was too good for him. Nikanoras felt he was wholly unworthy. And adding this turmoil to his already burdened mind, was overloading what sanity he still possessed. He was only seventeen. How was he to cope?

The longer Nikanoras' hesitation, the more devastating it became. As Meleagros hands held Nikanoras' arms, Meleagros' breathing changed to sobbing. If the dagger were in his fist, Nikanoras would have killed himself for the pain he was inflicting upon him.

As the first tear of frustration rolled down his lover's perfect face, Nikanoras broke inside. "Meleagros, never doubt my love for you." His words tore his insides to shreds, and as he spoke them he knew they must be true. "Though I cannot pretend this is what I would have chosen, let me assure you, I no longer have regrets. Though you will never believe me since I made that grave mistake with that slave, I am yours body and soul. No two in our ranks are closer. Do not be deceived by my silence. I was not so enamored with my erastes that he taught me all I needed to know about love. Believe me. You are aware that he repulsed me."

With anguish tainting his lovely voice, he dropped his hands to his lap and said, "Yes, yes, I know. Nor I so taken by Sostios. But, our erastes were only there to begin our lessons. It is up to us to learn all we can about love. Unless of course, I repulse you too."

"No. Stop this. I am trying. At seventeen years, I am no sage. You expect too much of me." Nikanoras was busy trying to keep alive, to avoid an assassin, to stop his mentor from ruining his family and home. This was much more than he was able to handle and he needed Meleagros to just silently support him and understand, nothing else.

The argument was upsetting them both unreasonably. And it was Nikanoras' secrets that haunted him to distraction.

"Do you mean it when you tell me you are mine? Body and soul?" The strain began to lessen in Meleagros. It was as if he needed it repeated again and again, so vulnerable had Nikanoras' lapse in judgment made him, at times Meleagros felt as fragile as a virginal maiden.

"What more must I do?" Though he knew Meleagros' doubts were his own fault, it was Nikanoras' turn to shed tears. He was worn out, mentally and physically. His very being was battered, his emotions in shambles, he felt helpless to deal with his mother, his father, and in fear of being shot down by an anonymous arrow ordered by Persepolos. It was too much.

In that dim sliver of light, Meleagros raised his hand to Nikanoras' face. With a gentleness of touch, one that greatly contrasted the swift strike of his sword in battle, Meleagros sent a shiver down his back and whispered, "You never caress me. It is a platonic relationship." His lip quivered. "I am sick of lying to our friends, of pretending we make love."

"No, you are wrong. I am just spent. If you knew the mess in my mind, Meleagros-"

"You cuddle, you pat my back in gratitude-" It appeared as if Meleagros' own words sickened him. He was not one to whine, nor appreciate it when someone else did.

Nikanoras knew, for Meleagros to complain thing must be unbearable. Here Meleagros was, near a man he was so hungry for he would devour him noon and night, and in return, nothing. Excuses.

Nikanoras said, "And you have the strength to make love after marching twenty miles, or fighting until we drop?" After training he could hardly keep his eyes open, let alone gather up strength for a night of passion.

Pushing the wool blanket off his body, Meleagros hissed seductively, "Make love to me now."

Never taking his eyes from the gaze he was receiving, Nikanoras felt his pulse rise. It had been since before battle training began, while they were still at the palaestra. In the back of his mind he knew Meleagros was testing him. His loyalty and commitment. And what Nikanoras had told him, it had been the truth. He was giving all he had to the battles. Any sexual tension was drained out in his sweat. In the few mornings when he had woken up hungry, the time was gone and they had scurried out to practice. It was no longer on his cluttered mind. He had no time or strength for it.

Inching closer, Meleagros' hands in his hair, he drew Nikanoras to his lips. At the contact of that lush sweet mouth on his, he remembered what he had thought he had forgotten. Desire.

And his taste, it was succulent honey. Sweet forgetfulness of all his problems.

When Meleagros' tongue touched his, a shock raced through Nikanoras. A whimper escaped his lips as everything he had been missing came rushing back over him like the heat of the sun when the clouds disperse.

Allowing Nikanoras to be the aggressor of the two, Meleagros had been waiting for his lead patiently, knowing from past experience, he would repel advances if they had not been his own. When they had first met, he had learned that lesson well. Forgetting his own advice, Nikanoras had begged him not to treat him like a female. And with much self-control and frustration, Meleagros waited. But, it had seemed to him, the waiting was in vain. Nothing he did stirred him as of late. Nikanoras missed his signs continually as he paraded naked before him, licked his lips in longing, or reacted coyly as he brushed past. It was all was lost on Nikanoras' preoccupied mind. And as tales of the others coupling reached him, Meleagros' sadness and isolation grew.

Fool was Nikanoras to think it as passive acceptance of the kind of friendship he had anticipated and thought he had wanted. For what were grown men called that played the eromenos role passed eighteen years? Pathics. Not a pleasant title.

But this was not pederasty. This was two equals bonding. And Nikanoras was not cruel enough to label his lover something distasteful.

What he had thought in him dead, had become aroused. Pushing Meleagros back violently, Nikanoras climbed over him and pinned him under him, never releasing that sucking mouth.

Nikanoras stared at his lover's beauty in the dark. Only the firelight from beyond the tent shone in. Nikanoras ran his fingers down Meleagros' chest, every rippling muscle and sinewy fiber made Nikanoras shiver. Meleagros opened his thighs and pushed the wool cover down, exposing himself.

Nikanoras' pulse accelerated. He held his lover's length, feeling it throb. As with all their contact, Nikanoras became the master. He made for Meleagros' mouth and sucked at it as he squeezed Meleagros' cock. Tiny sounds of pleasure escaped Meleagros as he dug his fingers into Nikanoras' hair, deepening their kiss.

His lover's hips rising, his body tensing to steel, Nikanoras cupped the spilled seed and used it on himself as lubrication. While Meleagros recuperated, Nikanoras knelt over him, parting Meleagros' legs further with his knees.

Without hesitation Meleagros held his shins and opened his body.

Blocking all thoughts of war and death from his mind, Nikanoras penetrated his lover and hammered into him, losing himself on the pleasure and the strength of their bond.

"Nikki," Meleagros whispered as Nikanoras drew closer to the climax.

A shiver washed up Nikanoras' spine and he came, clenching his jaw and pressing as tightly to his man as he could. As the sensations subsided, Nikanoras dropped down on Meleagros.

Nikanoras had finally convinced his lover, he was truly his. But, unburden himself to him with his problems, he did not.

Spent, satisfied beyond his expectations, Meleagros asked sleepily before he closed his eyes, "What did Antakinas want when he drew you aside?"

Hearing the question, choosing to avoid it, Nikanoras merely snuggled closer, and fell into a very deep slumber.

CHAPTER 13

The next morning they were roused from a deep sleep. The next battle they were to fight was a real skirmish. Whispers began to blossom in speculation, until their commanding officers quelled their rumors to advise them that the enemy was a band of slaves from Thrace, who, upon defeating them, would gain their freedom. The slaves were to be well armed, but obviously, not as organized as were the band, nor trained. It seemed to Nikanoras the Sacred Band were merely supplied as an order to kill these men. If any of the band perished in the assault, it would be highly humiliating, to say the least.

Their fears calmed at so bland a foe, they geared up and were supplied with their steel weapons and shields.

Though Meleagros desired the thrill killing, Nikanoras wondered how he would react to the taking of a human life. Obviously if it is the enemy or him, or any of his regime, then it is they who must die. But, death for the sake of death? He wondered what the gods would think of such an act.

Luckily this was to be staged in daylight. Their commanders treated it as an actual battle and they spoke of strategy and timing.

"Are they armed with sarissa?" Nikanoras' comment was heard over the rest.

Meleagros rolled his eyes at the folly.

General Coninious' stern gaze found the guilty party, registered who it was, then immediately ignored his question. Throwing his hands up in frustration, Nikanoras was about to argue a point he had argued since he came to this band.

Meleagros elbowed him in the gap in his armor, shutting him up. After Nikanoras closed his lips he received more attention in the form of direct eye contact from that general when he spoke aloud to their troop.

A shiver ran through Nikanoras at the warning of Antakinas. How many generals were in league with Persepolos? His paranoia ignited like dry wheat in heat lightning. Suddenly this small trial skirmish took on another meaning. *Why am I to fight so many battles at once?*

The isolation of all he knew was weighing heavily on him. He was just a boy. Just a young male from Thebes. Nothing special, nothing noteworthy. Why was he to carry this burden of a death threat when all the other young average males didn't have this same curse? Why him? Over and over he asked that question and still could not understand how the act of his being caused too many such cataclysmic distress.

As his orders rang in their ears, General Coninious mounted his horse and went to check on their 'enemy' to see if they were armed and ready.

Grumbling in his head with his saber in his fist, Nikanoras wanted answers. And by the gods, before this battle with Macedon, he was going to get some.

A bonk on the helmet stopped his brooding. Meleagros, fresh with memories of their night of passion, laughed at him.

"You laugh now." Nikanoras warned, "For what you do not know."

"Shut up and kiss me."

Nikanoras frowned into his pucker.

Long nosed, Xenorus, heard as he passed and cracked, "If you won't kiss his gorgeous mouth, than I shall."

"You shall not." His lover, Parmitheus, shoved him hard enough to make him stumble as he paused.

Breaking into laughter, Nikanoras softened up and pecked those irresistible lips. "Now do your job and protect my ass."

"I will. It means the world to me." Meleagros' perfect white teeth shined under his helmet.

115

The hilarity over their sexual banter was not lost as several men within hearing distance roared with laughter.

It was the fun before the blood, and Nikanoras thought the stress of even this mock battle was beginning to emerge. The enemy was armed after all.

It was not long before they found the slaves, shackled at the ankle as they were led to their starting point looking fierce and hungry for a chance at freedom.

After making sure they had all they needed on their person before they started, their commanders escorted the men to the open field.

"How do I look?" Nikanoras stood tall for his lover. "Everything in its place? All my bindings bound? I don't want to lose a piece of me come the battle."

Grinning devilishly, Meleagros walked around him slowly on the pretext of checking his gear.

When a hand reached under his kilt to his bottom, Nikanoras scolded himself at not expecting it. After his jump and gasp, he found those wonderful light eyes. "I take it I am fine."

"Oh, yes, dear Nikki. The finest they make."

"Just get moving." Nikanoras shoved him to walk in front of him.

Called to form ranks, they stood shoulder-to-shoulder, shield-to-shield, like some type of reptilian creature with impenetrable armor. As horns and shouts commenced, the battle began.

They marched into a roaring crowd of slaves that was set loose with the carrot of freedom dangled before their blue tattooed noses. The Thracians were known for their colorful faces, but Nikanoras found them grotesque and barbaric. It did, however, make them appear less human, and easier to skewer.

Sadly, all of the wooden sword battles did not prepare them for this. When Nikanoras was faced with actual armed men with spear and sword wanting his death very badly, the surge of sensations in his body were unlike anything he had yet experienced.

But, like a true war machine, the trained group kicked into battle mode and the slaughter began. As taught, Nikanoras kept his vision all around him, including his back. Meleagros was amazing to watch. As the body count mounted before him, the smile on his face made Nikanoras think he was actually enjoying this nightmare.

Not to be outdone by either his lover or the pairs around them, Nikanoras increased the power of his sword and decided to best the others around him out of sheer pride.

Grinding his teeth and convincing himself this was the way to survive Philip's army, Nikanoras plowed before the rest, cutting down the advancing hoard in their tracks.

As the blood spurt from their amputated limbs and open throats, Nikanoras squinted at the spray and stepped over warm corpses, thinking only of winning the body count.

Unknown to him at the time, his fierce progress kept the arrows from his back. Two Scythian mercenaries were to be paid if he was killed in battle. Since he was up front of his regime and his comrades were crowded behind him to fight at his side, no opportunities arose. This time.

As if his impetus had spurred the rest, just like Antakinas had said it would, a collective roar emerged from the well-trained group, and they did indeed become savages. So frightening were they that the few Thracians who had stood at the back, turned to flee in panic.

Breaking the line, Nikanoras flew after them. Only after he had hacked down the enemy before him did he realize he was far out in front of his own group.

Nikanoras allowed the men to catch up, until the entire legion had flown along like a flock of Titans to his aid.

Meleagros rushed to be directly beside him showing so much pride, he was about to combust.

After the last living Thracian was hacked to death, they straightened their backs to search for more. That was it? They could keep killing all night.

Three hundred enemy bodies lay in bloody piles while their three hundred were unmarred. Not one of their regime suffered an injury. Nothing more serious than chaffing from armor. It was almost beyond belief. As Nikanoras stood panting, checking again for any sign of more to battle, an arrow whizzed past his face.

Spinning around and raising his shield, he searched for the source. Meleagros as well, ducked and then rose up to find who may have been responsible. In the chaos, it was almost impossible to tell.

"Nikki!" Meleagros yelled in horror as he realized it must have come from one of their own Thebans.

Nikanoras' heart pumped hard under his ribcage. More frightened was he to be stalked and killed by a hired assassin, than to face hundreds in a legitimate fight.

The rest of the band had no idea what had passed. When the reality hit them, that they had conquered the 'enemy' and not suffered a loss, cheers and laughter were heard echoing among the hills.

All around Nikanoras the men were patting each other on the backs for a job well done, almost forgetting the human carnage. They had hundreds of dead bodies to be burned and buried.

Sheathing their swords, the men built pyres, finding wood and stones for the task. They began a more solemn job that is also a part of their training. One must always treat the dead with respect.

After dragging the last limp corpse to the wooden piles, the generals lit them as they began to dig the ground so they may bury their ashes with their swords.

What had taken thirty minutes to rid in battle, took three hours to bury the dead. Nightfall was looming and they were starving and blood-stained.

For their reward, Antakinas himself led them to a tributary river that dumped its contents into the Mediterranean Sea. At the sight of that crystal clear water, the Sacred Band stripped eagerly and plunged into the chilled water, refreshing in its rejuvenating properties, and washing the blood of their enemies downstream.

Three hundred naked boys, thrilling in victory, splashing and horse playing like they'd not a care in the world.

And north of them, the orator from Athens, Demosthenes, was

begging Thebes to join them to defend against Philip, for the monarch's power had grown even further, like a thunderhead about to rain down lightning bolts.

It felt wonderful to laugh. Awakened as if they had found some new source of energy, the boys of the Sacred Band bobbed and jumped in the clear waters.

Nikanoras was atop Meleagros' broad shoulders and trying to dislodge Lysos from his massive lover's, Chasathenes', stocky frame. Not to miss the fun, Mycandor, his legs around Argo's neck, reached to tear Nikanoras from his perch.

Nikanoras was laughing so hard he found it impossible to actually topple anyone at all. But the fun was in the trying. When Mycandor and Lysos ganged up on him, Nikanoras was gasping for air and choking with hilarity.

"Aye! Two on one! Unfair!" Nikanoras said as he battled, Meleagros under him trying to keep a solid footing.

"Easy, Nikki," Meleagros yelled, almost losing him from behind. "Watch. Lysos is coming again."

Turning over his shoulder, Nikanoras spotted Chasathenes struggling to walk upstream with his blond lover on his shoulders. "Faster." Lysos urged him, as if he were on a horse.

"The current is strong. It would help if you leaned forward." Chasathenes grumbled.

Seeing the opportunity, Nikanoras grabbed Lysos upper arm and shouted to his own mount, "Backwards, lover."

Meleagros powered back and Lysos began flailing his arms in panic. A large splash was heard and up came the fair-haired male through the water's surface, sputtering and wiping his face.

"Well done, Nikki." Meleagros then turned his attention to Mycandor, who was approaching him like a raging bull. "Over here." Meleagros made sure Nikanoras saw their advance.

"Right. Move in, Meleagros." As the other men watched, laughing in delight, Nikanoras and Meleagros met up with the other two to battle.

Clasping his arms around Mycandor's head, Nikanoras twisted

him like a top as Meleagros swept under the water at Argos' legs.

"Cheating!" Argos said when he felt the kick.

But, down they went as the tactics worked. When only Nikanoras and Meleagros were left upright, Nikanoras shot his hands into the air in victory.

At the same time, their commanders began calling them out to get back to work.

Hearing the order, Meleagros lifted Nikanoras off his shoulders and set him on his feet. As they waded out of the water, they shared a wonderful smile knowing they were the true crowned victors of the squad.

****

That evening, they passed through camp en route to their tents, wine flasks in their hands, the blush of victory was still fresh in their faces.

The oil lamps were lit surrounding their little makeshift homes. The three pairs of lovers once again made a ring to sit and reflect on the day's battle.

Meleagros and Nikanoras had still not discussed the arrow incident. Nikanoras was trying to forget it, and he imagined Meleagros felt he just didn't have the right moment to bring it up.

A light pat on Nikanoras' rump told him his lover was about to explode in pride, reflecting on his courage in battle. As Nikanoras stared at the rest, setting his shield and helmet near their tent, he met Meleagros' stare.

"You were glorious," Meleagros said, "I had a Hades of a time keeping up. Who would have thought my own Nikki would show me up?"

Though Nikanoras knew Meleagros was as proud as a Spartan mother whose son had just stolen a purse of gold, he could not help but feel a little embarrassed by the attention. In his opinion, he did no better or worse than his peers. And with this nagging in his heart of treachery about to take his life and snuff it out, it was difficult to rejoice.

Lysos made himself a comfortable spot next to his lover. "And you think we shall have trouble with Macedon." He scoffed.

"An army of slaves, does not a Philip make!" Nikanoras replied in anger.

Nudging Lysos to a more comfortable position against him, Chasathenes agreed with him. "If you believe this was what a war with Macedon will be like, then you are sadly mistaken."

"There. You see." Nikanoras pointed to Chasathenes in gratitude.

In Lysos' defense, Mycandor said, "But the rest of the Theban army will be alongside us. We do not go three hundred against three thousand."

"More like thirty thousand," Nikanoras warned.

Meleagros grabbed Nikanoras' long hair in his fist and dragged him to the dirt to sit down. "Nikki has a way to diminish the celebration, does he not?"

The laughter did not amuse Nikanoras.

"Let us worry of that battle when the time draws near, yes, Nikanoras?" Stocky Argos smiled at him kindly, then passed the skin of wine.

Meleagros wrapped his arm around his lover's neck in a headlock, preventing him from taking the much needed drink.

As Meleagros tilted him off balance and ignored his protests, Meleagros spoke over his head, which was now simply a mass of his long hair over his face and eyes. "He is a born worrier. I need not bother, for he spends the day pacing for the two of us."

Both of Nikanoras' hands were on Meleagros' muscular arm as he struggled to pull him off while on his knees beside him.

Meanwhile Meleagros sat comfortably, ignoring his lover's discomfort.

In rage Nikanoras said, "You shall see! You think we have prepared for that war. But, you shall see." Getting very tired with the effort after a full day of battle, Nikanoras moaned, "Get off me!"

Everyone was enjoying this game while Nikanoras felt like Perseus battling a Gorgon.

Not hiding his amusement, Mycandor said, "He paces all the day, pray tell, Meleagros what he is like in the night?"

"At night he is Eros," Meleagros purred, nuzzling into Nikanoras' hair.

"Agh!" Nikanoras broke his lover's strangle hold, pushed the hair back out of his face, panting and blowing like a beast.

"Eros with the temper of Hera." Lysos laughed, slapping his thigh.

"Do you think this a game?" Nikanoras could not be calmed. It was the stress of the unknown assassins taking their toll, and that didn't even count the mess he was leaving at home for his father.

To his amazement, every one of them stopped laughing and gave him serious gazes.

"No, lovely, Nikanoras," Chasathenes began, "By my father's ghost, I assure you it is not a game. But, we must rejoice while we are living and cheer our small victory, lest it be our last."

At that sobering remark, the wind was expunged from Nikanoras' sails.

They all knew what was ahead. Make no mistake. One would have to be both deaf and blind to not hear the murmurs of Macedon's might.

But, Mycandor was right. Here they had slain three hundred without so much as a scratch to their Sacred Band. Surely that was cause for celebration.

Nikanoras was more humiliated over casting a shadow on their group than he was when his lover boasted of his prowess. He thought of how to bring back the laughter he had so unfairly quashed.

He looked to see Meleagros' pout and glazed eyes staring at the flickering lick of flames. Nikanoras grabbed Meleagros in a head lock this time and rubbed his knuckles through his long thick hair to his head. "It is well I worry for two. For you, my Pan, are nothing but a sexual beast!"

As Meleagros flailed to free himself, Nikanoras was glad to hear the amused chuckles coming from the crowd.

"That should be all our luck. A 'sexual beast' with the beauty of Ganymede." Lysos coughed as he laughed.

Through his captivity, they heard Meleagros growl, "Who are you calling Ganymede?"

"Shush, my lovely thing." Nikanoras wrapped both arms around his head to squash him. "The boy thinks he's a man, simply because he shaves."

Chasathenes seemed to just get what his lover, Lysos, had said, "All our luck? You are calling me ugly?"

As they roared once again with laughter, Nikanoras released his lover's trapped head, but held onto him long enough to whisper, "Your beauty makes me the envy of all."

His turn to clear his long locks from his face, when Meleagros glanced up at the ring around him of admiring eyes, he laughed. "So? You think I am prettiest?"

"Oh, do not feed his ego," Nikanoras teased.

"No. No, feed it. Feed it." Meleagros waved his hands, trying to encourage comments.

Once again the group was filled with a delightfully lighthearted repartee, and Nikanoras tried to be content to have the fears set behind them for the time. They'd enough to trouble them as it was.

CHAPTER 14

In the night Nikanoras tossed and turned with horrible dreams. Though they had jested and rejoiced over their victory, in reality, he had killed men. Dozens of men with families, wives, children…and it was as if their death was haunting him. That, and the threat of his own murder from some foolish mistake he had made, insulting so powerful a general.

When it was too much for his mind to handle, it woke him with a start. As he sat up, his heart pumping like mad, Meleagros stirred groggily and tried to understand what was happening.

"Nikki?"

"Nothing. Go to sleep."

Meleagros sat up and leaned over Nikanoras in the dimness. "You are soaking wet. Are you ill?"

"No, a bad dream. Please, go back to sleep."

As he wiped the damp hair from Nikanoras' forehead, Meleagros asked, "Do you remember it?"

Nikanoras calmed himself enough to speak of it. "It was as if I were in the midst of a great swirling mass of spirits, Meleagros. Warriors with swords and helm, all moving around me. So many I could hardly see through them though they were translucent. It was horrifying. I knew I had been the one to slay each of them. It was then I dropped my sword and looked down at my hands. Lover, they were dripping with blood."

"Shh, all right. It is the first time for all of us, but we will get used

124

to it." He gently caressed Nikanoras' long dark hair.

"But you seem so accepting. How do you do it?"

"You must think me cold and callous."

"No. I know you better," Nikanoras whispered, holding him tight.

Inhaling deeply, his large lungs expanding his smooth chest, Meleagros said, "All I can say is that I convince myself they are the sacrifice of the gods. That we are ordered by Athena to vanquish her enemy. Then they are killed in her name, and she rewards us with victory. You see?"

"Yes...I do see. It is for her we go to war."

"Of course. And she loves us like her own sons."

"That is it. I need to pay tribute to her."

"I am sure if we ask, we will be allowed. Lysos said they are going to sacrifice a bull in the morning anyway."

Grateful to hear Meleagros was leaving the death in war in the hands of the gods, and not mortals, it did take some of the guilt away. "Thank you, lover."

"Sleep, my pet. We have another day of hell tomorrow."

Nestling in once again beside him, Nikanoras was not quick to fall back asleep.

With a twitch of Meleagros' thigh muscle, Nikanoras thought Meleagros was well on his way to slumber.

But sleep did not come his way as it was Meleagros' turn to lie staring. Then he whispered, "That arrow, Nikki-"

At having to come to terms with it, Nikanoras covered his face with his hands.

Meleagros tugged them back. "Who has your death on their mind? Tell me."

"So many. What is the use?" Nikanoras breathed out loudly in defeat.

"That pompous general." Meleagros growled as he spoke, "I know I am right. But, who else?"

Reluctant to reveal his mother's despicable conduct with his erastes, Nikanoras refused to answer.

It angered Meleagros. He sat up straight and gripped Nikanoras at the wrists. "Talk to me. You cannot survive this war without help.

And I am not only talking about the one we face in Macedon. Trust in me. Let me help you."

Through the dimness, Nikanoras could make out the silhouette of his lover's face. He dreaded burdening him further.

They were too young. The expectation level of a city was already weighing upon their shoulders. Why did he need to share this pain with anyone?

Softly, sweetly, Meleagros crooned, "Nikki, lover, your Euridises is gone. Who else can listen to your heart? Ease your pain? I am here. Believe in me."

As his words sunk in, Meleagros asked, "Where did that arrow come from?"

A catch formed in Nikanoras' throat. He was of two minds. One was enlisting Meleagros into the knowledge for he was so powerful an ally, the other was not dragging him into a mess, which ultimately may claim him as victim as well.

To Meleagros' agony, Nikanoras chose silence as his answer. But to satisfy his lover, Nikanoras offered his body. He got to his hands and knees and stared at his lover until he got the message.

Meleagros didn't hesitate once he realized what was on offer. He knelt behind Nikanoras and caressed his bottom lovingly.

Nikanoras lowered to his elbows, hearing Meleagros spit into his hand. As pressure pushed into him from behind, Nikanoras closed his eyes and, though he could not find it in him to climax, he was happy to allow his lover the opportunity.

Meleagros held Nikanoras' hips and thrust inside him; it was quick and worth everything to Nikanoras to give pleasure to his lover.

As Meleagros' body shuddered and he made a deep noise in his throat, Nikanoras felt him hug him from behind. Once Meleagros pulled out, they both dropped to the matting and held each other tight.

****

Trying to cope without enough sleep, Nikanoras went through the motions of dressing in his metal coverings as if he were in a trance.

126

Through the night, he lay still, but never drifted off. He wondered how he was to cope with the day of marching ahead. He had several regrets for not getting enough hours rest and dreaded another bloody battle in this state.

His luck was riding high as he was informed they would indeed be marching, but, not into another bloody fray, at least not until they rounded up enough men to slaughter.

The tent and bedroll stowed with his pack, Meleagros assisted him in shouldering his load, making sure nothing was chaffing or loosely hung.

Back in formation, their little group of six friends was about halfway from the front and the same from the back. They were headed up to the highest hilltop of the Cithaeron range to sacrifice to Athena. From there, it was said, they could see Mt. Olympus. If this were the case, Nikanoras thought it was worth the effort to climb.

Through wooded switchbacks, they toiled uphill, thinking only of the rest and tribute at the top. Meleagros was behind him, Argos in front, as Nikanoras dazed off to the hypnotic movement of the sway of Argos' backpack, marveling at the size of his calve muscles.

A tender melody drifted in the air and it took Nikanoras some time to realize it was coming from his lover.

As he sang softly, Meleagros took Nikanoras' mind off the miles and aches. Perhaps Meleagros was unaware that his lovely sweet voice had lightened the hearts of all those around him. Through the fatigue in his limbs, Nikanoras felt both love and envy for him. Love because of the strength he gave him and the complete loyalty and devotion, but envy, for Meleagros' acceptance of his fate with almost joy. Being where he was meant everything to Meleagros, and he would choose no other path for his life.

Savoring the battles, drinking up the victory like Dionysus' wine, Meleagros was so utterly content with his life, it killed Nikanoras. What must it feel like to be where you want to be, and doing precisely what you want to do? Was he the only member in three hundred to have wants, other than that of the Sacred Band? Everyone was honored, chosen, elite, respected, valiant; the number of adjectives used to describe them was endless. As they paraded around the city, citizens bowed to the ground and hailed them as heroes even before they had seen any war. If he would speak to Lysos, Mycandor, or any of the rest Nikanoras would hear their pride, their lust for battle, and watch their heads held high in glory.

Was he alone then in his thoughts? At times, he felt, it did seem so. And best he kept them silent.

"You've a lovely voice," Nikanoras spoke over his shoulder to his lover.

"You inspire," he replied.

Curious as to his impish giggling, Nikanoras gave some thought to the comment, then asked, "I am flattered, Meleagros, but, tell me, how do I inspire?"

"For the last ten miles your kilt has been tucked under your pack."

Registering his comment, Nikanoras stopped short, making the line behind him do the same, and when he spun around the expressions on the faces following him were explosions of hilarity about to burst. "It took you ten miles to inform me of this?" Nikanoras was not pleased.

A crowd was forming to see what the hold up was. The line ahead had not stopped for them and was advancing into the wood.

"Go on!" they shouted at Nikanoras, for the path was single file and none could pass.

"Fix my kilt." He growled. "Do me the favor."

Sensing the irritation behind him, Meleagros reached under Nikanoras' pack to straighten him out. When he was decently covered there were hisses of disappointment and not less than a dozen comments on how boring the rest of the march would be.

Losing sight of the rest, Nikanoras had no time to argue and had to run with the weight on his back, clanging and bruising with every loping step.

Chasathenes was breathless, rushing with the rest of the line behind Meleagros. "You needn't have told him. It was passing the time."

"I regret it. What a bore the rest of the hike will be." Seeing Nikanoras had opened a gap from his speed ahead of him, Meleagros shouted, "Come on!" to the rest and stepped up his pace with a great effort.

Catching up once again, Nikanoras regained his breath as Argos looked behind to ask, "Where did you disappear? A call from nature?"

"No, never mind." Adding to Nikanoras' feeling of exhaustion, fatigued, and sleeplessness, was *irritation and humiliation!*

Just when he felt he could not take another step, the line halted. It seemed they had finally reached the smooth rounded summit. As one of the generals rode on horseback, crashing through the underbrush to find their end, he shouted, "Move to the clearing and set camp!"

The slow process of filing to the bare cap of the mountain, almost took longer than the original journey up. It was the knowledge that they would get to rest and be fed that left them anxious to finish.

Once they had set their things in an enormous ring, ten deep, the aroma of cooking stirred Nikanoras' empty stomach.

Meleagros handed him some dried figs from his rations. Nikanoras thanked him as he stuffed them in his mouth. Before they were ordered to set their tents, a large black bull was brought to the center of their circle. Massive and thick, with white horns and a ring of bonze through its nose, it was a beautiful beast. The highest ranking officer, who was on their training march, did the honors. As they knelt down in unison in the dimming twilight, the bull made a belching, trumpeting sound and then collapsed onto its knees with a cut throat. As it died, a chant rose to Athena, begging her to accept it with their humblest gratitude.

At appeasing the gods, Meleagros leaned against Nikanoras gently to show his support. With that task behind them, they lined up for some well deserved mash and wine.

His hunger sated, yet never actually feeling full, Nikanoras located a grassy spot to lie back and view the heavens, which were crystal clear and spattered with brilliant points of light.

With more wine he had confiscated from some unknown source, Meleagros lie beside him, overlapping him as he tried to recognize the constellations he had been taught.

Nikanoras passed the wine and said, "There is our hunter."

"Alas, poor Orion," Meleagros whispered, then took a generous mouthful and passed it back.

"One should never underestimate the aim of the gods. Especially Artemis. She is more highly skilled with the bow than the rest."

"Was a dirty trick of Apollo. How was she to know it was Orion swimming?"

"She was not to know. That was why Apollo challenged her. He was insanely jealous of her love of him."

Meleagros propped his head up in his hand, leaning his elbow against Nikanoras' shoulder. "Jealous, gods." He clicked his tongue in sympathy. "One forgets he did rape Metrope. So perhaps that is why he deserved death."

"But, he loved her so, and her father refused her hand in marriage. I still feel pity on him." Nikanoras' focus came upon the brightly lit belt with its three blazing stars, Alnitak, Alnilam, and Mintaka.

"Yes, you would. You have too much heart, Nikki, that is your problem."

Changing his direction to gaze at Meleagros' grey eyes, he said, "I have never been told that."

"About time you had." That sly glimmer appeared in Meleagros' expression.

"What is wrong with too much heart?"

"Sympathy is a deadly feeling in battle. It will make you pause."

"I do not feel sympathy for my enemy."

"But, you do. Your dream. It is from guilt."

Those words that brought pain, whether or not Meleagros had intended them to.

Meleagros pressed closer, wanting his attention back. "There is no way to purge it of you. So, you must be content."

Stifling a grumble at the notion of 'being content', Nikanoras was deciding whether to be irritated with him at the patronizing or just put his mood down to his exhaustion and constant preoccupation.

"You need sleep." As if Meleagros read his mind, he nudged him. "Go."

"Will you join me?"

"Soon."

After his peck on the cheek, Nikanoras crawled into their humble tent and collapsed, falling asleep before he remembered lying his head down.

Meleagros walked through the camp solemnly, keenly aware of the others around him. As he gazed discreetly at the affection and laughter, the sheer joy and elation of partners sharing mutual excitement over being where they were at that time in their lives, his heart grew heavy.

After passing some time alone, he returned to Nikanoras, physically worn out and mentally spent. With the help of the gods, Meleagros accepted his place under the star lit heavens, and no longer pressed Nikanoras for more than he could give.

Crawling into the cozy tent, Meleagros stripped of his armor and moved behind his lover, inhaling his fragrant hair. Meleagros wrapped his arms and legs around his sleeping lover, holding him tight.

CHAPTER 15

At morning light they were greeted by some new arrivals. Coming up from the hills on horseback, their group of almost three hundred mentors arrived to check their progress.

When he had found Nikanoras, Arybos opened his arms to Nikanoras for an embrace that was purely for show.

Meeting eyes briefly with Meleagros to see his reaction, Nikanoras gave Arybos a quick hug, and then backed away, his gaze lowered until he had given them some distance.

"Your father sends me to see you. For the past week he and Persepolos were busy in the debates. The Amphictonic council is about to declare war on Amphissa."

"War? Why is that?" Meleagros asked.

"They have cultivated the land that belongs to the gods against the writings of law." Arybos' attention was diverted as Meleagros stepped closer to listen to the news, blocking his view of Nikanoras. "Sostios is looking for you at present. Surely you should seek him out in this mob. We split up to find you knowing you would be together, or so we'd been told."

Meleagros had no choice but to bow silently, and go on his way.

The moment his lover had vanished into the mulling crowd, Arybos handed his horse off to his slave after unpacking one of its bags. He then gestured to Nikanoras' tent, holding a parcel.

Nikanoras raised the flap to allow him to pass.

"You've kept well. We heard about your victory against the Thracian slaves. Well done, Nikanoras." This was spoken with

132

Arybos' back to him as he was busy unfolding something.

Keeping silent, wondering the purpose of his visit, which left Nikanoras highly agitated after the mention of his father and the memory of this snake with his mother. He peered over Arybos' shoulder as he unwrapped his things, hoping it was not his own kit with the audacity to announce his intentions to stay with him. Nikanoras was pleased when Arybos handed him some gifts.

Nikanoras' expression softened, knowing it was expressing his suspicion a moment earlier. He graciously accepted the new sandals, kilt, and cape, which Arybos claimed, were from Nikanoras' mother.

"And from your father." He raised a wrapped parcel.

Looking around him for an appropriate spot to open it, Nikanoras set the things Arybos had given him aside and took it, bowing in thanks. He carefully unrolled the cloth, feeling its weight. The moment he released it in his hand he knew it was a weapon.

But a sword so fine was a treat to his eyes. "Arybos, it is magnificent." Then he recognized it, it was his father's own sword. Allowing the dim sunlight that filtered in to shimmer on its highly polished surface, he admired the skill of the maker. "You say this is from father? But, it is his own. Why does he give it me?"

Until Nikanoras' attention was drawn to him once more, Arybos kept silent. When Nikanoras' fascination with the fine weapon waned, he found Arybos' gaze. "Your father, Nikanoras."

The way it was said, Nikanoras knew what would follow. It was the same way he had been told about Euridises. In his mind his father was already dead, but didn't Arybos just say he was debating at the council?

"I am sorry to bring you news that he is ill. Though a fever has its hold, he continues to go to work and battle it. But, I fear, sweet Nikanoras, his battle is in vain."

An image of Saliukos drinking a glass of toxic wine flashed through Arybos' mind like a strike of an adder.

The night before, kneeling in front of Thessenike in the courtyard, Arybos' had whispered, "Your irascible daughter is dead, her equally irritating brother soon to be. It is time, my lovely Thessenike, it is time."

She whispered back, "You have it with you?"

From under his cloak he produced a small vial, showing her.

"Will it kill him immediately?"

"No. Not in one dose. But, I should think, my love, two shall do it."

"In two or three, lest someone think it is anything over than a fever." She tapped his hand to hide the vial. "I shall have Nazabine serve it to him."

"The slave knows?" Arybos panicked.

"No. Don't be a fool." She breathed in irritation, then calmed herself. "I shall place it in his wine without him becoming aware. Give it here." Her greedy claw reached for it.

"What shall we tell Nikanoras?"

"Bring him gifts. Things he will surely need. Tell him it is from his father and I. Then casually, bring him the news he is ill. There is no way, Arybos, that he shall suspect a thing."

As she cupped the poison in her fist, Arybos rose up to allow her to pass. Like a wicked gorgon, she crept to where Nazabine was preparing the dinner and wine, slipping behind him to pour half the contents of the vial into the chalice.

When the slave felt her presence he spun around. "Madam?"

"Just checking you are taking care of him. Carry on." She nodded, hiding the vial in her hand. After he had left with the elixir tainted wine, she walked back to the courtyard and a fretting Arybos.

In anticipation he waited for her words.

She handed him back the vial, and whispered, "The traitor shall have his doom. One more day shall do it."

Taking back the bottle, his eyes widened in awe at how cold and calculating she had been. Not a hint of pain, or remorse showed in her hardened features. Clasping her hand in affection, he whispered, "You are the perfect woman, Thessenike, a killer, and a lover."

Smiling affectionately at him, she squeezed his arm to remind him, "Come, let us get some things to pacify Nikanoras. Help me pick out what he shall need."

Arybos noticed Saliukos' sword resting on a wooden bench. "Look, Thessenike, his sword."

"By tomorrow he will not need it." She scoffed and turned away.

"Then, I shall make it part of the gifts."

Smiling perceptively, she said, "Clever as a fox, you are. Yes, tell him it was from his father's hand."

Arybos smiled wickedly.

"What of my father?" The way Arybos spoke without the slightest hint of feeling, made Nikanoras wince with pain. One by one something had set out to extinguish his entire family. It was too soon. No one had given birth to the next generation and he was too young to decide his own fate.

Arybos drew close. "I can get permission for you to see him. They will allow you to come home with me."

His seductive purr sent the goose flesh rising on Nikanoras' skin. He backed away and asked, "Temporarily?" This needed clarification.

"Yes, of course. They will not ask you to leave your men."

"But if Father dies, who will run the household? Mother? On her own?"

Before Nikanoras received his answer, Meleagros poked in his head into the tent. "Excuse the interruption. I just wanted to invite you out for some wine with me and Sostios."

"Then you have found him." Arybos pretended all was well. "Good. Yes, we shall be out to join you presently."

Once Meleagros checked Nikanoras' expression, the tent flapped closed behind him.

Arybos clasped Nikanoras' shoulders to get his undivided attention. "You do not have to worry for your mother. She will be well looked after. Nikanoras, you can remain here with your pretty partner. Have no fear that you will be forced from him."

So many thoughts passed through Nikanoras' mind, the foremost being, how wrong Arybos' assumptions were. By law, he could now leave and stand in if his father dies. It was not expected for an aristocratic woman to be alone, especially if she had an adult son. He was not yet eighteen, but that was only months away. Yet, this would mean his father's death, and leaving his lover, half of a couple.

Not to mention the gleam of malice in Arybos' eye at the thought of having his mother all to himself, that, and his father's palace and purse of gold.

Arybos appeared surprised at his silence. "Do not think of these things now. Let us have a drink." He nudged him.

Nikanoras came back aware and ducked through the tent flap, knowing none of this talk was final.

Already seated on a mat set out in the sun, Sostios and Meleagros were busy catching up. Though he tried to be polite, Meleagros could not concentrate until he had discussed what was being debated between Nikanoras and his mentor. As Nikanoras approached, Meleagros could read pain in his face. It appeared Nikanoras was stricken with worry. Meleagros knew his feelings about Arybos and what had passed at the marketplace with his mother. The man was a viper, there was no mistake.

Handing off a flask of wine, Sostios smiled at Nikanoras, greeting him warmly.

"Thank you," Nikanoras spoke softly as he took the flask and made a seat next to his lover.

His patience tried, Meleagros could not stop himself, "Are you all right, Nikki?"

Lost in his thoughts of finding a way finally to get out, marry, become a statesman, and claim his inheritance, he was slow to hear his Meleagros' question. When he asked it once more, Nikanoras raised his lowered chin to find his grey eyes almost tearing up in worry. "Yes, fine..." He nodded in assurance.

Sostios continued where he had left off when he and Meleagros were interrupted, "Athens has broken the terms of the peace treaty by sending ships north to Cardia and Thrace. Demosthenes has been very busy. He sees to it himself that Macedon is surrounded by enemies."

Arybos was stroking his beard, which he did habitually, as he listened.

When Sostios paused he added, "The actor traveled to

Propontis. He has sent word that Byzantium is no longer in an alliance with Philip."

"Is it true Philip was once a hostage of Thebes?" Meleagros asked, reaching out for his share of wine.

Sostios said, "When Philip's brother was king, he and thirty children of noble families were sent to Thebes, yes." He nodded. "A mistake it was to show the Greeks their good nature, for Philip lived with Pammenes and was able to watch and admire their beloved Epaminondas."

Arybos added, "In my opinion it was his time with our great general that taught him the art of war. As far as the rest of Epaminondas' many loving characteristics, none has been passed to that wretched creature."

Meleagros' eyes widened. "King Philip of Macedon was trained to fight by the leader of the Sacred Band?"

"You see." Nikanoras pointed to him. "It is useless to try old tactics against him." His fears were not imaginary.

"Calm yourselves." Sostios raised his hands expressively, like a high priestess over a sacrifice. "Do not come to this war with doubt. Have faith in Athena."

Nikanoras rubbed his face tiredly. Hoping your own father dies so you may take his place is tempting the gods to do terrible feats. But, he could not help but have them.

****

As Nikanoras packed a small kit in their tent for his ride back to the capital city with Arybos, Meleagros sat beside him in tears.

"You will not be back."

The agony of his words was pressing down on Nikanoras' chest as if a horse had rolled on him after a fall.

"You have your way out, do you not, Nikki?"

"What am I to do?"

"I will not survive it. I swear to you by Apollo, I will kill myself if you do not return to me."

"Shush. Stop this talk." Opening his arms, Nikanoras beckoned him. It was flagrantly rebuffed. As Meleagros sought to control his sobs, Nikanoras sat next to him, leaning on his shoulder.

"Why are you so sure I have chosen to live with my mother? You know how she behaves. I would sooner stay in a den of harpies."

"Why do you lie?" He cried, "You have your escape from me. You have your life in the council and your wife waiting. Do not lie!"

It was as if he were pierced with that treacherous arrow, the pain in his chest was so sharp. Moving to face him, both of them seated cross-legged on the floor, Nikanoras caressed the long hair back from his face to see those fiery eyes.

"If I do not fight with you in battle, and win, then the council will be useless. Macedon will come storming our gates and murder all those in power. So, my love, you choose my fate. Would you rather I die in battle, or be killed by an invading army of thieves?"

"Liar!" he thundered as he stood, shoving Nikanoras back. "Once you leave here, I will never set eyes on you again!"

Was he a liar? Or could he convince himself he belonged here, with Meleagros?

"I cannot stand the sight of you!" Meleagros sobbed, then blind with tears, left their tent.

As Meleagros shoved his way out, Arybos entered, filled with concern. "Nikanoras? What has passed between you?"

Wiping at his own wet eyes roughly, Nikanoras could not begin to explain it for fear of choking in agonizing sobs.

Arybos sat beside him, his hand on Nikanoras' shoulder. "Does he think you will choose to not come back to him?"

A nod was all he could give in response.

"And? What were your reassurances?" He asked anxiously, as if it were he leaving his beloved.

Covering his face to hide, unable to contain the pain in his heart, Nikanoras wept like a baby.

Arybos shook him in fury. "You will return to him! Reassure him you will be back!"

Sobbing in misery, Nikanoras said, "How can I? What if Father dies? What then? Do you plan to take my place before me?"

With the power of his malice and hatred toward him, he let loose yet a back-handed slap across Nikanoras' face.

Nikanoras was stunned and held his cheek at the sting.

Arybos said in fury, "As your mentor you shall treat me with respect. How dare you speak like this to me?"

Nikanoras growled in anger. "I have seen you with her! At the market! Do not act as if you had my best interests at heart!"

This appeared to shock Arybos. "But, you are very wrong, my lovely eromenos. Of no other do I think. You see, it is I who brings you now to your family in the time of need. I who cares for your mother when she is lonely and craves a compassionate ear. Do not think I have other motives. For, my beautiful Nikanoras, your well being has always been my first concern." His hand reached to caress the cheek he had punished.

Nikanoras flinched and leaned away. If Arybos expected him to believe in this nonsense he was more lame than a Spartan beggar.

As Nikanoras packed his things onto a horse, Meleagros, still sobbing loudly, was hiding in a small huddle of friends. Mycandor, Argos, Chasathenes, and Lysos, patted him and cooed soothingly to him. Meleagros could not be consoled.

With four sets of furious eyes burning into him in hatred, Nikanoras shied from their glare and mounted, turning the horse in the direction of home.

CHAPTER 16

To see the city coming into view again, retracing his regime's steps, but this time on horseback, Nikanoras was home in half the time. Arybos, destined to accompany him against his will, stood behind him as he approached the front door of their lavish palace home. It was as if Arybos were afraid he might say something to incriminate him to his father, so he shadowed him if *he* were the one who could not be trusted.

Nazabine bowed as he opened the door for him from within.

"Where is Father?" Nikanoras wanted to see his state for himself.

At his slave's expression, Nikanoras felt as if ice filled his belly.

"Are we too late?" Arybos shoved passed him and rushed to see for himself, an almost joyous excitement to his gate.

There beside Saliukos' bed, knelt Thessenike with his hand in hers.

And at a vision sickening to see, as if he were her true love, Arybos raced to her and cradled her in his arms. As he rocked her gently, she lay her head down on his chest and crushed against him.

At that sight, Nikanoras was wretched. Not wanting to speak his suspicions out loud, he cleared his throat, at least to let his mother know he was there.

When she heard it, she looked to see who it was.

Nikanoras felt as if were angry he had been sent for. Was he a roadblock set before her from now on?

Averting her disgusted gaze, Nikanoras tread on soft feet to look down on his father's corpse. His father was pale, still, and yet continuing to emit some power Nikanoras could not explain.

If Nikanoras expected his mother to react, to rush to his arms like

140

she had to his father's best friend, he was mistaken. It seemed suddenly he was the outsider in this house, not the rightful owner and heir. It would most certainly be in Arybos' best interest to get him off to battle. The snake had laid claim to the family fortune. Nikanoras had no doubt. But, could he be betrayed like this? From his own erastes? One whose own hands taught him the nature of love?

"Get some food and wine, Nazabine," his mother ordered, her strength returning after the initial show. She still had not spoken a word to him. Standing on her own, brushing her clothing straight, she daintily attended a loose strand of hair, never meeting his eyes. Nikanoras was about to explode in anger at the slight.

His tutor knew him well, and this behavior from Thessenike was beyond suffering. "Thessenike, your son is before you."

"Save your breath, Arybos. My mother shares no love for me. I came here to see Father, now I have seen him. Perhaps I need to consult with the senate to find where my duty lies."

As Nikanoras spun on his heels to leave the room, Arybos grabbed him from behind. "Do not be hasty. Sit, eat, and rest. Tomorrow we shall see more clearly and we can debate where you are best needed."

Spoken like the true man of the house. Nikanoras sneered to himself. So, it was Arybos' intention to sleep under his mother's roof as well as be the one who comforts her.

As Nikanoras gazed back on his dead father, he had graver suspicions than that. "Why was no doctor summoned?"

When that question brought another flash of rage across his mother's face, Nikanoras knew his answer. Crossing the room to confront her, his father's sword at his hip, his hand on the hilt, he was about to finally voice his thoughts and reveal what the truth must surely have been about his demise.

Arybos once again, restrained him. "Do not say things that will soon be regretted. I ask it again, wait until the morning."

It was getting to the point where Nikanoras did not know who was his ally and who was his enemy. He knew well the fate of a young boy, crowned as prince when he is not yet a grown adult male. Though he was seventeen and trained as an elite killer, he had not yet the experience under his belt of a true man of the world. And they all knew it. This left him with two options; he was either to leave, powerless, or kill everyone. In other words, he had one option.

And whom should he hate? Arybos for wanting to further his fortunes and love an attractive woman, now available and in need of a man? Or his mother, for her cruelty and neglect of him, pushing him into the arms of his sister, who was the only love he knew in that house? In reality, it was only himself he loathed for he was powerless to change or do a thing to help himself. And the one man who had some care in his heart for him, was lying there, still, the end of the line for their family tree. For it was no longer imagined Nikanoras would ever live to see through this treachery. He was going to suffer his father's fate if he stayed, or die in battle if he left.

Pondering which choice to make was one of the hardest decisions in his life. He had no allies in the senate that he knew of. And a very powerful enemy, General Persepolos and his peers. Who could he seek out to right this wrong? Accuse this close friend of his father of murder? Point to his mother as villain and co-conspirator? No one.

At the dinner table, he ate more in one sitting than he had in all his marching and camping meals combined. Never one to gorge himself on food and wine, he did with a hunger he could not quench. It was *his food, his wine,* yet Arybos ordered his servants around like he had already possessed them, and this, with his father, still on his deathbed.

And of course his mother was already thinking of giving Arybos all. Last she wanted was to be a widow and chase off unwanted suitors, like Penelope torn from her Odysseus, who suffers to house the wretched while her son is too young to defend her. Is that he then? Pathetic Telemachus? Too young to defend her? Yet old enough to fight in a war to end all wars?

It was a joke. His mother needed no protecting. This was her will as it was Arybos'. Now with his father dead, they did not have to hide their hideous affair.

142

After cramming all he could into his mouth, and drinking all her wine, Nikanoras left the table without a word to lie in the bed he had once claimed as his own.

There, against all the richness of his cushions and blankets, he cried. Though he was a man in his own eyes, strong and capable of leading a regime of fighters behind him with his zeal, he could not even find the voice to defend what was rightfully his. And no stronger was the presence of his beloved Euridises anywhere more than in that house. If she were here she would kneel by his bedside, comforting him, and assuring him that what was his will be his, as she herself would guarantee it.

The scuff of Arybos' sandal alerting him, Nikanoras jerked his head to the doorway. Lit by torchlight, Arybos set the flame in a wall holder and sat on the bed near him. "Do not cry, lovely Nikanoras."

"You tell me not to cry? When I see your intention is to take what is mine from me and my father?"

"I do not want it in quite the way you think. I merely care for your mother."

"Do not talk to me of my mother," he warned.

"She is helpless, Nikki, helpless."

"You! Do not call me 'Nikki'! Only one has that right," he roared in fury.

"Yes, forgive me, Nikanoras." He lay his hand on Nikanoras' thigh through the blankets. "Believe me, I do not want your fortune. When you return from battle, it will be here for you, safe. Your mother asks me to stay. I do what she wishes."

"And what of me? You expect me to die in battle. Do not deny it."

"No. On the contrary. You, my lovely, are one of the best. The Sacred Band of Thebes. No one can defeat you. Once Philip is vanquished, you come and claim your place. You have my word."

"Your word?" He sneered. "How do I know you both did not plot to kill Father?"

Arybos' face contorted in rage before it regained control. "You speak before you think. Do not accuse so freely. There are many things you do not know, Nikanoras. Some things about your father.

143

Secrets he kept close."

"What things? What secrets? If you know something vital to me, you cannot keep it from me." The power this man had over him was virtually destroying him.

"Past indiscretions. Deeds that would have seen him hung if it were not for my silence. So, you owe me respect and gratitude."

"Things you know? Is that why my father has always been submissive to your every demand? Turned a blind eye to your affection of my mother, and then he handed me to you so you could devise your plans and make me one of the Sacred Band?" Panting to catch his astonished breath, Nikanoras asked, "What did you know of him to torment him so?"

"Since he is now with the gods I will tell you. This is something he kept close to his heart for the last thirty years, Nikanoras." Leaning closer, he whispered, "Your father was a spy for Sparta when he was but thirteen."

"Liar!" Nikanoras roared, cowering back from him as if Arybos were the god of Hades, his heart pounding. "Father loved Thebes! How could he rise to the senate? Own land. Liar!"

Gripping his shoulders to calm him, Arybos said, "Only twice did he bring news to the King of Sparta, then with news from them he returned to give their secrets to Thebes. It was then he was given riches for his information. Never again did he betray Thebes."

Shaking his head in denial, Nikanoras could not help but see it fit into some puzzle as Arybos always seemed to have his father under his thumb. And surely, this knowledge would have ruined all of them.

Arybos moved his hands to a more personal spot. Nikanoras shifted away from it and said, "So. You have exposed your secret over him. What is it you intend to do now? Do you admit you are in love with my mother?" Nikanoras knew Arybos was deciding what he wanted to hear.

"I loved your father, your sister, and your mother and you. You are all my closest friends and family. You know how I adore you, Nikanoras, like my own son."

"Stop touching me like that." Nikanoras brushed his hand back again. "You are not my erastes any longer, so do not caress me like you have claim."

"But, you are still so young. A baby in my eyes. You've not the whiskers of a man."

As Arybos checked his cheek for stubble, Nikanoras swatted his hand away. "I shave. I am no baby." This talk was enraging him. What did Arybos take him for? Someone he could use? Like a whore?

"Come, lie with me for one last time, then you shall love me like your mother does."

As Arybos enveloped him in his embrace, his mouth attempting to find his, Nikanoras roared in anger and pushed him away, stumbling off the bed. Nikanoras searched for his sword, and wished he had not consumed all that wine with dinner. He was far from clear headed. "Do not touch me!"

Calmly, Arybos sat on his bed, watching him. "I am simply a man asking his eromenos to behave and listen. You know very well I have the knowledge to destroy your family name, and still you defy me?"

"I am not yours. I have a new lover. As Father commanded, I have formed another bond. I am true to him. So, do not threaten me with your venomous tales."

"Are you? And of this 'bond' why are you so eager to leave it? You obviously do not love this boy." Standing up, his robes falling straight around his heavy bones, he approached Nikanoras where he stood, his back against the wall, naked under the torchlight.

His chest heaving with his rapid respirations, Nikanoras was being trapped by logic. They were right. He was no man of the house. He was merely a confused little boy with no direction, no conviction. Lost, he wavered between decisions like a balance on a string.

"I know what you need, Nikanoras...come here. I command it."

When Arybos reached out, the revulsion Nikanoras felt almost made him heave in sickness. "No. I am the one thing you cannot have. Move away." Finally spying his saber with his kilt, Nikanoras shoved passed him and grabbed it, raising it up menacingly.

"You dare to lift a sword to me in the house of your mother? Threatening your tutor and mentor?" Arybos thundered in rage.

"Not of free will! You are cornering me! Leave me!" The blade in Nikanoras' hand lacked the conviction to do Arybos harm as it trembled in his clenched fist. It was all for show, and both of them knew it.

When he spotted his mother's pale face at the doorway, Nikanoras' skin turned clammy in fear.

"What is going on?" Her long hair was out of its clip and her sleeping dress brushed the tiled floor. "Nikanoras! Put away your sword. How dare you?"

"But...Mother..." Nikanoras couldn't even begin to tell her what had passed.

"You have seen your father. Now leave us." She pointed to the door. "Go and make a man out of yourself. You are useless, Nikanoras. At least die valiantly in battle."

Seeing the gleam in Arybos' eye, Nikanoras wondered if he had played well into his hands. He had no choice. As they watched, he lay down his blade and dressed for travel, in his armor and shield, hoisting his kit to his back. With tears running down his cheeks, sobbing at everything he had ever loved and lost, Nikanoras didn't look behind him. Mounting his horse in the blackest of night, he headed back up the hills hoping to find his way.

****

Meleagros did not hear him lift the tent flap as he slept.

Unburdening himself inside the tent of his kit and his clothing, Nikanoras was relieved to come back and set eyes on the only person who truly loved him.

Eager to hold him close for some much needed comfort, once Nikanoras stripped off his gear, he snaked his arms and legs around Meleagros' nakedness.

Meleagros moaned softly, as if half in dream, half awake.

"Nikki?" his voice was gravelly and distant.

"Go back to sleep, my lovely Eros." He squeezed him close, inhaling him and wrapping his legs around him.

"I never expected you back. Why so soon? I do not understand? We all thought you were gone from me. Gone for good. Please, what has happened? How is your father? Are you here to stay? Or—"

Exhausted from the journey, Nikanoras hushed him. "I am here to stay, in your arms where I belong. Sleep."

Nikanoras closed his eyes and rested his lips against Meleagros' neck, releasing a sigh that kissed him like a butterfly's wing. Soon after they both drifted off.

CHAPTER 17

With the view of Mt Olympus at their backs, shimmering with the rosy dawn on its snow-covered surface, they headed down the hills once more. They were to meet up with the regular army to go through maneuvers with them as they would in the real battles.

Having had little time in the morning to discuss the events of the night before, Meleagros was still wondering what his lover had been through. He did not even know yet he what had transpired with his father. It seemed to Meleagros, that Nikanoras needed to calm himself emotionally before discussing things with him. And on march, with so many other ears to eavesdrop, this was neither the time nor the place.

The descending trip less wearisome than the one up, they were down quickly, even with almost four hundred in the procession. North of their city of stone columns and gates, they paused at a field to meet with their cavalry, two-thousand horse; their hoplites, thirty thousand; and their light-armed troops, numbering five thousand.

It was an impressive gathering. Nikanoras looked to see Meleagros' expression. Nikanoras knew the sight of so much manpower would light him up like the eternal flames at an altar.

Antakinas called over the chaos for them to set aside their kits and come armed.

The men tossed their packs on the growing pile and rushed

excitedly to find their place in this unordered mass of confusion. As they stood impatiently, in perfect formation, they were the only regime to have such instant discipline and obedience. Around them as they remained at attention, the rest were slow to find their way.

The mounted generals were growing hoarse shouting for their men to come into line. When it was taking what appeared to be a disastrously long time, Nikanoras leaned on Meleagros' shoulder to whisper, "I do not believe this lack of organization."

Overhearing his comment, Chasathenes said out of the corner of his mouth, "It is an embarrassment."

Argos leaned in to the discussion, "We have only three hundred to organize, they have thousands. What do you expect?"

"I expect them to know their place." Nikanoras' comment was the loudest. One of the generals caught it giving him a warning and hand threat of punishment if he did not stay silent.

Biting his lip as he watched, standing stiff and as perfect as the other two hundred and ninety-nine of them, they must have appeared wooden soldiers by comparison.

What seemed to Nikanoras as hours of waiting, the mass of men finally calmed down to a silent army. In that large flat expanse, they stood tall as the captains instructed the troops on what was to be expected of them.

Nikanoras strained to hear. His men were to remain in the background until the light-armed troops opened a gap, then the band were to rush in. The aim was to kill either Philip or his son.

The powers that be thought they knew how the Macedonians would fight. Spies who were sent out to gather information and observe the battles involving Macedon, seemed to feel confident on their method.

The sudden sound of a horn blasting and their general's raised sword startled Nikanoras out of his daydream.

Roaring as they went with the light-armed troops before them, the men pretended to advance against an invisible foe in perfect formation; through the center, and what would presumably be the heart of the Macedonian army.

Rushing at air, slicing the wind, they practiced this pattern again and again. Try as he might, Nikanoras could not understand how this 'light' army would surpass those pike-men, and open up a thing, other than maybe their own chest cavities with the sharp sarissa. That was it.

And as far as Meleagros' strategy of coming in from behind, Nikanoras saw nothing of the sort.

By mid-day the sky opened up on them, drenching them to the skin. It mattered not to the captains, as they had them repeat the performance over and over. The churning on the grass became a muddy swamp within an hour, slipping and sliding them around like they were deer on ice.

By dusk Nikanoras could hardly see through the heavy torrent. The torches would not stay lit.

Finally the generals ordered them to halt their exercise. The men had an opportunity to catch their breath.

Nikanoras narrowed his eyes through that blinding sheet of rain. The crack of Zeus' lightning lit up over their heads.

They were released from battle to find their way back to their quarters. The plain clearing quickly, Nikanoras lost track of Meleagros. Checking every face under the concealing helmets, Nikanoras began to get a little upset that he had moved away from his side where he had been for the last nine hours of practice.

Bent over from the strain of the day, he foolishly became distracted staring at his mud-slopped feet when someone bumped him in the crowd. Jarred from the impact, Nikanoras raised his chin quickly to see through the dusky shower. A glimmer of silver startled him.

Nikanoras gasped at what seemed to be a knife moving swiftly toward the gap in the side of his armor. He managed to raise his shield, knocking the blade free from the clenched hand. When he unsheathed his sword to defend himself, only the splatter of soaked sandals met his ears as the assailant vanished into the murky blackness.

Sheathing his sword, Nikanoras picked up the knife. A short curved blade with a bone handle was almost his doom. After another glance around him, he swallowed his fear. How did he come to be where he was now, with so many wishing him dead?

When it appeared almost all of the soldiers had found their way home, Nikanoras heard some noise that caught his attention. A familiar thrilling shriek and giggle led him back to the field to find the rest of his comrades were doubled over with laughter.

Their shields set aside, their armor in a pile, they were sliding on the mud as if it were a sheet of frozen lake.

To his astonishment Nikanoras spotted, Argos, Chasathenes, Lysos, and Mycandor, Xenorus and Parmitheus, covered in shimmering mud from their toes to their chins. And who was sliding on bare feet as he approached? None other than his lovely Meleagros. The white of his teeth shone through his brown clay covering as he shook with such silly laughter, Nikanoras was instantly lightened at the sound.

"What on earth are you doing?" Nikanoras asked as he doubled over with laughter like the rest. "Look at you all. Like wild boars rolling in sloppy mud."

"We wondered where you were," Argos replied. "Meleagros was convinced you left us all behind to get clean."

"I see you had intentions of the opposite." Crossing his arms, Nikanoras shook his head at their state.

"Come. You must try it." Meleagros rushed at him.

"No. And get as filthy as a hog? Are you mad? I am beyond famished, and in need of some wine and a soak. I desire not, a coating of mud." He cringed away from Meleagros' sticky fingers.

"You see?" Mycandor gestured his way. "He is too serious. He knows not how to have fun."

"Then we shall help him get less serious." Meleagros began advancing on him.

When the others guessed his lover's intention, Nikanoras found himself surrounded by mud-covered fiends.

"No. No! Stop this. Can't we just get clean and eat? I am too tired." He whined pathetically.

As if on command, Nikanoras was jumped by seven and pinned to the ground as his gear was stripped off. And through it all, the rain battered and the thunder blasted overhead. No amount of protest could stop the attack.

Once his coverings were ripped off, Nikanoras was raised up and carried to the deepest of mud puddles. Though he flailed violently, he could not break the grip of so many.

They dropped him in the mud and then landed on him, making sure he was coated in brown, for they missed not one bit of clean skin.

A slithering pile they had become, and Nikanoras was laughing so hard he could not breathe.

Though he had a mind to admonish their dirty deed, it felt good to laugh. Nikanoras forgot the near tragic act of only a moment before.

As the squirming became arousing, Nikanoras found his lover had maneuvered to the top of him, sliding along his slimy length, the gleam of his lovely light eyes like the fire of an eternal torch. Using the mud like oil, Meleagros rubbed his excited body over Nikanoras.

"You are a very naughty boy." Nikanoras giggled seductively into his grin. Most of the men who were rough-housing were sporting a stiff cock.

"And you are a very perceptive one." Meleagros laughed, kissed him, and held him tight, rolling them over so Nikanoras was on top. When Meleagros spread his legs, allowing Nikanoras to fall between his thighs, Nikanoras looked around. None of the other friends were paying attention, having fun with their own lovers in the downpour. When Nikanoras met Meleagros' light eyes he smiled. "Yes."

"Yes?" Meleagros' expression lit up.

"Yes," Nikanoras repeated, as if it was clarifying.

Meleagros nudged Nikanoras off his hips and grabbed both of their stiff lengths in one hand, pressing them together.

As Meleagros pleasured them, Nikanoras closed his eyes and felt the cleansing rain pelt his skin as he heard Meleagros' pleasure moan in his ears.

CHAPTER 18

Clean, fed, and sated with wine, the three pairs of men sat together in one of the common buildings attached to their quarters; a modestly decorated hall with columned and arched walls that opened in all four directions to the rest of the complex that housed the soldiers. Unadorned except for the a main frieze above the columns of the battle of Troy, and a lone statue of Athena in her helm near a fountain, it was a calming place to come and share ideas before bed.

Oil lamps flickered and shivered on an invisible breeze, as they sat on stone benches and finished the wine they had brought with them. They had been given the night off after their muddy battle to do as they wished. Most of the boys had gone home to their families. The four of them chose to stay at the barracks.

Out of their confining armor for once, they dressed in their casual white mantles and sandals, relieved of the chaffing for one night. Meleagros seemed more himself in the dress, his brown chest and right shoulder bare, his long washed hair dusting it as he spoke.

The others too, appeared more at ease for once in a long while. The wine and food had been well deserved after what felt as if it were a year on that mountain. Wars were generally fought in the summer, so they knew they had some time yet before they would be called into a real skirmish. Though Nikanoras could guarantee they would not lavish in that place for long, for if they were allowed to stay in some place warmer than a tent, it would be only after ten to twelve hours of practice.

As he sat and sipped the wine, the conversations of his companions like a pleasant hum in his ears, Nikanoras thought about going home, almost defiantly. But, what would be the point? To see his mother in Arybos' arms? Or perhaps she had shorn her hair for his father's funeral. He laughed spitefully.

If he did not go, he would not find out the truth. And his imagination was enough torture without that knowledge. So, here he sat, with his closest companions, sharing a moment of peace and harmony.

One knows too well, peace does not last forever, for it is in men's nature to seek some kind of turmoil and fight for a parcel of land. Sparta ruled for four hundred years before they destroyed her. Those savages raped and pillaged to their hearts' content, until the power of Thebes put a stop to them. They continued to stick their chests out proudly at that feat though it had happened decades before they were even born.

The thought of his own father revealing secrets to that race of barbarians curdled Nikanoras' blood. It is best he learned these things after his death, for he would have shunned him like a leper had he known prior.

Having Arybos' will over him must have made his father's life torture. Nikanoras knew it had his own. Some relief he did finally feel knowing Arybos could no longer offer him any harm. He had succeeded in isolating his mother to remarry and claim her wealth. And she so readily eager for his company, what more could they want of him? It was agreed that he must die in battle. Of that he was ready. But, of this other threat? The one that wanted to kill him from behind, he worried more.

That Persepolos had bribed or had power over his own Thebans to order his death, premature of battle, was more troubling than all else. Could everyone not be content that he will die when they battled Macedon? Why the rush?

His lover too silent for his liking, Meleagros kept a wary eye on him. They had discussed nothing. Not since he returned in the night from his home. And that silence drove Meleagros mad. It was as if he were closed out of Nikanoras' life. That Nikanoras had tiny doors in his head and chose where and when his lover could enter, while Meleagros knew he gave all to Nikanoras without hesitation.

There were no secrets he harbored, nothing he could not reveal. The wall needed tearing down, and Meleagros was only biding time for the moment to destroy it.

As if Meleagros' brooding had penetrated his own mind, Nikanoras still had not had the chance to speak to Meleagros alone.

Unaware of Meleagros' thoughts, Nikanoras wondered if he had given up wondering what had passed on his trip home. Or was Meleagros content to wait for the right moment for him to reveal it? If it be the latter, Meleagros surely was learning quickly.

"What of the method? It is what they had used against Sparta." Mycandor appeared like the god Hermes, for he was very thin and tall. Especially in comparison with his shorter partner, Argos, whose profile was outstanding with such a fine nose.

"You all go on about something you can do nothing about," Meleagros said.

"How do you know we can do nothing? If half of the Band act up, then they must listen." Nikanoras was not to be told he could have no opinion in something that risked all their lives.

Lysos tossed back his blond mane, a color that was rare for this city of tanned skin and black hair. "To die in battle is a gift to Athena. Epaminondas and Pelopidas did not flinch, yet died proudly."

"True, but to live victorious is more my liking." Nikanoras growled. "What use are they to us dead? We need them both here alive. Have you no idea of what those men went through to secure Thebes? And look at us now. Are we secure?"

This chronic debate over tactics was upsetting Nikanoras. The evening had begun on a more passive note of conversation about food and wine.

"Change the subject lest Nikanoras storms off for home," Chasathenes said.

"Enough." Meleagros shook his head.

155

Finishing his last gulp of wine, and wishing he had still more, Nikanoras met each stare, one by one, as they stared back at him. "My father has died."

The exclamations of astonishment followed, with Meleagros the worst, infuriated he had waited so long to tell him.

"I am so sorry, Nikanoras. Forgive me for not knowing." Chasathenes frowned sympathetically.

"Nikki." Meleagros turned to face him. "Why did he die? What cause?"

"A fever, or so I am told. By the look of their attachment, you needn't ask if it would surprise me if Arybos and Mother planned his murder." Nikanoras stared at the empty cup, pleading it would magically refill itself.

"Do not say such things." Argos shook his head in admonishment.

"Thessenike and Arybos?" Argos' lover mused at the odd couple. "No. You have no reason to suspect that."

"Don't I?" A laugh erupted from Nikanoras' throat. "He brings me there to see my father on his death bed. Too late. Says Arybos that my father had been debating only a day before. How can I believe this when he is lying dead and cold? He hisses venomous lies to me. Then, my mother seeks comfort in his arms. Before my very eyes. And at the markets. Remember? I spied them together." Nikanoras was near tears, but this burden needed lifting.

Meleagros reached out to touch his lover's hand.

As for the rest, they were studying him silently. Nikanoras was not one to reveal his feelings, or family secrets easily. So, they gave him the most respect they could. Silently allowing him his say, and giving him their complete attention and sympathy for it.

It is sometimes a hard lesson to learn who your truest friends are, but Nikanoras was surrounded by the truest comrades a man could hope to find.

"Then," he continued, "When it is obvious he has been living in my house, orders my slaves like he already owns them, he comes to me, like he is still my erastes, angry when I shun him."

This news enraged Meleagros to a new height. Nikanoras heard him curse under his breath, and his fingers gripped his hand tightly. "If he touches you, I shall kill him," he said.

"You need go back," Chasathenes said, "Though you loathe the idea, you must, Nikanoras. You must claim your house."

"I cannot." The lump in his throat almost choked him. "My mother, herself, expelled me from it. If I go back, I will again be sent away. Or poisoned."

"You must fight," Lysos said in anger.

"Fight? And kill my mother and mentor? Are you drunk?" A cool sweat had broken on Nikanoras' face. The damage this conversation was doing to his insides was beginning to surface on the outside.

On the edge of his seat, Meleagros heard the arguments. He knew what leaving that house and staying with the Band would bring to his lover. The decision Nikanoras had made to stay with him astonished Meleagros. If he had heard this story before this night, he would have laid bets Nikanoras would never return to fight with them again. Even with Thessenike's imposed exile, Meleagros would have thought Nikanoras would demand his inheritance, and begged the senate to intervene on his behalf. And they would have.

But, only Nikanoras knew, if he chosen that way, Arybos would expose his father's past and not only would Nikanoras lose all, but his name and his father's name would be spat upon.

"But, you have so much to lose," Argos said, his own anger mounting. "Let us go with you. Together we can rid Arybos from your house. I shall slay him for you."

"Listen to yourselves." Nikanoras replied, "Yes, what if. Say it is how you dream, we go there. Chase him out or murder him. To what end? Then if we leave on practice, or to battle, and in grief my mother either kills herself or sets a trap and poisons me. What use then? You do not see. She loves him. It is my guess she has always loved him in spite of my father's existence. If I bring Arybos harm do you believe that leads me any closer to owning what is mine?"

Taking a few deep breaths, he spoke more softly to say, "For men who are born of aristocracy and diplomats, you are all spouting nonsense. Your plans of murder will bring me back to Thebes in chains."

In the following quiet moment they all thought of ways to combat the problem. "What if you were to go to the council first?" Lysos asked. "Seek help there."

"From whom? Xenophos?" Meleagros laughed sarcastically as he mentioned his father.

"No. Perhaps not your father, Meleagros. But, there must be someone who knows you, Nikanoras, who will hear your plea." Lysos sat up straight.

"No one knows me. You do not understand. Father bred me for war, not politics. What purpose would there have been for him to bring me to council? No, forget this. I did not bring it up to debate. It is merely a fact." He had enough. His head was beginning to pound with the frustration.

After some careful silent deliberation, Mycandor whispered sadly, "If his mother wishes to marry Arybos, then there is naught Nikanoras can do. I am afraid he is right."

"We are too young." Lysos sighed loudly. "Old enough for battle, but still too young to assert ourselves. Surely, Nikanoras, you are not the only one this has befallen. Others have walked your path."

"I wish Euridises were alive." Nikanoras held back a sob of anguish. "She would have her say with mother. At least she would make her promise to leave something over to me, and not to all of Arybos' heirs to come."

Feeling Meleagros' warm hand on his back, Nikanoras felt comfort from his lover. Meleagros' grey eyes were filled with emotion and complete empathy for his plight. Nikanoras managed a smile for him.

In the silence around them, the two couples nudged each other to take their leave and let Nikanoras and Meleagros alone.

The whispering sounds of their sandals vanished through the stone archways into the darkness.

Meleagros scooted closer to Nikanoras on the bench, wrapping his arm around his shoulders. "You have sacrificed so much, Nikki. I am so sorry."

Trying to rid the strain in his body, he straightened his back and said, "No, I don't feel I have sacrificed a thing to be here with you. The more I learn, the more I realize you are the only person that means anything in my life. You and our friends." He tilted his head to the direction they had left in. "It only makes me believe this is where I was meant to be. To fight with you, to win, and to then come home victorious and claim what is mine."

"And I shall be beside you, Nikki. After we defeat Macedon, I shall come here again with you and we shall take back your inheritance."

As far as Nikanoras was concerned, kinder words were never spoken. Nikanoras rested his hand on his lover's bare shoulder feeling unbelievable warmth emitting from it. "Thank you, Meleagros. I do not know what this world would be like without you in it. I would be lost."

"But you are not lost. And I am here. I will always be here beside you, Nikki. No one will ever tear me from you."

Meleagros' blue/grey eyes catching the last of the flickering oil lamp's light, his long dark soft hair covering his forehead and dusting his shoulders, Nikanoras gazed in awe at the ethereal beauty of him wondering why he had been chosen. Why and how he had found a friend who was better to him than was his own mother.

After giving Meleagros a light kiss, Nikanoras rose up and reached out his hand, bringing him back to their room for his reward.

CHAPTER 19

A day off was like a blessing from Dionysus, sweet and luxurious. The blackened clouds had parted and the sun shone bright on that crisp fall day. For once they cared not to hear the rumblings of war and Macedon, and decided on hunting after giving a votive to Artemis at her shrine. With a quiver filled with arrows, and a bow, they headed into the woods, not far from the trail they had taken up to the top with their squadron. In the tall tree-lined canopy, the sun flickered and danced on the leaves that were still falling from the branches stubbornly refusing to let go of their birthplace. The sounds of birds flocking together at the highest of limbs filled the breezeless air with a wintry song.

Hungry for the game of stalking, they made for a likely spot where Meleagros had seen a herd of deer prior to joining the band. It was long ago, four years, but he remembered well where his father had led.

"A herd like I have never seen, Nikki." Meleagros adjusted the quiver on his shoulder. "The bucks had enormous antlers on their heads, like crowns of royalty." Pushing some low scrub aside, he paused to listen. "Nikki." He waved him over. "Look. A cascade."

As Nikanoras drew closer Meleagros said, "No. More like a crashing river." Waving in excitement, Meleagros shouted, "Come look!"

On feathered feet they crept to the edge of a chasm that dropped off to a rushing waterfall to peer at the depths. The sound was inviting, so they stood still, taking in the presence of the goddess and the natural beauty around them.

"What a vision." Nikanoras crouched down to enjoy its tranquility, almost falling prey to its hypnotic powers. "The sound, it is like a sweet melody, do you not think?" The smile on his lips, Nikanoras glanced back to see Meleagros standing away from the edge.

"Do not get too close, Nikki." Meleagros took a wary step back.

Turning again to the pristine view, Nikanoras sighed, inhaling the fragrant plants and flowers around him. "Do you think it a good omen? The goddess will lead us to her herd?"

"Perhaps." Meleagros gazed at the silent woods around them.

Hypnotized by the sound of the water and the intriguing patterns of the white foam as it roared over the cliff, Nikanoras relaxed, contented to stare, drifting off at the delightful combination.

Meleagros said, "Time to continue on."

Sighing at giving up such a lovely spot, Nikanoras rose from his crouch to join his lover. Standing too quickly from such a low position on the grass, lightness came to his head. Following this dizziness, a strange darkness plagued his sight as his senses drew to a close narrow tunnel.

As he tried to clear his vision, shaking his head, Nikanoras' footing slipped at the edge of the ravine. With the surge of adrenaline that followed, his senses returned just as he fell. Hearing Meleagros shout his name in terror, Nikanoras grabbed savagely at anything he could to stop what he knew would be a murderous plunge. His left hand grasped a protruding tree root just before his momentum had dragged him into oblivion. With his feet dangling, he used his toes to kick and dig into the sandy soil trying to find a hold.

Meleagros tossed his quiver and bow to the ground and lay flat, extending himself over the edge to reach him. "No! Nikki! Hold on!"

At the sound of some tearing, Nikanoras could see the root he was gripping was raising itself out of the earth. Craning upwards, he witnessed Meleagros' panic, as he reached as far as he could, coming within a breath of his hand.

After his fall, Nikanoras' bow had slung back over his right shoulder freeing his right arm. Desperately Nikanoras felt around for anything he could to raise up that small amount he needed to touch those outstretched fingers. "If I pull you, we shall both go!" he cried.

"No! Do not despair. I can haul you up."

"I will not pull you to your death!" Nikanoras shouted over the sound of crashing water under him.

"If you let go, I shall never forgive you!" he yelled, "Can you get your feet into anything?"

His right hand clenching that lone root as well, Nikanoras peered over his shoulder to see the height, which was not a good decision, for it sent a terrible flutter through his mid-section.

"Do not look down!" Meleagros scolded in fury. "Nikki, concentrate."

Knowing Meleagros would most likely jump if he fell, to certain death, Nikanoras felt around with his feet for anything sturdy enough to press down on. The sound of sand raining frightened him as he imagined he was digging a hollow to undermine the piece of dirt Meleagros was occupying. It was all very dismal, and he could see no pleasant end. Finding a patch of blue through the thick canopy of trees, he called to the gods, "Is this how you want my demise? To die here and never see battle as you have asked of me since I was born?"

"Nikki! Shut up and climb!" Precariously Meleagros edged even further out.

Nikanoras used his feet to hunt for a foothold as the root was making horrible snapping noises. Nikanoras moaned in defeat, "By the gods...it is the end, lover."

"No! No!" Meleagros lowered one end of his bow, almost poked Nikanoras in the face with it. "Grab it!"

With his right hand Nikanoras did, squeezing the bent wood in a death grip. "Do not get pulled over!"

Meleagros grunted at the strain.

Nikanoras was edged up just enough to give him new hope. Trying not to tug on the bow with the amount of force he really needed to get up, for he knew one good yank and Meleagros would sail over his head to certain death, he kicked his feet once again and to his astonishment he felt his foot find a solid hold.

Pressing his weight on it, he was gradually being pulled over the lip of dirt he had fallen from. Just as his left foot lifted off that stone, he heard it crash to the bottom rocks, ricocheting with high-pitched notes like plucking a lyre.

A very strong hand grabbed the material of his mantle from behind his head. Between the scrambling of his arms and legs, and Meleagros' brute strength, Nikanoras was pulled up from the precipice of death.

Once over the top, Nikanoras lay on his face on firm ground. Meleagros was seated, legs splayed, panting for air. They were frozen for the time, trying to recuperate. When he could move, Nikanoras raised his head. Sweat had coated Meleagros and drenched his skin. His pupils were constricted, and he could not catch his breath no matter how hard he tried to stop gasping.

On his elbows and knees Nikanoras crawled to him, wrapping his arms and legs around him. And when they embraced they cried.

"Thank you. Oh, Meleagros, thank you."

"I would not let you go." He sobbed. "Not like this. We are not ready yet. Not like this." Meleagros ran his hands over Nikanoras' face and hair, touching him as if to reassure himself he was truly there and in one piece.

"I do not know how it happened. All I did was try to stand and—"

"No. Do not speak of it. I cannot endure it. You are here in my arms, safe."

Sighing with relief, Nikanoras lay his head down on his lover's chest and closed his eyes to hear the chirping of the birds and that near fatal song of the waterfall in the background, not nearly loud enough to cover the throbbing beat of his heart.

Nikanoras didn't know how long they stayed there, silent, except for the pounding of their pulse, but when they opened their eyes it was late afternoon, almost dusk. In that moment of destiny Nikanoras decided to trust in Meleagros with all his heart, and that meant with all his secrets as well.

When Nikanoras leaned up over him to see if he slept, Meleagros' eyes were wide and unblinking, gazing at the patches of sky seen through the towering trees. "Meleagros."

He nodded at the serious tone. "What is it, my dearest, Nikki?"

Nikanoras tugged on Meleagros to get him to sit up so they may face each other. Nikanoras inhaled and revealed something he never thought he would burden him with. "Twice now someone has tried to take my life."

"The arrow," he said like he was revealing the answer. "When else?"

"The other night, in the mud-filled field. I was attacked with a dagger. This dagger." He produced it from his waistband, handing it to Meleagros.

Taking it delicately, Meleagros studied it as if he were trying to identify, then met his eyes. "Who?"

"It must be the general."

"Persepolos."

"Yes. With Arybos feasting on his father's wine, I doubt he will hurry my death. He knows my fate is in battle, but—"

"But, your sister's widower will not wait." The anger rose in Meleagros appeared to rise.

"I am helpless, Meleagros. I cannot accuse him."

Stabbing the dagger into the grass, Meleagros growled. "Why do you not tell me these things?"

"I am telling you now." Nikanoras tried to hold his hands to stop his anger.

Meleagros let go a sigh and appeared most unhappy. "You trust no one. Are all your companions so unworthy, Nikki?"

"No. I trust you, my lover. Only you." Gently Nikanoras caressed his jaw, making sure Meleagros met his eyes to judge his sincerity.

"Maybe we can reveal his plot to one of our own commanders. Surely there is someone who will listen and believe."

"Don't be a fool. Believe us? Against a man so powerful? No, it is useless, my love. I simply must remain vigilant."

Biting his lip in anger, Meleagros then said, "You have enough to deal with battling the enemy. How are you to mind your back as well? And what of another arrow? One closer to the mark? I say we set a trap with our comrades and find this menace, getting him to tell the tale."

At the idea of others knowing his personal problems, Nikanoras shivered in fear.

Seeing that tremor course through him, Meleagros gripped his arm. "The faith you have in me you must also have in the two hundred ninety-eight others. They are sworn brethren, and have only loyalty to one another. If you believe in me, believe in your fellow Sacred Band members. They are not traitors, they will not fail you."

An army of three hundred seemed mighty against such a tiny threat. But the guilt of using his men to watch over him, when each had more important things to deal with, seemed humiliating at the very least.

Meleagros touched his lover's face tenderly. "Believe in me," Meleagros whispered.

The stress dropping off his shoulders at the burden released, Nikanoras said, "I do, my lover. I do." After receiving his kiss, Nikanoras added, "There is one ally."

"Whom? Please, Nikki, we need all the help we can muster."

"Antakinas. Remember after he spoke to us of the war of Leuctra?"

"When he asked you for your help? Yes, of course." Meleagros appeared annoyed at yet another secret that had been hidden for weeks.

"It is he who warned me. Beware Persepolos he said, though I already knew to watch my back from that day on."

"Then you have more friends than you think." Meleagros made like he would stand, readying them for some decisive action.

"Wait." Nikanoras grabbed him, dragging him back down. "Not yet. Let the world wait another moment, my lovely Eros."

Meleagros lay beside him.

"Come to me." Nikanoras reached out hungrily. "Come, let me somehow show my gratitude."

A soft contented smile forming on his lips, Meleagros moved into his embrace, finding his mouth. At his kiss, Meleagros choked up in emotion. When he could he whispered, "I love you, my beautiful Nikki, never doubt the capacity or purity of that love."

"Oh, my gorgeous Herakles." Nikanoras sighed, squeezing him

tightly. "It is the same for me. I love you."

Nikanoras inched his way down Meleagros' body, kissing as he went. Hearing Meleagros moan and feeling his response made Nikanoras happy. At least he could do something right. He took Meleagros' length into his mouth and sucked.

Instantly Meleagros' hips rose off the ground and his fingers clawed the weeds and rocks.

Nikanoras couldn't deny he enjoyed contact with his lover, and the more he appreciated Meleagros for his honor and kindness, the more Nikanoras chose to please him.

"Nikki!"

Chills washed over Nikanoras' skin at his lover's pleasure. He caught the seed on his tongue as it shot into his mouth. Once Meleagros slowed his thrusting hips, Nikanoras spat the seed into his hand and used it as lubrication on himself. Meleagros parted his legs and bent his knees.

Nikanoras kissed his way back up his lover's body, and penetrated him. Kneeling between Meleagros' powerful thighs, Nikanoras claimed this man again. *You are mine.*

He shivered as he came and threw back his head. When he opened his eyes, Meleagros was staring at him with so much adoration, Nikanoras knew there would never be another one like him. He pulled out and embraced his partner, rolling with him on the forest floor, exchanging kisses.

****

Their hunting expedition gone awry, they decided to head to the top of the mountain to give thanks to the gods. It seemed important to show their appreciation. They were so near it only took moments to find the peak which consisted of a clearing with a large stone stained with blood from previous sacrifices. Not wanting to come empty handed, they had gathered some brightly colored leaves which Nikanoras had woven into a crown.

As he set it on top of the boulder and knelt down to give homage, Meleagros grabbed his arm in alarm and pointed. The land faced west across the inlet of water that separated their hilly mountains from the peninsula they had held training on. There in the distance was a very distinct line of torches. An army was on the move.

"Macedon?" Nikanoras gasped.

"Who else? Back to Pella." Meleagros squinted, trying to see clearly at such a great distance.

"Do they march here?" His heart was back in his throat again.

"I don't think so. Look. The torches disappear west. They are not bending with the land south."

"Maybe they were asea. They have a fleet." Nikanoras could just make out the last few flames as they vanished into the depth of the woods.

"Not as strong as Athens. No, Philip will not want a sea battle. His power is with his cavalry and phalanx."

Feeling drained completely, Nikanoras sank to the dirt with the sacrificial stone at his back.

Meleagros raised the ring of red and gold leaves and set the crown on Nikanoras' head. "King Nikanoras, I bring you great gifts."

Slanting his eye at him, Nikanoras smiled at the thought.

In his booming voice Meleagros said, "Tell us, oh wise King, what is it you would like, most in the world? If it is in my power, I shall give it to you."

Playing his game, he said, "Very well, kind soldier, bring me the head of the King of Macedon. And then there will be peace in all of Thebes."

"Your wish is my command, oh Great One." Meleagros bowed with a flourish and they giggled at each other. Twirling around, his white chlamys flaring, Meleagros raised his hand high. "Behold, King Nikanoras. The head of the King of Macedon."

"Are you sure that is his head?" Nikanoras scratched his jaw and stared into the empty air under Meleagros' fist.

"Of course, Your Highness. You see his fat goat face and blinded eye."

"How do you know he has a blinded eye?" Nikanoras had no idea whether to believe his ravings.

"It is common knowledge, Your Lordship." He bowed again, still keeping the imaginary head aloft.

Nikanoras rose to his feet and pretended to have a closer look. "If you say this is indeed the King of Macedon, then this means Alexander is now on the throne. And what shall we do about him?"

The light of the growing full moon sparkled in his grey eyes, "Do? With pretty Prince Alexander? Why, invite him for wine. After he is drunk, we shall do as we wish with him."

"I see. Toss that thing. It sickens me." Nikanoras pointed to the imaginary head.

Giving a very good impression of one spinning for a shot-put toss, Meleagros heaved it over the side of the mountain. As he brushed off his hands from the deed, he said, "Thus ends the cruel reign of Philip of Macedon. Long live King Nikanoras."

A sound was heard in the dense wood behind him. "Shush." Nikanoras warned and waved him closer.

Immediately Meleagros armed his bow. "What did you hear?"

"Something shuffling. I do not know."

"With one scare enough for the day, let's head down the mountain. There are some rogue hill tribes about, and I've no doubt they would seek these woods as cover."

Standing silent to listen before they moved, they gathered their possessions and headed back to the city. Before they did, Nikanoras left the wreath of leaves on the stone, then unsheathed his saber and began their descent with very sharp eyes and ears.

****

Once they had made their way to their quarters, Nikanoras and Meleagros made the effort to find food and eat. The day had drained them horribly, and Nikanoras did not want to tell their friends of his near miss with death on the cliff. Luckily, Meleagros was no braggart, and kept his private life just that. He didn't need to boast about saving a life. Meleagros had too much ego and needed no more acclaim. A boy of so much beauty, he was well guarded even at an early age by his nursemaids.

Though sometimes his conceit emerged like the rocky shore from a receding tide, he pretended to be humble and even feigned embarrassment when complimented. Maybe Meleagros' insecurity with his lover was because Nikanoras had never fed him those words. Never fawned over him like some others had. Not blind, Nikanoras knew Meleagros was perfect, what need had he to remind him over and over, like some sycophant hoping for gain.

Nor was Nikanoras envious, for he never considered himself unpleasant, and in Nikanoras' mind he knew if he could attract and hold someone like Meleagros, he must surely be on his par, though he would never openly ask if he were. It seemed useless folly, all this talk of beauty.

Beauty was held with such esteem, Nikanoras couldn't walk a step without some image carved of marble in the likeness of a god. In reality he knew it was sculpted from a lovely male or female that had lent their form to the maker. Ideal beauty means nothing, if inside the outer shell there is bitterness or hatred. Luckily for Nikanoras, his lover had only the mildest of tempers, except in war.

Walking wearily passed the image of Apollo towering over them in an arcade, Nikanoras glimpsed at that marble profile quickly, then at his own hero. By far his was the fairest. "I can barely walk. I fear I am more exhausted now than from the battle practices."

Meleagros smiled, but looked tired. "It is the fright. It has drained the life from us. I swear, Nikki, I have never felt a surge through my body as I did when you slipped off the edge of that ravine."

Nikanoras caught up to walk by Meleagros' side not even realize his fatigue was dragging him behind. "Maybe it was another type of surge that wore you out."

169

Meleagros' light eyes shining brilliantly with the tease, he wrapped his arm around Nikanoras' waist to purr. "Mm, Nikki, I crave you like wine."

"And I crave you, you pampered pet." Nikanoras rested his head on Meleagros' muscular shoulder.

A soft chuckle emerged from Meleagros at the label. "Yes. I was."

"Still are." Nikanoras winked at him.

Allowing his lover to enter their quarters first, Nikanoras set his bow and quiver against the dry mud wall by the door. When he straightened his back to find Meleagros doing the same, he said, out of thin air, "Do you think of your mother?"

"At times." Meleagros began disrobing, taking his tunic over his head. When he was naked he sat on their bed, waiting for Nikanoras to join him. "I loathe speaking of her, Nikki."

"Do you?" Nikanoras draped his clothing over Meleagros' and then cuddled with him on the small bed. "Why?"

Meleagros said, "Because she is kind. More like Euridises than Thessenike, and I don't want you to be jealous. But it does me no good to mourn our separation. My departure from her home was not like the events at your palace, Nikki. No." Meleagros hesitated before continuing, making sure Nikanoras wasn't taking this explanation the wrong way. "I wanted to be here. I had loving support for it from both my parents, and even from my brother, Ephisomines. Well, he was such a disappointment to mother, I had to see to it she had one son about whom she could stick out her chest in pride."

Remembering that effeminate man clearly, Nikanoras said, "But it seems likely your bother will not marry. What if you are to be slain in battle? Who will carry the family name?"

Smiling sweetly, caressing Nikanoras' long locks, Meleagros answered, "He will marry, lover. Though he detests the touch of a woman, he will marry. Father no doubt has that plan already in place."

"Are you jealous? Do you wish it were you that had the future of a wife and family?" Nikanoras was so envious of that limp-wristed aristocrat he could scream at the injustice.

And Meleagros knew he was. "No," he said simply.

Lying back with a sigh, Nikanoras stared at the dank ceiling of their tiny quarters to stew about that eternal question. Why could he not be happy where he was now?

Running his hand from the nape of Nikanoras' neck to his pubic hair, Meleagros exhaled a breath that was a mixture of his exhaustion and his contentment. "I do not envy my brother, Nikki." Delicately he brushed his hand over Nikanoras' crotch. "For I would not trade places with him for all the gold in Thebes' treasury."

Nikanoras whispered, "I would imagine that is not very much."

Meleagros nuzzled into his hair. "I would continue to praise your virtues all night, Nikki, but forgive me. I am so weary, I cannot keep awake."

"Good night, sweet Meleagros. May the gods grant you peace in the night."

Their long day off, slowly at an end, they felt the coming dawn with a sensation akin to dread, for the new lessons of battle they would endure would surely leave scars.

Days of leisure were soon passed into memory, and over the next two years they had too few to count. But, of the ones they shared, that day had, with all its peril, brought them as close as any two humans could be.

CHAPTER 20

Unknown to Nikanoras, his lover had taken no time at all to alert his closest companions to his plight.

They were shocked to find out that a general so trusted and honored would stoop as low as to send paid assassins into battle with them. They were more than happy to watch over Nikanoras and find the general's minions who were so bold as to threaten to kill one of the Sacred Band.

Once again at night, fighting their mock battles armed with wooden swords and shields, they were made to work until exhaustion.

Half the Theban army boasted feathered crests on their helms to differentiate one side from the other; the brilliant red of his own battalion against the white of their faux enemy.

No one was to get injured seriously, as again, if one struck a simulated blow that was fatal, one was supposed to fall. Most were happy to drop down to the ground, getting to rest after so grueling a day. But not the Sacred Band. No one would be accused of falling, or even worse, pretending to get injured to be out of play.

Meleagros at his side, Argos and Mycandor not far from his left, Lysos and Chasathenes near the right, the group plowed over the enemy soldiers like battering rams. Their progress was forcing a gap behind them as the rest of the squadron battled their left and right flanks as they were attacked by the cavalry.

Because of their progress Nikanoras' back was exposed. It didn't take long for someone to take advantage of his vulnerability.

When a live arrow, complete with a metal point came from the dark, it cut through Nikanoras' left shoulder, grazing him. He screamed in pain, spinning around wildly, trying to find the raised bow.

"Nikki!" Meleagros spotted the blood oozing from the slice and called to the men, "Behind! The assassin is behind. Live arrows!"

With Nikanoras' head still spinning at the turn of events and the pain, forty men in hearing range pivoted on their heels and roared like lions as they ran into the rest of the Sacred Band. When Band members faced Band members, the chaos was extreme.

In the darkness, Meleagros was leading the group passed their astonished comrades, and sniffing out the odd one. The one who would be fleeing with a full quiver of arrows.

Their commanders noticed the disarray. On horseback they were trying to understand why half the Band was advancing backwards against itself.

The mass of tangled lines and wooden swords was blinding it was so disorganized.

With his teeth snarled in fury, Meleagros was shouting his intentions to the rest of their squadron as they gaped in awe at this backwards advance. "An armed quiver!" he yelled, "Find him!"

Three hundred men strong and angry didn't wait to ask who or why. But hunting like a wild pack of bloodthirsty dogs until they finally knew the reason for the madness.

The commanders called a halt to the exercise, trying to locate the centre of the confusion. They attempted to stop the action and separate the two sides. When they met each other on horseback they shrugged in bewilderment, for none of them could determine why the entire Band had seemed to retreat in on itself.

With Meleagros leading the way, pushing stunned players of the battle aside as he sought out the one, the men of the Sacred Band caught a single male fleeing through the darkness. A Scythian mercenary.

With several alerting the rest of their discovery, the entire band veered and crashed through the thick trees, pitch dark, but for the peeking out of the moon's face from the drifting clouds.

As their group came to a halt, someone indicated a man had been caught.

Nikanoras caught his breath, bending over his knees to recover. It wasn't until he stood straight that he realized he was completely surrounded by his closest friends. All facing outwards, like wild animals that guard their young, they were protecting him with their lives. Too stunned to speak Nikanoras could only swallow the dryness in his throat in awe.

When one of their generals, Coninious, finally corralled them to scream in anger, the Scythian was produced for him; a stranger to them all. This man was thrown on his face before the general and his full quiver was produced with bladed tips.

General Coninious dismounted his horse and approached this prisoner. "I demand to know what is going on!"

Meleagros grabbed Nikanoras' arm and dragged him front and center. "Sir. May we have a word?"

Nikanoras shivered at the intimidation he felt to be the cause of so much trouble. He lowered his eyes humbly as his lover relayed his information.

"Nikanoras was his target. You see how close he came." He moved Nikanoras so the general could see his sliced skin. "A paid assassin is here. Make him tell you whom he works for."

The general stepped closer and studied Meleagros. "Why do I get the impression you already know this, Meleagros?"

"I want you to hear it from him." He pointed to the captive, his teeth showing in his fury.

The general was now surrounded by almost three hundred angry warriors of the Band. He had little choice. He kicked the captive man to get his attention. "By whom were you paid?"

When the captive refused to answer, the general warned, "If you tell, you live, if you do not tell, I shall let all three hundred get a piece of you."

As the whites of the prisoner's eyes showed to this mob of soldiers, Nikanoras could see him swallow in a large gulp. "General Persepolos paid me. By the gods he will kill me now himself."

A murmur rushed around the perimeter. Nikanoras lowered his head in shame.

His commander appeared to have no idea what to do with that knowledge. He looked stunned.

Meleagros was not going to let the general off easily. "All this murderous planning, simply for that day of the funeral of his wife. My Nikki, in his distress over missing his sister's funeral rites, insulted the general in public. Surely you remember."

Nikanoras could see that day did ring a bell with the general.

"Seek Antakinas," Nikanoras finally said, "He knows."

"Take him away." The general waved to his staff to get the captive out of the crowd, then he walked closer to Nikanoras to speak quietly. "I am not sure what I can do with this knowledge, Nikanoras."

"You see. They protect the guilty when it is each other," Meleagros said, pointing an accusing finger and making sure the rest of the squadron heard.

Though Nikanoras reached to calm him for fear of reprisals, he, himself, was no less angry.

"But," General Coninious continued, "I assure you this will be the last attempt on your life by him."

"Thank you, sir." It had to be good enough. What else could Nikanoras do?

"Assured?" Meleagros coughed in disbelief. "You assure us? That is it?"

Reaching for him to shut him up before the wrath of the commander was aimed his way, Nikanoras grabbed his lover and shook him. "Enough, Meleagros. Let him deal with it."

"He 'assures' us," he muttered, getting nods in agreement from several others close by.

As the general headed off on horseback to resolve the ordeal, the commanders cancelled the rest of the mock battle and told the men they were free to go.

While Meleagros inspected his lover's cut skin, which had stopped bleeding and dried to a crackled smear, the men of his Band touched Nikanoras in reassurance that no one would harm him that way.

With tears in his eyes, Nikanoras nodded in thanks, knowing he had two hundred and ninety-nine blood brothers. It was more than he could have hoped for in all his life.

As the pack waned and only his very closest friends were left, Meleagros said, "You see? I told you we would take care of you."

Looking down at his bloody shoulder, Nikanoras winced. "Yes. I only wish it had been a few moments sooner."

"Poor baby. Come, to the infirmary." Meleagros hooked his good elbow. "Time to get you cleaned and bandaged."

Behind him he heard Mycandor whisper to Argos, "If Persepolos were not of rank, he would hang."

"True," Argos answered. "But, as they say, rank has privilege."

Lysos snarled. "I would put my own death curse on him."

Chasathenes said, "Let us first let the commanders handle it. Then, if another attempt presents itself, we shall take it into our own hands."

Overhearing every word, Meleagros leaned on Nikanoras to whisper, "You see? I told you their allegiance is to our band first."

Nikanoras was not happy about the other men getting into any trouble because of him. "I just hope it is over. For all our sakes."

Meleagros escorted him in the darkness, back to the camp. He pushed through a tent flap of the infirmary and stood tall. A few men who had been wounded in the skirmish were being tended. One of the medics noticed Nikanoras and nodded to him he had seen him as he finished up with another man.

"Sit, Nikki." Meleagros nudged him to a cot.

Sighing in exhaustion, Nikanoras sat down heavily and tried to look at his arm again in the torch light. "How bad is it?"

Meleagros took a seat beside him, moving Nikanoras' arm to face the brightest flame, then he inspected it carefully. "It is a gash. A gap. But, I don't think it is very deep. The blood makes it look worse. Once they clean it up, we shall see."

As he said this, one of the medics approached to take a look at it, wiping off the caked blood with a soft cloth.

Nikanoras winced as it ran over the opened part of the wound, then turned away in disgust.

"Will he be all right?" Meleagros asked as he watched the process from over the medic's shoulder.

"If he keeps it clean and changes the poultice." He pressed some soaked herbs against it, then wrapped it. He didn't spend too much time on it, having more urgent men to attend to.

"You hear?" Meleagros warned, "Kept clean and changed."

Cracking a smile, Nikanoras said, "That is your job, as my nurse maid."

As the two men exchanged loving smiles, the medic moved on to another injured man.

Seeing all that could be done was done, Meleagros reached out his hand to haul Nikanoras back to his feet. Once again out in the cool night air, Meleagros asked, "Some food or wine? Or are you too weary?"

"Some food and wine would be fine, Meleagros."

"Good. I am famished." Holding his hand, throwing his shield over his right shoulder, Meleagros squeezed Nikanoras' fingers tightly.

While they walked in silence, Nikanoras imagined Meleagros was replaying the night in his mind.

Staring at Meleagros' serene profile as he walked, head lowered, Nikanoras knew some unpleasant images were filling his lover's thoughts. "Do not fret, Meleagros. I do think it will not happen again."

Meleagros smiled. "I know you will be all right." Though it sounded like he was referring to the current wound, Meleagros sounded as if he were actually speaking of the fights to come, trying to find comfort that nothing would harm them.

The way it was uttered, Nikanoras knew it meant more than just a well wish for a cut arm. Returning the gentle squeeze of his hand, they spotted the rest of their group already eating and sating their thirst.

338 BC

CHAPTER 21

Thebes being the capital of Boeotia, Nikanoras had no idea how powerful his home had become. Second only to Macedon in thunder, everyone attempted to win them to their side. Nikanoras found that a bit ironic considering only thirty years prior, Epaminondas had attempted to enlarge their empire and bring in some smaller cities as allies. This failed sadly because the senate had not let them carry on with their own oligarchic governments. But they had never built an empire before, what did they know?

It seemed Philip was a much more strategic ruler, for he was engulfing the entire region, state by state. Whether it was through diplomacy or intimidation, Nikanoras was about to find out.

Almost the entire fellowship of the Sacred Band had turned twenty years of age making them real men, men to be reckoned with.

The efforts of the actor from Athens, Demosthenes, to unite Athens and their own powerful army were nearing a desperate plea. On his knees he was begging for support after Philip had threatened Athens again, demanding them to capitulate. And again Athens would not yield to the gluttonous king. In horror Demosthenes imagined Thebes allying with Macedon, giving that tyrant unimpeded access to Attica. If that were to pass, the King of Macedon would smash their city to pieces out of anger, they had no doubt.

In front of the Theban council, the actor again pleaded to join hands with Athens, only then, he said, would they have a fighting chance against such a great army.

As they argued and wasted time, Philip moved his forces without a fight through Thermopylae and Elatea, tactically securing the land that fell between him and Thebes.

Envoys of Philip stated their case as Demosthenes quaked in terror. Would Thebes, they would ask, care to join ranks with the new ruler of the Greeks? In return, King Philip asks only allegiance. Only? And when he comes to collect the men of the army as his mercenaries? Or their families as slaves? Removes the gold from the treasury? What then?

The council was not convinced, turning up their proud noses at the idea of being dictated to and bullied.

And as if he could smell it in the air, Nikanoras and his colleagues of the Sacred Band knew they were getting closer to a colossal war. The training had intensified. They were marched around ruthlessly, committed their skills to the test until they could not raise their hands up any longer from the fatigue. Their bodies were hardened to steal, their weapons merely an extension of their arms, and their need for human comforts, minimal.

They had succeeded as did Pelopidas before them, in creating a master race of warriors, '...*a band cemented by friendship grounded upon love, is never broken, and invincible.*'(1)

'Grounded in love- never broken- invincible.'

Mature, tall, and very powerful, they believed everything their commanders fed them. They had endured every torture they had put them through, every enemy had been destroyed that they set before them, every doubt had been vanquished that they had created. They were the answer to a city's prayers.

As the robe-clad men stood before the council, swaying their might to and fro, they paraded for their fellow Thebans, marching one last time in peace before their steps took them to their fate.

So secure were the people of Thebes in their power that they never thought once of failure. Call it brainwashing or propaganda, the men of the Sacred Band dared not deny they were everything they promised they would be.

After seven years of excruciating exercise and training, they could not fail.

As Nikanoras stood in formation, proud and ruthless, he glanced around at his fellow soldiers. Stone faced and hardened, they were men, not the boys he had first played with, dancing and kicking up their heels in folly.

Staring down his line of comrades, Nikanoras studied stout and solid Chasathenes with his tall blond lover, Lysos right beside him. Next, there was rugged Argos and at his left shoulder his massively built Mycandor.

On Nikanoras' right was his very own warrior. Meleagros had grown enormous. His shoulders were wide and flared, his back a rippling flag of muscles tapering to narrow hips and solidly placed thighs. His grey eyes had lost their sweetness and only a soldier's glare did they emit.

He would not want to face this group. Not without thousands to stand behind him.

At the end of the parade the men of the Sacred Band stood at attention as one of the prophets sacrificed a bull to Apollo in their honor.

Absorbed in the deed, Nikanoras' attention was diverted by a general in full armor tilting his head to his captain. When he recognized Persepolos, his sister's widower, a pain shot through his center. Nikanoras peeked at Meleagros, wondering if he had spotted the man as well.

With his lover's stern gaze still on the bull being slaughtered, Nikanoras knew he had not. In the last two years he had been spared, as Coninious promised, of any more attempts on his life, but he knew Persepolos would not be content to wait as he merely searched for another opportunity to seek his death.

The blood of the bull pouring onto the shrine, they knelt down in unison, their horse hair crests bowing, as they murmured their prayers.

Before they were dismissed for the evening's festivities, their captain held them in attention in place. Keenly aware of Persepolos watching, Nikanoras held his breath as his captain came directly to his line and barked orders that they were now to be the front rank.

No longer in the place they had trained; the mid-section of three hundred, their line of men was to lead the charge into battle.

Silently obedient, they all faced left on a pivot of sandals, in immaculate marching formation to the head.

Nikanoras was surprised at this unusual turn of events. The perfect warriors, his group of men moved out of the mass to dress directly in front of the rest of the Sacred Band.

Blackness was inside Nikanoras at the sight of that wicked grin. It had taken Persepolos three years to seek his revenge when his plans to assassinate him had failed. Nikanoras knew. In the general's deranged mind, he wanted Nikanoras first into battle before the rest of his men.

Biting his tongue, knowing an outburst would most certainly be his doom, Nikanoras said nothing though his thoughts were homicidal. It was not for him he worried, but for the rest of the group whom he took with him. The guilt was creeping in him like a thieving Spartan boy nearing a bakery filled with bread.

He wondered if they all knew why they had been chosen to die first. Nikanoras wanted to shout out in anger, *'Let it just be me. Do not sacrifice all my loved ones!'*

But, the wicked general knew Nikanoras. He also knew the workings of the Sacred Band and their loyalty not just to the partner they shared, but to everyone else in the group as well.

This man knew it would be torture for Nikanoras. All this agonizing pain suffered for a teenager humiliating him before his peers. Anger released the Furies, and Nikanoras was its victim.

With his captain making certain they were fully accustomed to the new set up, he dismissed the men to enjoy the last of the evening and the games to come.

The moment he was released Nikanoras made a straight line for that wicked man. He would have it out once and for all. If he was shackled and murdered, so be it. But the rest of his men would not suffer from this revenge.

The general waited for him with a smug grin on his lips.

A strong hand held Nikanoras back.

"No. Nikki. Do not approach him like you did so long ago. Surely you will not be spared. I will tell you with all seriousness, he will crucify you. The men do not care, front, middle back, what difference is there?" Meleagros said, shrugging his shoulders.

"What difference?" Nikanoras yelled, "Are you mad? First in line into battle?" Breathing fire, Nikanoras attempted to break Meleagros' grip and keep his eye on the general so he could go after him.

"Yes. I would prefer it to waiting for half to be killed to react."

Nikanoras threw up his hands in complete frustration. "That is you. What about the rest?" Continuing to free himself from Meleagros' iron grip, Nikanoras whined, "No. Release me. I will not allow his grudge to endanger the ones I love. I shall be the one. Not them. In the name of the gods, release me."

Meleagros tightened his grasp on Nikanoras to a vise-like hold.

It was then Nikanoras realized the men of his rank listening to their every word.

Meleagros said, "You want to know their mind? Ask yourself." Meleagros gestured to them.

Thirty men knew what Nikanoras' reaction would be to this altering of their position in the squad. Knew he would take it to heart and be wounded by it. With Lysos, Chasathenes, Argos, and Mycandor the first to comfort him, they all told him it was where they preferred to be.

"It is an honor to go into battle first." Argos patted Nikanoras' back, smiling. "I would have it no other way."

Mycandor knocked his knuckles into Nikanoras' helmet to get his attention. "I should thank you. I was very tired of having to get on my toes to see what came before us."

As he heard their comments, a jumble of words to his ears, Nikanoras knew this was what they had bred in them. Bravery. Like a lion they all wanted that place. All craved to fight best, to be first into battle. Being last in the Band was like a curse to them.

Nikanoras was numb with disbelief as the men patted his back thanking him for allowing them to lead the charge. When the crowd thinned Nikanoras scanned once again for Persepolos, but he had vanished into the throng like black poison into blue veins.

Meleagros stuck his chest out proudly and said, "You have heard your answer. So, that is the end of it." In an effort to get him to move,

Meleagros held Nikanoras' elbow. "Which do you want first, wine or games?"

The warmth of his brothers washing over his skin like summer rain, the guilt of being their demise, Nikanoras continued to fight his internal anger and breathed a sigh in defeat. "Need you ask? Wine."

"Wine it is." Meleagros escorted him to the nearest ewer.

Nikanoras and his friends sat at a table near the crowded streets and markets. The games had begun and the younger males had replaced them as the center of attraction. In no mood for joviality, Nikanoras drank his wine thinking bitter thoughts.

"Speak to me, Nikki." Meleagros' hand touched his arm as it rested on the table between them.

Nikanoras said, "All my life I feel things have been placed against me. From my birth to this day, nothing I have wanted has come to pass. I should have known my fate when I lost my sister to that hideous man. That, my love, has set the tone for the last five years. From that moment, I knew all hope was gone from my heart. I would not marry, not inherit my family fortune, and now, here I am again beleaguered with guilt over deciding the destiny of my loved ones."

Patiently, Meleagros listened. After living, sleeping, playing, and suffering with him day in and day out, he was so attuned to his lover's moods he allowed Nikanoras them. Not trying to change them like he did before. On the cusp of war, Meleagros knew, things would not get better before they got worse.

"I am sorry to drown in my self-pity. It seems I should be more thankful for my place. Many desire to be with our fighting group but are not high born and cannot dream of entering our ranks. And you, dear Meleagros, have always been my rock. You have not complained nor detested your appointment, but instead, you have flourished, rising like cream to the top of the Band. You are worshiped. Men gaze at you in awe."

Meleagros smiled. "Do not go on or you shall make me conceited."

Reaching both his hands to him across the plain of the stone slab, Nikanoras wanted the attention of his eyes. When he was granted their gaze, he said, "Like Achilles, you are the hero who goes into battle. Your size and strength will send them all running in every direction. You, my friend, will reign victorious."

"Not without you," Meleagros said, giving a shy laugh. "And you underestimate yourself, Nikki. I hear the comments. Do not compare yourself to me as if you are less than I."

A commotion was heard in the street. As the soldiers were enjoying their moment after parading, they rose up to hear someone shouting out news.

"Philip's troops have taken Elatea!"

Gaping at Meleagros, Nikanoras knew that that was the road leading directly to them.

A soldier in the crowd yelled, "Call to arms?"

The crier replied, "Demosthenes has declared alliance between Athens and Thebes."

Not waiting for the messenger to answer whether they should prepare for battle, all the armed men who were relaxing, hurried to their captains whom they knew would be at the games.

With their shields and swords at the ready, Meleagros and he rushed into the stadium. The games had been halted by the same news they had just learned.

A high ranking general was trying to calm the masses and be heard. Standing atop a stone stage, he waved for the mob to be silent. Finally, the army could hear him order, "Get to your regiments!"

The crush of leather on stone and smashing of shields roared in a mad rush. They had all thought this was their moment, a call to war.

Their sides brushing as they sprinted to the staging area, Nikanoras knew his lover's heart was beating quickly, yearning this day, this hour. But, in Nikanoras' own mind was a seeping dread.

Three hundred in position, the Sacred Band stood at attention, ready for war. Their anxiety peaked, waiting for the order.

Now first in line Nikanoras and Meleagros had nothing obstructing their view as the regular army gathered, along with the horsemen. After some initial panic, calm had fallen. It seemed the danger was not as imminent as was first assumed. Macedon was not marching down that road. At least not at the moment. Spies were sent off in fast relays, coming back in the dead of night to report, no army was advancing.

The spies had met with envoys on the road, escorting them back to the city. Again Philip wanted peace. Drawing a collective sigh, they were instructed to rest as a force of mercenaries was dispatched to protect the road from Amphissa.

Unknown to them, they were falling into a well-laid Macedonian trap. Athens strength was its navy. Last thing Philip wanted was a battle at sea. So, like a fisherman with a lure, he was dangling little worms for them to snap at. Drawing them north by land was his aim.

With what the leaders thought was a situation well at hand, they released the Band for the night. Tired and fatigued, they were not in the mood for anything more than a brooding sleep. This game of cat and mouse with the King of Macedon was wearing on their nerves.

As they scuffed back to their barracks, silent and angry, they heard the soft goodnights of their close friends, returning it with a nod or a small wave.

Inside their quarters, Nikanoras could read Meleagros' fury. If it had been up to him, he would have led the Theban army himself into battle, right then and there.

As Meleagros tore off his armor, tossing it in complete frustration to the floor, Nikanoras stood back, handling his shining metals with more honor.

Usually drowning in his own black pool of self pity, Nikanoras often forgot the anxieties of his lover. So good was Meleagros at covering his anger and fears, that no one thought this handsome powerful warrior needed a thing. How wrong they were.

Watching him as he stifled the snarl of fury in his large muscular chest, Nikanoras thought of his own life. Though his father and he were never best of companions, they did not hate each other. When he died he could not say they had parted on bad terms.

But, Meleagros and his father, Xenophos, though they had gotten along when Meleagros was a child, as Meleagros matured they began to despise each other. Having that effeminate weak older brother, Meleagros was neglected by his father, who set all his faith and guidance in Ephisomines, knowing he would be the most needy.

The elder child was schooled by the finest tutors and brought up to be the statesman and educator. Why, Nikanoras could only guess. The boy was so homely and delicate his father must have feared if he did not educate him to be a scholar and statesman, he would amount to no more than a thing to mock.

On Nikanoras' first and only meeting with him two years ago, he was stunned by his frail nature, such a contrast from his masculine lover/soldier. From what he had revealed of his childhood, Meleagros, though he had convinced himself he was the pampered brat of the palace, in reality could only struggle for attention in that household where he was placed second best.

Ironically, since Ephisomines was homely, one would have thought the pretty child would be so honored. But it was not so. Having not been graced with the beauty of the gods, Ephisomines sneered down his pointed nose at his lovely little brother with so much distain it was painful for Meleagros to endure.

The moment they could rid of this younger pest, they sent Meleagros off to military school, seldom seeking him out again. Meleagros, though wounded to the soul, never shared his pain, nor looked back. As for his mother, who adored her beautiful baby boy, she was powerless and overlooked by all of the males in the family in favor of his father's concubines.

Embarrassed to be associated with that brother, or even the father who coddled the creature, Meleagros had given up on his family and devoted all his hopes and dreams on his lover and war. Wanting nothing to do with any of his kin, Meleagros found his new family with the boys of the Sacred Band. Having more faith in the gods than anyone Nikanoras knew, Meleagros released all his anger and channeled it into a more purposeful life. The contented aura was not a façade.

Meleagros knew he possessed one thing his brother did not; beauty. Meleagros allowed his chest to swell in superiority, completely happy to be with the most elite army in the land, satisfied with his skill and strength, and madly, passionately in love.

But on occasion that shell would fracture, and the anger and frustration would emerge. It was Nikanoras' turn to nurture him, as his lover had done countless times for him.

"I know you wanted to march. Soon, my Meleagros, very soon."

Bare-chested, his hands clenched in rage, he faced him to say, "They waste time. Philip is no fool. He can move an army overnight. Look at them. Sending a pathetic ten thousand mercenaries to defend a prominent road against his power. Why are they so complacent? Do they not see? Suicide. It is suicide to trust the envoys. To not prepare. What are we? Can we not see this disaster coming?"

The agony of Meleagros' words, was that Nikanoras agreed with him. Speechless, he had no lies of comfort. It was not in their hands.

Needing something to tear or smash, Meleagros looked around in vain for an item to destroy. "By land!" Meleagros shouted near tears, "By land we will not win! Why is it Demosthenes continues to push our forces in front of Athens? We will take the beating not they."

As his voice edged to sobs of frustration, Nikanoras moved across the room to calm him.

"Fools." Meleagros cried. "Fools who think they understand what we do. And they believe an actor. Why, my own father could do better, and you know what I think of him."

"All right, my Herakles...shhhh.'" With his hand on the back of Meleagros' neck under his long hair, Nikanoras could feel the boiling heat of his skin.

"Nikki." His name emerged as a whimper. "Why do they delay? Why do they not allow us to march? Surely the time we spend idle will only help Philip."

Weakness was the one emotion Nikanoras had never seen in him. But, Meleagros was so tired and spent, so drained from the expectations of battle, dashed again and again, that even this huge man had his limits.

Embracing Meleagros to comfort him, the smooth skin of their chests connecting, Nikanoras rested his chin on his shoulder as he urged Meleagros to do the same. Then he cooed softly to him like a mother to her child. "Remember Athena. Allow her to make decisions."

As if the stress had been released from Meleagros, like a steam cloud from a boiling pot, Nikanoras felt his body relax against his own. He knew reminding his lover of the gods was the way to ease his spirit.

As Nikanoras rocked him gently, he said, "Soon. The time is near. Very soon you will get your wish and see Philip face to face."

Raising his head from Nikanoras' shoulder they met gazes. "And when I do, I shall be the one who slays him."

A shiver like ice water passed down Nikanoras' back at the venom. No one wanted to murder the king of Macedon more than Meleagros. His hatred of that greedy tyrant knew no limits.

"Okay, my lover, you shall be the one to slay him. But, for now." Nikanoras finished undressing him and led him to the bed, crawling beside him.

Nikanoras had to drag him down to make him rest. Reluctantly, Meleagros relented and let go a very long stressful sigh.

Shifting on the bed so he may lean up and see his face, Nikanoras caressed his fine features and large rounded smooth chest, trying to soothe him. "You, my Herakles, shall be the slayer of the snake, just as the mighty god had done for his brother, Iphicles in their bed."

Nikanoras smiled, knowing comparing his lover to the gods and heroes was an easy method to pacifying his soul.

"Thank you, Nikki."

Nikanoras met his lips for a kiss. He judged the level of response to see how exhausted his man was. When he was met with enthusiasm, Nikanoras moved his hand down Meleagros' body to his groin, finding it growing ready for pleasure. He moved closer and opened his mouth for Meleagros' tongue, hearing him moan and feeling his body harden.

Knowing both of them would wear out quickly from the stress and physical day, Nikanoras fisted his lover's length quickly, parting from the kiss to see his expression. Meleagros' gray eyes met his as his breathing grew heavy and raspy.

"Nikki…" Meleagros showed his teeth just before he released his seed.

Nikanoras milked him a moment longer, taking the slippery semen to use as lubrication. Meleagros parted his legs and reached for Nikanoras.

Nikanoras mounted his muscular lover, staring into his beautiful features. It took no time for Nikanoras to reach his peak. He slowed his hips and closed his eyes, savoring the bond they had made, which was like no other.

As Nikanoras recuperated, Meleagros held his cheeks, bringing him back to his mouth to kiss. Nikanoras pulled out, falling heavily against Meleagros and they stay that way as they drifted off to sleep.

CHAPTER 22

A week they waited for orders. None came. Renewing their exercises with unmatched fervor, they practiced their charge and slaughter with a heightened sense of urgency.

Their patience tried to shreds, word came that the mercenary troop they had sent to protect the approach to Thebes, had crumbled.

It seemed the King of Macedon had sent a messenger to that group of soldiers informing them he was leaving for another battle up north with Thrace. Why they believed him, no one knows. But, assuming the information was correct, they let down their guard, drank too much wine, even played games to pass the time.

Like a panther, Philip crept up in the night and killed them. Those that could, fled back to Thebes, shrieking in terror that Macedon was on its way.

The Theban army was infuriated they were spending too much time waiting, and not enough time attacking.

Once again they were called to battle.

Dressing in their armor yet again, in that tiny room they had shared, Nikanoras was strangely silent. When at other times they chatted quietly of the latest gossip in the ranks or the frustration they felt to be put off time and again, this time, it was happening.

Meleagros was covered in metal, sword in hand, helm on head, grinning. "Victory so sweet, I can taste it in my veins."

Nikanoras picked up his helmet from the floor and placed it on his head. Though he wanted to agree, to make some sort of cheer at their certain success to encourage them, Nikanoras found the words stop short in his throat. 'From behind', echoed in his temples. No, there was never a method of breaking the Macedonian line to attack from behind. That was a doomed fantasy.

Though Meleagros waited for some comment of inspiration from him, when nothing came, Meleagros said, "Come, lover, to our finest hour."

Nikanoras could not even fake a smile as he passed by out of their door to find the others.

In formation, looking down the front line, Nikanoras could tell by the expressions around him, the men of the Sacred Band were sick to death of being put off. Shifting their weight from side to side, inhaling deep massive breaths of air, stiffening their backs, the three hundred men of the band were like charioteer horses before a race.

The waiting, it seemed had come to an end. They were so tightly wound they wanted blood, the sooner the better. A yell of a command to march rung out and at the sound, Nikanoras' blood pumped painfully under his chest armor.

Loud crashing stomps of heavy legs and feet in perfect rhythm behind him lit the fight in him. Moving in flawless timing, each step identical, the elite of the army moved out, the cheering of the crowds behind them ringing in their ears.

The army of Athens met their own, as they number thirty-five thousand infantry and two-thousand cavalry, they marched north with Thebes.

Nikanoras sensed they were finally coming closer to their goal, the relief was almost palpable. Under those crested helms the men were smirking. Nikanoras glimpsed down the line, passed his lover to the rest, thinking, *This is what we have been trained for. All that hard work and sweat had come to this.*

Moving through the Kerata Pass the military was making for the plains of Chaeronea. The Cephisus River on their right, and beyond that the Moutain Akontion, they had enough open space to spread their troop out. On the right flank, with some flair, their Band came to a halt. Through the brilliant noon sun they caught their first sight of the cavalry led by Prince Alexander.

The silence around them, with so many voices quieted, made Nikanoras think they were in some eerie burial ground. When the King of Macedon himself road to the front of his army, Nikanoras gasped in amazement. Not that he was a thing of awe, for his son outshone him like Helios compared to Luna, but, the fact that he was so bold to ride in front of them that way was an indication of his confidence.

If Meleagros had a quiver of arrows and a bow, he would have shot that bloated king down. Hatred burned in Meleagros' light eyes, and it was all he could do to remain passive and still as that monstrous creature rode by.

In reality, the King was assessing Thebes' strength, having second thoughts. Once he had seen their entire force, he sent again an envoy to negotiate even as they stood on the battleground.

"What is happening?" Nikanoras asked Meleagros out of the side of his mouth as he watched strange comings and goings.

"The pig has seen his doom in our eyes and is frightened," Meleagros said.

Mycandor overheard and said, "He has underestimated us, is my guess. And seeks talks."

"Talks." Meleagros snarled in disdain. "His time for talk is over."

Hearing the murmurs, General Coninious rode down the line on his brown charger. "Silence!" he ordered, then raised his head back to the plain and the meetings.

Seeing a signal from someone, he shouted to the army to stand at-ease.

Nikanoras exhaled and sheathed his sword as every man in line did the same identically, like mirror images.

When the general rode off once more, the muttering resumed.

"He is chicken." Argos scoffed. "He did not bargain for us."

Chasathenes spat onto the ground in disdain. "The beast assumed we were nothing to meet. That he would run ragged over us. What arrogance."

"He is not boasting now." Meleagros' white teeth showed under his snarled lip. "I would sell my virtue for a bow and arrow."

"Virtue?" Nikanoras laughed. "You lost that more than five years ago, my love."

A deep basso chuckle surrounded him as those around him heard.

"Oh, shut up, Nikki. You know well what I mean." Meleagros clenched his fists. "Look at the ease he rides by. No fear. As if he is a god and no blood will pour from his veins."

Lysos squinted into the sun's glare for another look at the king. "I fear there is no blood there, Meleagros."

The men paused to see what Lysos would say, staring to him.

"There is hog fat!" he yelled, then laughed.

A roar of hilarity passed from the front to the back of the band as the line was repeated to all those who had not heard it from its source.

Staring into the glare, Nikanoras whispered, mostly to himself, "We laugh now... oh, but if we will laugh when we have met him on the field."

They heard.

The men's smiles slowly falling, they waited, wanting for this stalemate to end.

Hours later, when their legs were stiffening from standing and their bellies began complaining, the general returned.

"Break ranks and pull back to the edge of the wood." He pointed as he commanded, "We shall camp there overnight as the debates continue."

"What?" Meleagros yelled in frustration. "Break ranks? You mean we are not attacking?"

As the horse snorted and stomped its way to him, General Coninious peered down at Meleagros' handsome features. "Not yet, Meleagros, not yet. Try and get some rest, for tomorrow we may not be as fortunate."

"Fortunate?" He puffed up in anger.

Before he annoyed the general, Nikanoras and Mycandor both reached to calm him. "Come, my wild dog." Nikanoras tugged on him. "There will undoubtedly be many more hours of debate."

"What is this? Debate?" Stomping his sandals as the other two dragged him backwards, Meleagros' disappointment was clear for all to see. "Have we not debated enough? We are here on a battlefield. What use is debating? He knows we are his match. He is afraid. Now is not the time for debate."

"Is he always this stubborn?" Mycandor gripped Meleagros' upper arm tighter as he and Nikanoras physically dragged him back to the woods.

"Oh, you do not know the half of it." Nikanoras rolled his eyes. "Come, Herakles, come to rest."

With Meleagros still kicking and mumbling about how impossible this situation was, they managed to get him to stop brooding and help gather wood for the fires.

"You watch," Meleagros warned, "He will attack us tonight whilst we sleep. Oh yes." He nodded to emphasize his point. "He cannot win fairly. So, he will send his assassins in the dark."

"We have a guard." Nikanoras held a bundle of sticks under his arm as he gathered more. "Will you give it a rest, Meleagros?"

Finally closing his mouth on his protests, Meleagros snapped a dry twig and brooded as he threw them on the growing pile.

Fed a very slight meal of grains and bread, they sat in circles around the campfires, knowing they needed to sleep, yet too keyed up to get any.

"He plans to exhaust us." Lysos yawned, rubbing his face. "Sleepy soldiers are what he wants."

"We should go to bed," Chasathenes agreed. "Lysos is right. If we are not refreshed by morning, we will not do ourselves any favors."

With Lysos' yawn making the rounds, Nikanoras caught it and stretched lazily. "Sleep. Yes. Come, Meleagros, though you will be tossing and turning like a plague of the Furies, come lay back and try to rest."

His mood dark and foul, Meleagros felt Nikanoras' hand on his arm. Giving in, exhaling tiredly, he lay back, trying to get comfortable in his armor. With only their helms put aside, for fear they needed to be at the ready if ambushed, finding a comfortable spot was not an easy task.

Lying on his side, Nikanoras stroked back Meleagros' hair from his forehead, as he heard around him the rest of his companions crushing metal on grass to try and rest.

As Meleagros' eyes grew heavy, Nikanoras wondered if this was the beginning or the end of their time together. "I do love you, Meleagros," he whispered, but knew he had already fallen asleep.

The commanders allowed the men to rest as peace talks were again attempted. Though they did not trust this king to wait for daylight, they gave him more faith than he deserved. Sleep did come to the army, who were under a watchful eye.

August 3rd 338 BC

CHAPTER 23

When the sun sank down in the western sky, its red glow casting an omen of doom over all who sat there to stare at it, they knew there was no turning back. No magic spell to speak to get the kingdoms of Greece to split or join peacefully.

Though Phocion, one of Thebes' statesman, was begging the generals to accept Philip's proposals lest they have a miserable war, Demosthenes refused to back down, saying that Philip was not a man of his word, and would enslave all who capitulated to his terms.

During that fateful night as the men in white robes debated, shouted, waved their arms in anger, none of the army slept well.

In the open field they lie as the infantry watched the enemy fires for movement.

Their Band in its spot, resting atop one another as pillows, staring at the star lit sky, Nikanoras wondered what the new day would bring. As he felt Meleagros' heart beating under his head, he tried not to imagine anything happening to his lover, nor to the rest of his men. Somehow they would pull through this battle, unscathed, perfect. Like they had with every mock battle behind them. They were the blessed ones. Loved by Athena. No harm would befall them.

In the silence around him, Nikanoras wondered what the thoughts were in the minds of so many. As some imagined their tactical

196

training, while others the thrill of the victory. Or the men of the phalanx, going home to their wives and children after, no one knew what daybreak would bring. To the day he died, Nikanoras wished they never found out.

Before the sun had lit the eastern sky, horsemen were heard approaching. An entire army rose to their feet at their arrival. The negotiations had broken down. The talks had failed.

At that news Nikanoras' limbs grew cold. It had come. A day they had trained for since they were thirteen-year-old boys.

As Meleagros realized the same thing, he met his lover's gaze. Locked to that valiant grey stare Nikanoras did not know what to do. When Meleagros' lips broadened into a smile, he returned it. "It is here," Nikanoras said.

"The gods be with you." Tears came to Meleagros' eyes.

"Yes, and you." They embraced, their chest guards clashing.

Men all around were wishing their partners well in the coming skirmish. But soon their encouragement would be halted as the captains ordered them into ranks.

Standing on the right wing, in front of twelve thousand Boeotians, the three hundred strong Sacred Band raised their shields and swords. As Nikanoras craned his neck left he could see Athens' ragtag army of ten thousand hoplites and beyond them a group of light armed men along with some troops from the Acropolis. Dead center were five thousand mercenaries while their cavalry remained behind the lines.

As the sun rose, the light revealed Alexander atop a black horse with his heavy cavalry directly in front of them, Philip with his phalanx of sharp sarissa on the left directly opposite that weak Athenian regiment.

The look of this darkened Nikanoras' heart. He knew *they* were ready. Their Theban army was powerful and prepared. But, judging the shape of Athens' soldiers, he could see why Athens had so desperately begged them to come along. Hardly more than farmers with spears, they were a mismatch of armor and helm. Of them he expected nothing. So, it was up to the Theban army to do all the fighting.

Against one of the best trained armies the world had known, what chance was there? As his skin prickled in warning, he knew Macedon had come prepared, yet Thebes had not. Had they practiced with Athens? Had they brought their skills up to par with their own? It was too late to worry. It was too late for most things.

Doubt growing to anguish, he looked down his line as if it were the last time. Standing proud and undaunted, Lysos' blond mane flowed from out of his golden helmet, Chasathenes at his side, trying to appear tall. Argos biting his lip in anxiety as his lover Mycandor strained to see over Alexander's line.

And his lovely Meleagros, pressing his shoulder against his wanting nothing more than to hear the order to charge. A lump grew in Nikanoras' throat as he wondered how the events to come would change his life.

As he pondered these trivial matters, Philip of Macedon knew where the heart of the battle would be. It was with them. He feared not the mayhem of the Athenians. But he knew with the Sacred Band he was fighting the fiercest of warriors, and with the experience of the Theban army behind them, they would be the only power on that field.

As the sun rose over that plain, both sides held their breath.

His heart pounding in his chest so loudly Nikanoras was deafened by it, that when the trumpets blared he almost did not hear. With their swords held high, they roared, advancing into the powerful cavalry, led by the crown prince Alexander III.

With the rushing Macedonian line, the Athenians raced into the fray, blindly hacking and advancing against Philip's army. Philip's right wing extended deliberately slightly passed theirs. He was slowly drawing the makeshift army away from the center.

As the Macedonians marched in reverse while still slicing and battling, the Athenians wrongly assumed they were retreating. One of the Athenian generals, cocky and self-assured, could not see the strategy before his very eyes. Thinking he was getting the better of them, he urged his forces forward, shouting at them to drive the Macedonians back to Pella.

Well disciplined and orderly, Philip's army was not retreating. With those pointed sarissa, the ones Meleagros had so long ago advised be attacked from 'behind', were stopping any full out assault. Macedon backing them into a trap, the allied line in the center had bent to breaking point. It was what Philip had hoped for.

Fighting against horse and rider was more of a challenge than they had imagined. But, undaunted by the task, the Band was doing very well. Sadly, they cut into the beasts to topple them, then the hand to hand combat could commence, and they were most effective that way.

As Nikanoras quickly glanced around, Meleagros was still there, as were the rest of his men, snarling and cutting savagely this line of horsemen, until they had hewed through hundreds.

The Athenian side of the battle was not as fortunate. The second they gapped the center of the field, the finest horseman of Macedon and Thessaly, the *Companions* led by the golden prince, smashed through the line separating the Athenians from the Thebans.

The moment that had been accomplished, Philip halted his 'retreat' and the carnage began. The pikemen roared with the charge and either skewered them or sent the Athenians running in every direction.

His shield taking blow after blow, Nikanoras felt arrows whizzing past as his sword cut through arms and legs, necks and chests of the men around him. The noise was a terrible mixture of cries of pain and the thunder of anger.

There was so much bad blood and hatred between Thebes and Macedon, they knew they had to win or be destined to hard labor or death. Macedon despised them. There was no way to lose this war. They had to win or die.

When Nikanoras heard Chasathenes cry out, he spun to see the reason. Lysos had been struck by an arrow in the neck. As he fell, Chasathenes went mad on a savage rampage of revenge. Though he wasn't the first of their Band to fall, he was the first of their small group. The rest of them heightened their assault to a new level. Nikanoras did not know what takes over when reason and human feelings leave. But he did know that from that moment, when Lysos fell, they were a pack of wild dogs set loose.

Without a way to look beyond their backs, for the battle before them was so intense, there was no chance to have seen that they had been cut off from the rest of the war.

As the mercenaries and Athenians fled in terror, only Thebes was left to battle the might of Macedon. And that heavy cavalry, led by Alexander was surrounding them like starving wolves net a lamb.

When even their own phalanx and hoplites deserted them, they were alone on that battlefield. But, they had no way of knowing it.

With two hundred of them still standing, their backs to one another, they battled on. With all his heart did Nikanoras want to shout out to Meleagros to take care, not to get hit, but if he had he would have diverted his attention, which at that moment was already split battling two horsemen at once.

Stabbing his own opponent in the chest, Nikanoras rushed to his side. Again as Meleagros hacked at the men above, Nikanoras slashed the legs of the steeds, which wailed in high-pitched terror. The injured horses reared up and tossed off their riders, or knelt down to the ground and rolled on top of them.

When they had hewed through still more, Nikanoras could not believe the amount behind them. For every two they cut down, ten were taking their place. Where was the rest of their army, he wondered in agony? Why were they so outnumbered when on the original field they had been evenly matched? It was blatantly obvious, something had gone terribly wrong.

Suddenly all his fears returned. How many times had he questioned their tactics? Too many. And who would be left alive to remind them he had told them so?

On one brief pause he was able to twist around to actually check his entire field of view. It was then he could see horsemen all around what was becoming a very small defense. When he spun back, out of the tail of his eye, he caught Meleagros drop to the ground.

Having no time to see the type of wound, or to halt even for a moment, Nikanoras went completely berserk. Throwing his shield at an advancing infantryman, he grasped his saber in both hands and used it like it was an axe. Blinded by his own tears and completely deaf to any sound, Nikanoras decided to take the whole Macedonian army on himself.

The few around him thought the same. They would sooner die than give up Pelopidas' legacy.

What began as slow motion to his distorted senses, for he could only see the blur of horsemen as they kept advancing, again and again, Nikanoras stretched his fatigued muscles to swing his blade, cutting deeply, fatally wounding so many he could never count.

As weariness gripped him, he was slowing his pace. Grating his teeth, he forced himself to lift his sword and swing it. But, he was just slashing at air. When something cut through his right biceps, his sword dropped. A spear slammed into his chest immediately after. And he went down.

****

In a nightmare of blood and flesh, Nikanoras heard the sound of bones breaking, armored men dropping to the hardened clay dirt. Over his head through the filtered sunlight, men still fought. As the siren songs called him to death he closed his eyes. Even through his lids he could see images and shadows clashing over him, the hooves of horses coming close to trampling him. Someone cried his name. Or he dreamed they had. Then all went black.

A thunderous voice called off the cavalry. Upon seeing the carnage, Philip signaled the victory, and the cheer of the remaining Macedon troops echoed across the plain. What Athenians they could capture were brought back as prisoners temporarily, until he could make an agreement to release them. He wanted no argument with Athens. The Theban army, however, he would sell as slaves or ask ransom.

The snort of a horse broke the eerie silence. As Nikanoras squinted open his eyelids, he wondered, *Am I dead?*

The whiteness of the light in his eyes felt like a noon sun. It was very confusing. It seemed almost that he was awakening from a bad sleep and Meleagros would be beside him to smile brightly at him.

Trying to move, he felt so much pain he lie back again. Both his right arm and his chest were throbbing horribly. He had never felt so exhausted. Even with all the practice and long hours, nothing drained him to the core like this had.

Sounds came to his ears as they cleared from the blackout he had suffered. Air escaping lungs, death gasps. He could not look. Where was his lover?

It came back to him. Meleagros had gone down after a blow. *Oh, lover....no... not after all we have been through. I cannot face this life without you.* He moaned silently.

Hot tears ran down his temples.

Another sound invaded his thoughts. Footfalls. As he opened his eyes toward it, a shadow fell over his face.

"One is alive, Father."

"Kill him!" That voice answered, so coarse and rough in crude Macedonian which Nikanoras could barely understand.

In formal Greek the son answered, "No. I will not. Not one so brave as the Sacred Band."

Nikanoras vaguely remembered asking the prince to honor him and kill him. That hour after battle was nothing but an unfocused memory to him. If he could have, he would have killed himself. But, his right arm was useless.

The prince asked him his name. The lovely crown prince of Macedon wanted to know who he was. So, Nikanoras told him. He was his now. He had no other master.

With the help of his closest comrade, Hephaestion, Alexander managed to get Nikanoras up on his feet.

Forced to stand, Nikanoras grabbed at his arm in pain, trying to close the wound. *I will lose it! Then I shall be crippled and useless.*

He dared not look down at their dead for he knew if he spotted Meleagros he would die. Hard enough was it to think of his best friends massacred, let alone look at their inanimate faces. A moan of agony passed beyond his lips no matter how he tried to prevent it. Why was he the one left alive to see this carnage?

A reassuring squeeze was given to him by both men.

They had set up tents for the wounded. Macedonian soldiers glared at him with hatred as they escorted him to a cot. *Why do they tend me just to see me murdered in the dark?*

All this was going through his mind as the kindness of this prince seemed extremely odd to him. They had been told he was a barbarian, a murderer. Yet Macedon's own doctors tended his wound. Little hope did he have for it, but they were encouraging.

Cleaning it, adding herbs, Alexander himself oversaw his treatment, stripping him of his armor. They located the puncture wound in his chest. The spear had penetrated his guard and poked through. Battered and broken, Nikanoras was a mess, though not as bad as to die from it unless infection sets in. And in August it was less likely.

The prince himself brought him a bowl of broth and a chalice of wine.

Nikanoras could not help but ask why he was being so kind to his enemy? Avoiding the food, for he had no stomach for it, he drank the wine like water as Alexander told him of his admiration for his Band and the burial of his dead.

With tears streaming down Nikanoras' face, he thought of his loss. All of his companions, and the one he loved most in life, torn from him. His world was in shambles.

"Eat, Nikki."

Jerking his head up at that pet name, Nikanoras begged the prince not to use it. Alexander bowed his head graciously and apologized.

As Nikanoras gazed out into thin air, something the prince had said came back. Asking him if he had actually told him, that two-hundred and fifty four were being buried, Alexander nodded, confirming what had made it through Nikanoras' dull senses. "Then there are forty-five others alive?"

"Yes, but we are keeping you separated for the time."

Nikanoras tried to have hope that one of his friends could have survived. Maybe Mycandor or Chasathenes.

"Sleep. Heal. I will come back to see you later."

As Alexander pet back his hair, Nikanoras looked passed him to the other one, the tall one. Handsome and proud, Hephaestion gave him a slight smile, leaving him to ponder his fate.

Nikanoras checked the bandages on his arm and chest curiously. It seemed he would come through this. But what would become of him?

CHAPTER 24

As he dozed in and out of consciousness, Nikanoras heard voices around him. Struggling to understand the crude Macedonian dialect, he squinted in the dimness expecting a knife at his throat. Surprisingly, he found Alexander making rounds to the wounded, the doctor at his side.

With a lit torch, one of the men cast him in its brilliance. Instinctively he shielded his eyes with his good arm.

"How are you, Nikanoras?"

"Unfortunately, I live."

The doctor opened the wrappings of his wounds and checked them. Redressing them with a clean poultice, something in the herbs was numbing the pain, and he was grateful.

"Are you hungry?"

Nikanoras' expression must have told Alexander of his confusion. There was a sense about this that was almost sinister in its kindness. "Why do you nurse me? Is it to humiliate me?" Nikanoras asked.

Searching the others around him at such an odd comment, Alexander knelt by the bed.

When the prince seemed determined to get an explanation from him, Nikanoras again held back his tears. "That I have survived is pure torture. Do you see? I should have been struck down in battle to show my companions I am no coward. Please, kill me. Drive a sword through my chest so I may not be an embarrassment to them."

His blue eyes sparkling in the torchlight as he finally

205

understood, Alexander replied, "But you are not an embarrassment. You fought bravely. When the cowards around you fled to the hills, only your three hundred stood and faced the force of Macedon. So, be proud, Nikanoras. You and your survivors should be held in honor."

Missing his Meleagros, Nikanoras' throat tightening in his grief as he asked, "Who…Who has survived?"

"Whom do you seek?" Alexander's warm hand clasped Nikanoras' left one.

Turning away to hide his tears, Nikanoras could not do it. He had seen his lover fall in battle. He knew his name would not be among the few.

"Get him something to eat," Alexander ordered one of the men standing idly. "They have sent word back to the city of Thebes and your statesmen. They know there are survivors."

Allowing a sad laugh to escape his lips, Nikanoras said, "And there is still a city called Thebes?"

"Yes, but do not expect Father to keep your empire whole."

"No. I would think not."

Reaching to push the long hair back from Nikanoras' face, Alexander asked, "Do you have family left there?"

Nikanoras knew if Arybos and his mother heard he lived though the army had perished around him, he would be branded a coward and a traitor. "No," he said.

Nikanoras knew Alexander would see he lied, for all the Sacred Band had been bred from aristocracy, he waited for a rebuttal. But Alexander allowed him to hide his shame.

When a bowl of food arrived, the prince insisted Nikanoras sit up and eat it, nudging him like a mother. Nikanoras managed to ingest most of it and sip more wine. "Where are the others?"

"Soon, Nikanoras, I will lead you to them soon."

"What will be done with them?" The empty bowl was taken from him.

"I do not know. Father has spoken of releasing Athens' captives, but the Theban prisoners are to be ransomed."

"And if there is no one to pay? Then what?" He knew, but he

needed to hear.

"Sold as slaves, Nikanoras. I am sorry."

"I should rather die."

"Surely there is someone back in Thebes with wealth."

"No one." *Who? His mother?* Whose hatred of him was plain to see when she kicked him out of his own home? Or perhaps Arybos. Who was certain this war would be his death and would most definitely kill him the moment he knew he was yet alive.

Alexander waved off the few around them. "Rest. Something will come to us by daybreak."

As the firelight passed out of his view, Nikanoras gave in to sleep, hoping in the night one of the wounded Macedonian soldiers would slit his throat.

CHAPTER 25

An army to be successful must be mobile. Philip had mastered this as with all his other tactics learned while hostage in Nikanoras' homeland. As the troops packed up to head back to Pella, they were being assessed for litters. As someone approached he shook his head no. "I can walk."

The soldier who asked, could care less if he could or not, for left without another word.

Nikanoras sat up carefully, his arm in a sling around his neck to keep it still and a bandage was wrapped around his chest. He paused to allow his strength to come back before standing. When he did, he searched for his things and found them piled at the foot of his bed. Reaching for them with his left hand, he grew frustrated quickly at his helplessness.

He threw them down in anger and dropped back to sit on his cot, hiding his face, shameful of his tears. Where was he going? To Pella? "Oh, Father Zeus, help me..." he cried.

A touch on his shoulder drew his attention. One of the Macedonian soldiers had seen his feeble attempt at dressing himself. A blood stained cloth wrapped around his head, he said in Greek to Nikanoras, "I will help you."

Nikanoras stopped the man from this pathetic attempt. "Kill me. I beg of you."

Though the thought may have passed through his mind before, he shook his head. "You will be all right."

208

The time was drawing near and they were readying to march. Nikanoras gave in and allowed the soldier to assist him. Like he was an imbecile or a baby needing a nursemaid, the humiliation burned like coal in his cheeks. Here is the mighty warrior, who cannot even tie his sandals.

Nikanoras emerged from that tent into stark daylight. He narrowed his gaze at the orderly chaos of the troops around him. The moment he showed his face, a general assigned a guard to watch over him. Nikanoras was very desirable property to the Macedonian King.

His mind unable to focus, Nikanoras peered through the dust to the direction of the battlefield. He moved in a dream to it, as if being on that spot could solve some riddles in his mind. A hand held him back. "Please...can I not look upon their graves?"

Seeing the tears threatening, the guard nodded, leading Nikanoras to the site.

With heaviness in him, almost as if he had swallowed clay bricks, Nikanoras dragged himself with a purpose to that place. The bodies that had lain in bloody heaps were gone. Instead, there were mounds. Seven rows of thirty-six, with two extra added to the first. Buried where they stood to fight. Gone to the realm of Hades. His comrades, his lover.

Nikanoras fell to his knees in agony, wailing in pain, beating the dirt with an awkward left fist.

He could hear behind his back the guard tried to hold back his own tears. The Sacred Band members were legends to them. Warriors so dedicated and proud, they thought nothing could stop them. They were wrong.

Nikanoras clawed at the dirt in grief, trying to understand how this could have happened and why he was left to deal with it himself.

"All right," the guard said, "I need to get you back."

He was helped to his feet awkwardly, forcefully, for Nikanoras was in no mood to leave that spot. Nikanoras pleaded again for him to kill him. "If I get you some money, will you do it then?"

With a low laugh the wounded soldier said, "You are worth more alive to my king, I am afraid."

"He will get no ransom for me."

"We shall see." He shrugged. "If not, you will be a slave then."

Nikanoras was led back to the main camp. A long line of prisoners was being organized into rows for marching. As the soldier put Nikanoras in his place, to his utter humiliation, they placed chains on his ankles. So. They must parade them through their hometown like trophies for the victors. Oh, he would surely have died in battle but endure this.

Head bowed in disbelief that no more than a day ago he was standing proud in the front of a very different kind of parade, Nikanoras walked with the other prisoners, back to Pella for an unknown fate.

****

Having been made to march before, Nikanoras managed to get through it, even with his injuries. He was wondering if he went crazy, if somehow his reason could leave his body, then the enemy could no longer hurt him. Either that or he needed to find someone who would kill him. Didn't they want their foe dead?

Nikanoras had never been to the grey stone city. He was unimpressed. His Thebes was lovely by comparison, filled with gardens and temples. This seemed as barren a wasteland as their ruler's intellect. It was simply ugly. Nikanoras hated it on sight and yearned to go home.

Will my mother pay for my return? How about Arybos? Was he truly an orphan now? An orphan among thieves?

Someone was moving down the line separating the Athenians from the Thebans. When he caught sight of a head of blond hair Nikanoras held his breath.

Alexander stood before him. "Nikanoras. You look well. Come, you need not stand with the rest."

The Crown Prince escorted him to other men that had removed from the mass.

Nikanoras could see Theban generals, captains, and some silver and bronze armor he knew by heart. As he passed, checking the faces of the others of his Band, they were doing the same to him, hoping against hope it was their lover or someone they knew well.

210

Nikanoras was taking too long for the guard at his back he shoved him to hurry up. He and the other special captives were brought to a deep, dim chamber to wait for audience with the King.

Philip was interviewing each, one at a time.

In that crowded room, Nikanoras tried to move from one end to the other, hoping to see someone he knew, anyone. And one in particular.

Most had wounds bandaged, some bleeding through. It was breaking his heart, he knew not a soul.

Exhausting himself, Nikanoras gave up and leaned against a wall for support. The general he was near smiled sadly at him. "You fought well."

"Seemingly, not well enough."

"Do not take it to heart. It is in the hands of the gods."

Nodding politely, Nikanoras wanted no more of this conversation. Besides, the guard was about to come over and tell them to be quiet.

As the chamber was emptied, one by one, Nikanoras was brought before the ruler of Macedon.

King Philip was seated on his throne with his son at his side. A show of force of their top officials was surrounding them, and there was a servant with a scribe.

After the king had a good look at him, he said, "State your name."

"Nikanoras son of the late Saliukos, Your Highness."

The fact Nikanoras had addressed him as his king out of respect impressed him. Nikanoras had heard enough of this goat to fill an arena. Ego being his most obvious attribute.

"Ransom of three talents," the king instructed the scribe.

"My father is dead, King Philip," Nikanoras said, as if by telling him the first time was not heard.

"Who then, shall we ask a ransom? Your mother? What is her name?" Alexander asked.

At the sweet comment, Nikanoras met Alexander's eyes. In them was a mixture of pity and admiration. What was Alexander to do for him? Nikanoras knew his fate.

"You may ask it of my mother, Thessenike, but, it will be in vain."

"A mother who will not ransom her son?" Alexander obviously

could not conceive of this for his relationship with his own mother was one of adoration, so the gossip went.

As bitter water rose in his mouth, Nikanoras lowered his head in shame. *Yes, pretty Alexander, a mother who wants nothing to do with her son. There is such a beast.*

"Well, you had better hope she sends your ransom, for the other option is by far worse." The king waved his hand. "Next."

Escorted out again, Nikanoras was brought to a hall where they had set up a food line. Macedon knowing the few selected for ransom were the aristocracy of Thebes, they would not be treated as common slaves and thrown into a pit, yet.

If nothing else, Macedon treated their captives to the honor that each deserved. Glad was Nikanoras not to be a common foot soldier at that moment.

With his bowl of food in his good hand, Nikanoras sat next to the general he had met in the room before he was questioned by the king.

This man was in his early forties with a finely trimmed beard. He appeared sturdy and proud, obviously a seasoned veteran that had seen wars before.

"Do they allow us to speak to each other?" Nikanoras whispered over the table.

"Only if you use Greek so they may understand."

Nodding, Nikanoras tried to eat with his clumsy left hand. After he had consumed a few bites he said, "I am Nikanoras, son of Saliukos."

The man's eyes lit up in delight. "Nikanoras. Yes, your father was a great man. And sorely missed. I am Deodoras, a general from the Boeotian league."

"You don't know how sorely missed he is. I fear I will not be ransomed and will be destined to be sold into slavery."

"What of Thessenike? Surely she will send your ransom."

Nikanoras could see one of the guards listening, no doubt as he had been instructed. "No, good Deodoras. She most likely has remarried by now and forgotten me. We did not part on good terms."

"Take heart. No mother wants her son to be sold to hard labor.

212

She will come through for you."

"And if she does? What then? Go back and live in shame? Shall I be proud that I have lived when all my companions have died?" As the lump grew in his throat, Nikanoras pushed his bowl away, looking away to hide his tears.

Deodoras reached for Nikanoras. "Do not think of this. You will return a hero. Everyone knows it was your Band who fought the hardest. The bravest. Why, even Philip was impressed. So much so, he is having a monument erected to honor your fallen brothers. Philip himself was heard to say, '*Perish any man who suspects that these men either did or suffered anything that was base.*' (2)

"And my Meleagros is among them." Lowering his head to his left arm, Nikanoras cried. Would the pain never leave him?

Deodoras put his arm around Nikanoras' shoulder to comfort him.

The few around who were listening paused in their meal to stare solemnly. It had been a tremendous blow to them all. All their hopes lay waste when this group could not fulfill their dreams. But, they did not blame Nikanoras nor hold ill thoughts against him. On the contrary, they knew it was only by their strength that they had any chance at all. Their frustration and hatred was directed at Athens for their debacle. A people who had sent almost nothing to aid their cause betrayed them. And now they would bear the brunt of the wrath of Philip. With kid gloves Athens would be handled and fawned over, their two thousand prisoners freed without ransom, no war would he wage against them, but in return, Athens was to dissolve the Athenian Maritime League, becoming Macedon's ally.

It was better than they had hoped at the hands of so powerful an enemy. Thebes was less fortunate. Its government was to be replaced, all they had fought for was to be returned, and each state would claim their independence from them.

The greatest losses in battle, and the worst aftermath. That was the thanks they received for their valiant effort. And as for Demosthenes, Nikanoras wanted to see him hanged.

"All right, my boy. Do not cry."

Nikanoras rested his head tiredly. His wounds had begun aching again. "I only wanted to die with him in battle. What would he think to see me now? Hmm? Alive? Healing?"

"He would thank the gods that you made it through. As you would for him."

"But he has not made it." Nikanoras raised his head and searched the room in a useless gesture. "Look. Do you see him before you?"

The fact that the general did not know who he searched for was unimportant. "He would want you to live on."

"Live on? How? As a slave? Hard labor? Is that a life?"

"You do not know they will not pay your ransom. Why do you not rest? I can see you are in pain." Deodoras alerted the guard who was well within reach, for he had been listening to every word. "He is weak. Can he rest and his wounds be tended?"

With a nod, the guard shouted to another, who came forward.

Gently, they got Nikanoras to his feet. "Deodoras," Nikanoras sobbed as they separated them. He could not lose a friend he had just made. His only friend.

"I will seek you later. Go rest." The general waved.

Trying to find some reassurance in his words, Nikanoras was escorted out of the hall. As he passed, all the eyes of the Theban generals, captains, and survivors of the Sacred Band were on him. Nikanoras knew in their hearts they felt anguish for his suffering, for he knew their own shame was the same as his.

After a long walk across the city Nikanoras was given over to another guard. He led him inside a dimly lit columned hall, which led to a house of healing. The guard seated Nikanoras on a cot, his chains were removed, and he was allowed to lay back.

In pain, Nikanoras began to feel as if he were feverish. After a fitful sleep, he was woken by a doctor who once against stripped his wounds and redressed them. With the new poultice the pain once again subsided.

During the night he shivered with a fever, sweating and chattering his teeth.

Through his blurred vision he thought he saw the prince

discussing his state with the doctors. A wool blanket was laid on him and he was given strong wine.

Like a voice calling in his head, Nikanoras kept wishing he would die. Wouldn't something come and put him out of his misery?

By morning light his fever had crested and drenched the bedding. He was helped to his feet, slumped over as they changed the padding and blankets as if he were someone of import who needed their constant care. More wine and broth was brought and he did manage to eat everything they gave him.

Nikanoras was spent and dehydrated. He could do nothing more than lie there even if they had forced him to move.

As they allowed time for the messengers to get to Thebes to give out the ransom lists, he was able to sleep and recuperate.

Around him, dozens of men injured in that battle, some mortally, slept deeply, hoping for eternal peace, or healing, whichever came first.

Woken up on the third day of his convalescence, again his wounds were tended. As his arm was unwrapped Nikanoras watched the layers unroll, curious of its state. Still unable to move it, he had his doubts. When it was revealed to him, he was surprised to see the gap had healed. There were hand-sewn stitches in it and that astonished him. He had never seen human flesh sewn like a fabric.

With a sharp razor, the doctor cut them away.

Thinking his skin would open up, Nikanoras turned his face so he didn't see it. Once the doctor had finished, Nikanoras dared to peek. The gap had not reopened. Slowly Nikanoras tried to extend his arm. Though it was painful, the doctor forced him to do it. Nikanoras winced at the tugging and aching from being bent and in a sling. He managed to get it to lie straight. Moving his fingers in sequence, he didn't seem to have lost any sensation in his hand. With the help of the doctor, he sat up. The doctor had him open and close his elbows together, judging to see how the injured one compared with the whole one.

"I am amazed." Nikanoras smiled weakly at him.

"Yes, but you will have a long way before you can lift a sword."

"If I ever lift one again," he mumbled.

"Let me see your chest wound."

Nikanoras sat straight for him. The doctor peeled back those bandages as well. The puncture did not ooze any longer, but the skin around the hole was still very red and inflamed.

The doctor had Nikanoras lay back and poured some of the wine over the wound. Dabbing it off, he said, "Let's let it dry out now."

Nikanoras nodded. Who was he to argue when he had never seen medicine like this in Thebes. If he were home, he would have had his arm amputated and died of the infection in his chest. He was very certain.

When the doctor had gone, Nikanoras rested once more, leaning up against his pillows to stare into space. As the doctor went from bed to bed, Nikanoras tried to listen to his words, from nothing else, boredom.

A voice caught his attention. He looked over to the direction it had come, and noticed the doctor sitting on someone's bed, nodding. Then he seemed to be unwrapping bandages once more.

A strange sensation passed over Nikanoras which he shrugged off as nonsense.

A servant was coming in to feed them. Nikanoras had no complaints for the treatment they were receiving. Of course if the ransom did not come through, he would see that change drastically.

Through the tail of his eye he caught someone approaching. Deodoras' smile greeted him.

Excited to see him, Nikanoras set down his bowl and patted the place next to him on the bed.

"How are you feeling?" the general asked softly.

"Look. I can move my arm." Nikanoras showed off his newly revealed scar and bent his elbow for him a few times.

"Very good. You'll be back to fighting fitness in no time."

"More like chiseling rocks." Nikanoras bowed his head in defeat.

"Nonsense, but speaking of rocks, I thought you would like to know. A stone lion has been carved to stand guard over your fallen comrades."

"Really?" He asked in excitement. "Philip has done that?"

"He has indeed. You see, you were a thing of wonder, Nikanoras."

"No, not I. My comrades were. My Meleagros was the hero, and the others, Lysos, Mycandor, Argos, Chasathenes—" he choked up as he recited the roll call of the dead.

Stopping him, Deodoras touched Nikanoras' hair gently. "Let's not get upset again. Soon you will be on your way home."

Nikanoras wiped his eyes. "Have any of the ransoms come through?"

"Not that I know of. They will. Slowly they will trickle up north."

"Who waits for you?" Glad to get off the topic of death, Nikanoras tried to appear interested.

"My lovely wife and daughters." The smile was warm on his face with his memories.

Nikanoras said, "I would love a wife. And family...one day. It is what I have always dreamed of."

"Very soon you shall have your wish." The kind general smoothed his hand down Nikanoras' shoulder to his arm, trying to comfort him.

Raising his lashes to meet those distinguished mature eyes, Nikanoras said meekly, "So you say, but you do not know my mother. She will not raise one stater for me."

"You know that is not true. Thessenike is a lovely woman."

"Yes, but now my erastes, Arybos, is living with her. And may have married her by now, I do not know."

"Arybos with Thessenike? But, he was your father's closest friend."

It was obvious this connection surprised the general as much as it did Nikanoras.

"So, you see it is useless. I am stranded. Destined for slavery." A deep sigh escaped him.

"When I get back to Thebes, I will see her for you."

"I wish you luck. Last I saw her was when I was fifteen, and she threw me out of her house."

"What of Persepolos?"

"Oh, surely you are joking." Nikanoras lowered his voice again, not realizing it had grown in volume with his irritation. "That man attempted to take my life twice while I was at training, then he made sure I was in front of the Band to meet my doom."

The passive-faced general replied, "Why, Nikanoras, do you have so many enemies?"

Nikanoras met his eyes again instantly. As Deodoras stared at him, Nikanoras wondered what was behind that trusting gaze. Suspicion, he would imagine. Why, indeed, did so many seek his failure? Or worse, his death? Did he know that answer? He wasn't such a bad person, was he?

It seemed if Nikanoras didn't react, explain the reasons, this affectionate man would think that inside him there lurked a plague like in Pandora's Box.

Struggling to get the words out, Nikanoras tried to explain that he was good. That it was the love of his sister that put him at odds with the general, and possibly, with his mother as well. That he hadn't meant to draw his sword against Arybos, but he had made advances he could not accept.

All this sounded so hollow and desperate in his mind he didn't say a word. If Meleagros were there, he could explain it better.

He would show Deodoras he was not unlovable.

As Nikanoras' words trailed off like the sand under his feet after falling from a cliff, he was left with Deodoras' suspicious stare. It had changed from one of kindness to one of mistrust. And Nikanoras hated himself for losing a friend of so much value.

"You...you will not go to my mother now?" It was almost a plea. Hardly something that would pass the lips of one of the Sacred Band. Maybe the general was thinking he was indeed a coward. That he had feigned death to avoid fighting with his comrades to the end. If he did think that of him, Nikanoras would sooner be hung from his thumbs over burning flames.

"I will try, Nikanoras, but, if you have left things as you say you have..."

Nikanoras begged him with his eyes to understand. "If I have given you the impression I am a coward and a cheat, please. Find a dagger and kill me."

218

"You have not. Only simply, a young boy, who has much to learn about being a man."

As the general stood, moving out of Nikanoras' reach, Nikanoras had no words to speak in his defense. If he were the general, he would look down his nose at himself, thinking he was nothing but a waste of his valuable time.

"Rest. Hopefully everything will turn out well for you."

"Will…will you come back and visit?" His voice was closing in his throat.

Without his answer, the general waved and left.

Nikanoras lay back down, closing his eyes as pain shot through his head. The frustration of his lot, his failure to communicate to the general, his loss of Meleagros, and now the possibility of no one caring for him enough to save him from slavery, was rising over him again like a tidal wave.

Thrashing on the bed in agony, wanting to die, he sat up suddenly and gripped the edge of the bed. "Oh, father-Zeus, help me!" he cried in anguish.

Nikanoras climbed from his bed and advanced on one of the armed guards who stood at his door, hoping he would do him the honor and put him out of his misery. As Nikanoras approached the guard, try as he might to seem a menace with only one useful arm and no weapons, tears streaming down his face, the guard did not grant him the pleasure of his saber.

Instead, he held him off, calling for help from his comrades.

"No! You must end this misery! I beg it of you!" Nikanoras sank to his knees, his senses gone haywire, his ears blocked and his sight blind. Nikanoras thought he had gone mad to have heard his name called. But not Nikanoras, *Nikki!*

Rough hands brought him to his feet and back to the bed.

A debate was occurring around Nikanoras on whether to bind him so he could not move.

So wretched had he become that he covered his face and sobbed like an infant. Was there no end to this torture?

There was a commotion at the entrance of the hall. Alexander had heard some disturbance. Strutting in, his cape flowing behind him,

Nikanoras was pointed out as the cause.

Alexander appeared surprised to see it was he who had turned the calm ward into a battlefield. The prince knelt by Nikanoras. "What is the matter?"

Nikanoras said, "Dear Honorable Alexander, Crown Prince of Macedon, please. I beg of you. Do not put me through one more day. All I ask is that you give me your dagger so I may end this constant torment."

"But Nikanoras, you are so near to freedom. Soon the ransoms will be met." Alexander caressed Nikanoras' hair away from his face affectionately.

"Not for me, fair Prince. No ransom for me." Nikanoras sobbed.

"We shall see." His smile was very knowing as he stood.

Nikanoras grabbed after him in desperation.

His arms were struck by the stem of a spear to stop him from touching the prince. In agony Nikanoras cringed back as it made contact to his scarred biceps.

After Nikanoras had been hit, Alexander glared at the guard who had done it. He moved on him in fury. "How dare you! Do you know who he is?"

The guard went bleached as white stone, shaking his head.

"He is a survivor of the Sacred Band. And you shall respect him and honor him. Get out of my sight before I have you beheaded."

Bowing low, the guard nearly sprinted for the door to get away. After he disappeared, Alexander knelt down again and inspected Nikanoras' wound. "I am sorry."

"No. It is I who owes you the apology." Nikanoras could not meet his eyes.

"Rest, Nikanoras. We do not know what tomorrow will bring."

"Thank you, Prince Alexander."

After he had gone, the guard once again at the door, Nikanoras rubbed the raw wound to comfort it. The sting had just begun to subside. A slave was bringing wine for them as the afternoon sunlight waned and angled into the high arched windows of that massive hall.

Thanking him, Nikanoras sipped it, then gulped it down thirstily as he watched him tend the next in line. Nikanoras settled back down again in the bed, exhausted and ready for more sleep.

As he dozed off to the buzz of conversations around him, he thought once again he heard someone whisper, *"Nikki!"*

****

Dawn opened her eyes for the world of Greece and brought with her the warmth of August's sun.

Nikanoras was outside on a stone bench, a sculpture of Apollo by his side. He shaded his eyes to see some horsemen rushing by. News arrived that several ransoms had come through and they would be announcing the names as they came. Meanwhile Macedon was readying its forces to ride to new frontiers.

On to Peloponnese, Philip would march, unopposed, and Sparta would kiss his feet for defeating such a hated enemy as Thebes.

Alexander was sent to Athens with the ashes of their dead. There the Prince was treated like royalty, since the Athenians were so relieved of Philip's terms. They dared not encourage his anger again.

As the rider returned with his list, after meeting with the council, he stood at the doorway and read out names. Those he called were free to go, having had their ransom's met.

Nikanoras slouched over on the bench. He didn't even wait for his name, for it would never be called. The men who could walk on their own left that hall free men, the ones who needed a hand were assisted into the sunlight.

There he sat, unloved, forgotten, wondering how many days of leisure he had left before he was to be auctioned.

When the list was down to the few lucky ones whose families cared, Nikanoras could not bear it another moment. He stood, turning away from the smiling, cheering and pats on the back. Then he heard that thin voice again. *"Nikki!"*

Looking back at the men who moved passed him, Nikanoras studied every one. None he knew. Was he losing his mind?

He wandered back inside the hall to see who was left. A few hundred did remain. The price was so high, it did take some doing to come up with the coins. Most families' wealth lie in their land, their home, their possessions. Not in silver and gold. One must decide how to raise the money or what could be parted with. This did take some time for most. Few had the resources to hand over such a fortune. The wealthiest of the captives, the ones with caring loved ones, were set free.

With some irony Nikanoras envisioned his mother walking around her palace eying the vases and statues, deciding what is worth more to her. Or possibly Arybos was beside her murmuring, "No, Thessenike, surely we do not want to part with that."

Oh, if only his Euridises were alive. He would be the first outside this hall, and she would bring the money herself.

That hissing sound. He must be going insane. It is as if someone was calling his name.

Planting himself where he stood, he carefully assessed each bed and occupant. Who was so cruel to play these mind games with him? Not here. Not now.

The few men in front of him were asleep. Two generals, a captain, a few sons of aristocrats he did not know...

Nikanoras peered behind him at the guard. He was watching him like a hawk watches mice.

Perhaps Nikanoras was singled out as the one who attacked a guard. This man was wary of Nikanoras' every move.

Nikanoras continued walking past a few cots, some he had never approached before. Most of these men were seriously wounded and tended to more regularly. They were from his regime. He could tell by their ages. Very young men with grave injuries. Quite a few men had died over the past few days and had been removed and carried out. Added to that graveyard mound at Chaeronea? He assumed not.

Just noticing someone with long dark hair, Nikanoras moved closer to try and see his face. It was tilted away from him and in shadow.

The guard was growing nervous and said to him, "Why don't you get back into your bed?"

Nikanoras replied, "I am not tired."

"I don't care if you are tired. Get back!" With that order, the guard took a menacing step toward him.

"What have I done? I merely come to see—"

"Now!"

Taking one last look at the soldier in that cot, Nikanoras decided to sneak back again when the guard was changed, or maybe in the dark.

Obeying the man before he grew violent, Nikanoras bowed his head and moved back to his place, sitting down. His gaze was now in the direction of that long-haired soldier. He wondered if he knew him. Something about him seemed familiar. Though the wounded man had been there since the beginning, he never stirred. Surely he was seriously wounded or he would have been on his feet by now.

Bored, frustrated, and trying to be patient and wait for the next shift of watchdogs, Nikanoras lay back to stare out of the windows, waiting for the direction of the sun to set and darken the hall.

He drifted off to sleep. It was the first time since he was a young boy he had been allowed to lounge in bed for any length of time. He wasn't used to being idle, and though his body needed the rest to recuperate from its injuries, he craved activity to keep him from going stir crazy. But the body sometimes knows more than the mind, and sleep came to him every time he lay back on that pillow.

The only position he could endure was face up, on his back. His chest ached miserably when he lay on it, and on his side, his arm was sore. Flat out, deep in slumber, Nikanoras' dreams were of battle, slicing men and their mounts, his companions alive and cheering as they reigned victorious.

"Nikki!"

Nikanoras woke with a start. It was pitch-darkness outside and the dim flames from oil lamps lit them up enough to be seen by the guard at the door. At his movement, the guard stared at him curiously.

Nikanoras recalled his dream, wondering what he had heard. It was clearly Meleagros calling to him.

As he sat up and rubbed his face tiredly, he felt dehydrated and craved wine. Knowing his request would not go over well with the sentry, he tried to be content and settle back down. He tuned into the breathing around him. At least a hundred were in that hall, trying to sleep and restore their health.

Just as Nikanoras began to drift off once again, he heard it clearly. This time he was not asleep. He pushed the covers off and sat up. As he expected, the guard approached.

"I am sorry. I need to relieve myself."

Nodding his head, the guard stood back, allowing him to pass.

As Nikanoras left the hall, dozens of guards were stationed along the way. Once he had taken care of that business, Nikanoras returned.

Just as he took a chance to investigate the rest of the room, Nikanoras was caught and brought back to his bed. No doubt did he have that they would be glad when he has gone and they no longer needed to baby-sit him.

Nikanoras gave up on the idea of solving his mystery. He went back to his slumber, knowing somehow he would come to his senses and the tormenting whispers would fade.

CHAPTER 26

It had been almost two weeks of waiting. Alexander was gone and Nikanoras dared not ask of a guard when their time was up and they would be sent away to be sold. Nikanoras was sure they had given their families deadlines. All hope in him began to fade.

As the doctor made his routine rounds, he spent only a moment with Nikanoras and instructed him to keep working his arm, lest it freeze up on him. Nodding his head, knowing the doctor was trying to do what he thought best, Nikanoras didn't have much determination in him to get it back to its full strength. He would only use it for hard labor from now on, after all.

While Nikanoras watched, the doctor halted at the cot with the long haired soldier. Nikanoras wondered if he could stretch his legs and make his way closer to them. Several men were up and mulling about, having quiet chats between cots.

Acting as casually as he could, he rose up and stretched, then step-by-step moved closer to where the doctor was seated. In his mind he was trying to express he was simply curious of his methods and words of wisdom.

Hardly believing he had gotten that far, Nikanoras was standing right behind the doctor's back as he peeled open some bandages from this soldier's chest.

Though a scruffy dark shadow of stubble covered his jaw, and his hair was wild and falling over his eyes, Nikanoras gasped in shock to see it was his lover.

225

"Meleagros!"

The doctor spun around to him. "You know this man?"

Nikanoras knelt down by him to see if he could be mistaken. When the doctor turned the wounded man's jaw to meet his inspection, Nikanoras broke down to see it was not his lover at all.

"He has not been conscious since he was brought off the battlefield. What did you say his name was?"

"No. I do not know. It is not who I thought it was. Only in my hopes did I think it was he. I am sorry, I cannot help you." Nikanoras returned to his cot as if he were an old man without his cane, stumbling blindly.

Lying back to try and calm himself from the initial elation, then miserable disappointment, Nikanoras knew, he would see Meleagros everywhere. Every man that passed near his likeness, he would grasp to inspect closely. But, it was a useless gesture. His lover was dead.

Hot tears rolled down his temples, then the agony burst forth, along with horrendous guilt.

Why didn't I appreciate him more while he was alive? Why did I mistreat him and not show him how much he meant to me? And why, oh, why, gods in the heavens, am I not dead with him?

The guard noticed the warrior of the Sacred Band once again in tears of suffering. Biting his lip as he stared, he could not imagine the prospect of being one of the sole survivors, the disgrace, the blame, it was no wonder he was constantly on the verge of tears.

****

Precisely three weeks from the day of the battle, only a few lingered behind that were awaiting ransom. Bored and knowing what lie ahead, Nikanoras offered to help the slaves sweep the hall and take down the cots as they were vacated.

When one of the soldiers called his name, he moved to him numbly, assuming the day had come that he was to be sold.

"You are free."

Tilting his head in confusion, Nikanoras asked him to repeat what he had said.

"Your ransom has been paid. You are free to leave."

"Paid? By whom?"

"Does it matter?" He laughed at him. "Go."

"Go?" Nikanoras was so stunned he couldn't think. Who had paid? Mother? Arybos? Had guilt gotten their better?

Gathering his things together, wearing his armor, which was as it came off the battlefield, a hole in the chest guard, covered in blood and filth, he wrapped his cape around his shoulders and stood at the doorway.

He looked back only once and began his walk, southbound over the great Kerata Pass. Before he took his leave of Pella, he gazed back in wonder at the hive of activity that was to be the greatest war machine in Greek history. He hoped never again would he be brought there, in chains or otherwise, for the memories that it brought back were pure agony.

Penniless, and needing to stop frequently on his return from the exhaustion in his body, Nikanoras passed the plain of battle once more intent on seeing this monument given to them by Philip.

As he made his way across the flat land, grass trampled, dried out from the searing sun of a summer which was all but vanishing, Nikanoras was astonished to see a lion erected. Proud and serene, sitting up with a grimace of a growl on its lips, it watched over the graves of his loved ones.

In tears, he could not think of a grander tribute. Gazing through wet eyes at each mound, wondering which held his beloved, he knew it was sheer torture to be there, remember the battle, seeing Meleagros falling over and over in his mind. Again and again he went over the scenario wondering what he could have done differently to prevent his death, but it was useless. Nothing he could have done, even standing before him to fight for him which Meleagros never would have permitted, would have saved him.

"Nikki!" the breeze whispered as it passed his ears. Hearing that sound, Nikanoras clenched his teeth and fists and shouted into the sky, "Stop tormenting me! I will be driven mad!"

Nikanoras quieted himself, pausing to listen. He knew that voice would haunt him eternally. A night hadn't passed that he had not heard that whisper, either when he was just waking or just nodding off to sleep. But, here, on the plain where Meleagros had died, he heard it very distinctly. Again raising his unshaven jaw to the heavens he cried, "I could not save you. I am sorry. Forgive your lover, Meleagros. Forgive him and stop this haunting."

Hearing no more sounds other than the dry reeds flexing in the wind, he tried to clear his mind. The wind brushing his long hair back from his shoulders, Nikanoras scanned in the direction of his home. What changes lie ahead? How would he find his city now? Ransacked? Burned? He had no idea.

His mother had obviously wanted him to return, why else pay? Or maybe it had been Arybos' pity on him, knowing he was helpless now that they had most likely wed.

With no desire to head south, Nikanoras forced himself to walk. He had no other alternative, but to face what lay ahead in Thebes.

Four days it took him. Walking through the Kerata Pass, relying on the kindness of those who recognized his armor and crest as one of the chosen, he was fed and given places to sleep along the way.

When he first stepped through the gates of his city, it surely had been changed. The hall of the council was in ruin. He caught the scent of burning as he passed. His people were still living here, but it was a joyless city of captives. Murmurs surrounded him that Athens had armed every man in its city limits, including slaves and children.

Good old Athens had their warships left untouched. When word came that Philip was still intimidated by the Athenians, and that all their captives were freed, they rejoiced with little celebration, not trusting the old goat in the least.

Thebes was not as lucky as Nikanoras found their streets filled with Macedonian soldiers. He passed them as they patrolled and they caught his eye suspiciously. They knew exactly what he was. One of the few. A survivor of the chosen. Branded, he thought bitterly, branded a failure and a scarred for life by the defeat. *'Chosen'*, he scoffed to himself angrily, "Thank you, Father, for your wonderful choice." He growled. "My father, the spy for Sparta." Spitting into the dirt in disdain, he could not think of a more fitting end to a family line of traitors.

Though some may raise their heads high, he was humiliated he came back to this. To see his city occupied by the enemy.

The halls of justice burned, the council replaced by Macedonians. It was his worst fears realized.

As his sandals padded his own cobbled street, Nikanoras dreaded coming home. What was he to seek here? Why had his mother paid his ransom?

Before he entered he touched the front door. In a quick memory flash he had a wonderful image of being a child, coming home to see Euridises' glowing smile. He would smell cooking from their hearth. His father would be seated at the table, a wax tablet before him; Mother in the courtyard, catching the last rays of the setting sun.

Opening the door, Nikanoras inhaled the familiar scent of the cool stone interior. He expected Nazabine to greet him, but maybe the slave was otherwise occupied.

Searching the eerie stillness, Nikanoras heard men's voices. He walked softly to not make a sound and located Arybos talking to a Macedonian aristocrat.

At that sight the bile rose in Nikanoras' throat. It looked so much like an act of treachery.

Before he passed his judgment like the great Zeus above, he listened. It seemed Arybos was bartering for the chance to keep 'his' palace and some of 'his' wealth.

He was offering this Macedonian emissary a percentage, as tax.

It was a diplomatic side of Arybos Nikanoras had never witnessed. The men did not hear him step behind them.

Before he was discovered and the Macedonian could spy him, Nikanoras was grabbed and dragged away from the conversation. To his utter astonishment, the strong grip belonged to his mother.

He expected her to embrace him, giving thanks that he was yet alive and returned to her. Unfortunately that was the last thing on her mind. The force of her anger tore him to shreds.

In a strangulated whisper, she hurled the most painful

accusations he had ever experienced from her. "Coward! Eunuch! Bastard!"

When he could get a word in he said, "Then why did you pay my ransom?"

As Nikanoras fended off her fists, which were attempting to punch his face and chest and do him bodily harm, she denied ever sending him a thing, cursing the day he returned to her as if he were Perseus come back empty handed from his task to the disappointment of the world.

"Who then? Arybos?" He allowed her to batter him because he had to know the truth, though everything in him wanted to push her back to stop her from assaulting him. Hadn't he been through enough?

Hissing like the snakes on Medusa's head, she seemed about to explode. "Why did you not die in battle like a hero? It is because of you that the greedy masses from Pella come to plague our city like vultures."

And then she spat on him! As if all the blood he had shed, all the pain he had suffered, the loss, the humiliation wasn't quite enough punishment.

At that instance, Nikanoras did indeed shove her back, wiping his cheek from her disgusting act. Towering over her, his armor, showing her who he was with pride, he snarled. "You! You stand there and judge me? How dare you! You think you know what I endured? The suffering? And this? From the harpy who has murdered my own father to marry her lover? I hope Macedon takes all of your filthy, bloody riches from you. You deserve nothing."

"Get out! Get out of this house and never return. You are a disgrace," she screeched so loudly his ears hurt.

Never had Nikanoras seen her like this; her veins protruding, her mouth foaming, her eyes wide and bulging. Like wild Cerberus at the gates of Hades.

Their shouting was soon overheard. Arybos came scampering in as pale as if he had seen a ghost. "Nikanoras!" He gasped in astonishment.

When the Macedonian realized one of the Sacred Band was

before him, his mouth hung open in awe. "Who is this warrior?" he asked.

"He—" Arybos looked over his shoulder at Thessenike, who was trembling in fear.

Arybos said, "This is the son of Thessenike and the late Saliukos. Nikanoras."

The Macedonians stood back, investigating Nikanoras' armor, which the Macedonian obviously knew well. He said, "I will take it under advisement that you are a kin of this Sacred Band warrior. I shall come back with a decision for you."

"Wait." Nikanoras tried to stop him, knowing his standing would help his mother and her wicked lover.

His mother's nails embedded into his skin. Thessenike prevented Nikanoras from going after the man. "Don't you ruin this for me. Don't you let them take what I have worked so hard for."

Nikanoras wrenched his arm away from her claws, and said, "Who in the name of Hades are you? I would never believe you bore me as your son. Or my loving sister, for you are like a poisonous serpent."

"Don't you ever speak to me that way!" she screamed, her face a brilliant shade of crimson. "The least you can do is pretend you live here so your family home and gold will be safe. It is obvious you could do nothing to defend us."

In all his life Nikanoras never thought he could be capable of matricide, until that moment. In reflex he reached for his sword, but he was unarmed and the gesture was harmless.

"It is a pity the Macedonian left before I could tell him this was not my home so he may destroy it." Nikanoras' lip curled. "They can raze it to the ground for all I care."

Arybos said, "Calm down, Thessenike. What good is all this shouting? Let us try and be reasonable. I am sure we can come to some understanding." Arybos nudged them, making a gap between them.

Nikanoras turned his back to his mother. He could not bear to look at her at the moment.

Arybos shook his head at Nikanoras' appearance. "By the gods..." he mumbled as if praying he could be mistaken. "We heard the Sacred Band was massacred, Nikanoras."

"A few have survived. Some were even welcome in their own homes." Nikanoras asked, "If you did not pay my ransom, who then?"

Arybos appeared too stunned to believe Nikanoras could have been one of the few left standing after such carnage, neither answered his question.

Nikanoras threw up his hands in disgust, moved past them and out of the door. As he left he heard his mother say, "I want him killed." Nikanoras stopped and hid behind the shrubbery to listen.

"Thessenike." Arybos scolded, "He is your own flesh and blood."

"He is a disgrace. I do not want to see his face again."

"Let us just wait and see. Surely he is harmless, and if the Macedonian government think he is ours, he may aid us in keeping our wealth."

When it became silent and the front door closed, Nikanoras moved on.

The streets of Thebes were dusty and filled with humanity moving out or moving in. A great influx of mercenaries from Macedon had come to occupy them as their own citizens left before they were sent from their homes or enslaved against treaty. Some citizens were angry at Athens and were headed there to rage at the council in disgust for their peace with Philip. Peace? After they had died to protect her precious Acropolis?

Numb and exhausted, Nikanoras simply did not care. Nowhere to go, no one to see, he sat down on the lip of a fountain to observe the movement. Laden donkeys and horses packed full, waddled under their heavy burdens to new lands. It was a city under siege. He had let them down. It was from more than just his mother did he expect to be spat on. But so far the people of Thebes had pity on him and turned aside once they recognized his armor.

No one thanked him. Not one. He had not expected thanks. Not really. He had failed them.

"Nikki!"

Nikanoras spun around with his heart in his throat. He could not believe he was hearing his name again. But, this time, he was wide awake, and the voice was not what he remembered. It was very nasal and had a twang of femininity that made him shiver.

The adrenaline rush that surged through him, nauseated him. Half did he expect to see Meleagros there, bright eyed and arms open. To his astonishment he found his brother, Ephisomines.

Ephisomines embraced Nikanoras and crushed him in his arms. "When Father and I heard you were alive I was so relieved."

Standing back from him to see his narrow hawkish face, Nikanoras said, "Thank you. Your brother, he did not survive. I am sorry." The lump in his throat almost choked Nikanoras.

"No, I assumed not when no ransom was sought for him."

"I grieve, Ephisomines, I am lost without him." The tears threatened.

"Come. You must eat and bathe. Look at you. Oh, dear, oh, dear, you are a mess. And need a shave as well. I almost did not recognize you. Where is that handsome boy? Under all that hair." He grasped Nikanoras' locks, giggling.

Avoiding the odd glances from civilian and guard alike, Nikanoras bowed his head low, trying not to be ashamed to be seen with someone of Ephisomines' nature. He was the brother of his beloved and deserved respect and most assuredly, sympathy.

Ephisomines held his hand and began to escort him. Nikanoras assumed he was being led to the family palace. He had never been to Meleagros' home before.

When they arrived and it was not the mansion that belonged to his father, Xenophos, Nikanoras was surprised. He realized this palace was Ephisomines' own home.

Servants hovered for his command as Nikanoras gaped at the interior, more lush and gilded than his own. Or should he say, than *Arybos'* home.

Taking in the lavish surroundings, awed by the wealth, Nikanoras paused as Ephisomines glided around the mosaic stone floors and brilliant painted frescos on the walls. "I am amazed. What a place this is. They will allow you to keep it?" Nikanoras said, as he was encouraged to keep moving to the baths.

"Yes, for now. I have struck a bargain. My tongue has once again been my saving grace. Beauty never has." As he said that, he smirked at Nikanoras teasingly, assuming it was obvious.

Thinking back to the time he first met this man, Nikanoras knew what Meleagros and he both thought of him. Nikanoras' cheeks blushed in humiliation. He was ashamed for those naughty thoughts in the face of his kindness.

Clapping his hands, Ephisomines called for a servant to help Nikanoras with his things.

As Nikanoras was stripped Ephisomines was able to see the wounds Nikanoras had suffered.

Ephisomines stood within a breath of him and touched the large scar on his biceps first, then his chest. Lastly, he met Nikanoras' eyes. "I am so sorry," he whispered, trying to convey his empathy.

"Not as sorry as I. These wounds should have killed me. I am devastated I am still here with the living. I should have been with Meleagros." Choking on a sob of agony, he cried, "I wonder...does he wait for me at the gates of Hades?"

As he broke down once more, Ephisomines rubbed his back gently, offering what comfort he could.

"Bring my guest wine immediately!" He made sure Nikanoras had a never empty cup in his hand.

Investigating the puncture wound on his chest, Ephisomines shook his head in awe. "How indeed did you survive two injuries that appear fatal?" He said, "Come, bathe, shave, drink your wine, and then, lovely Nikanoras, rest."

"Thank you." Nikanoras did not know what to say to express his gratitude.

****

As Nikanoras was cleaned, shaven, and fed a very wonderful meal, Ephisomines kept Nikanoras under his watchful gaze.

Nikanoras tried not to feel self-conscious as Ephisomines studied his every move, clothed him in his finest garments, and catered to him as if he were a king.

Suspicion had begun to arrive in Nikanoras' mind. Trained to be a highly skilled warrior, tactical to a fault, he knew, everyone had motive and trusted no one.

Once Nikanoras was sated, comfortable, and tended, it was as if he were finally able to see after being blinded. At the sudden realization he said, "You are the one who paid my ransom."

Ephisomines was seated on cushions in front of a glittering fire as his servants attended their every whim. Ephisomines smiled seductively. "Yes, it was I. In the senate's last days, the list was read of the captives. My lovely Ganymede, when your name was read, as father and I hoped to hear Meleagros', I spied around for your mother. She was not there. I am afraid I knew of her recent marriage to Arybos and put the two together. Father and I believed they did not want to send ransom for you. Needless to say I was speechless at that realization."

Nikanoras kept his expression blank. It was no one's business how much that pained him.

"Well, I thought about you night and day. You there, in Pella, sentenced to be a slave. Though the two of us do not know one another well, I know how my brother loved you. I remember it in his eyes the day he introduced you to Father. You meant the world to him."

Turning aside as a wave of anguish filled him, Nikanoras fought the tears with all his heart. And Ephisomines knew it.

"So, my lovely, rather than see you in that horrible place, your beauty being wasted by hard labor, I sent for your freedom."

Gaining control of his emotions once more, Nikanoras said what was expected in a mechanical tone, almost knowing the answer beforehand. "I am forever in your debt. If there is a way, you must tell me, how can I repay you."

A devilish smile widened on his ugly face. Sadly, Nikanoras thought it did nothing to improve his look.

"Several ways, pretty Nikanoras. Several ways. But let us not get into all that tonight." The man licked his lips and batted his lashes, as if restraining his lust.

Nikanoras figured it was all Ephisomines could do to not cross the room and sexually assault him. Nikanoras knew of the most obvious way he was to return the favor.

It was not a comfortable position to be in, owing someone of Ephisomines. Somehow Nikanoras needed to get money and repay him, clearing his debt and setting him free. Though he had been spared the slavery up north, another type of subjugation was brewing in Ephisomines' complex mind. Nikanoras wondered if it was somehow worse than what he would have suffered in Pella.

Ephisomines said, "Rest. You are worn."

As delicately as a lady, he rose up and reached for Nikanoras. While the servants either backed away into the shadows or lit lamps to shine their way, he held out his hand to receive Nikanoras' as he guided him to his suite.

When a bedroom, rich with mosaic floors and tapestry-covered walls appeared, Nikanoras was as impressed with this young man's wealth.

"You have done well for yourself. You should be proud."

This appeared to surprise Ephisomines.

Nikanoras had been spoken with complete candor, not a hint of jealousy or sarcasm, which perhaps he was more accustomed to.

As if it was meant as a sign, Ephisomines approached Nikanoras, waving the servants out to leave them alone.

When their two shadows met in the middle of the vast room, Ephisomines craned his chin up to Nikanoras' height. A hiss of air escaped between Ephisomines' teeth as he gazed at him. Nikanoras was no fool. He knew what part of this payment would be.

Suddenly becoming as obedient as a slave girl, Nikanoras inhaled courage he needed for this task. He lowered his head and removed the fine garments, dropping them to the floor.

The years of satisfying Arybos' sexual cravings returned. Nikanoras did this out of duty, detached himself from where he was, and allowed his body to become hollow and vacant.

Only when he left his physical self was he able to give out what he would never do voluntarily.

As if he were some hungry mongrel being fed raw meat, Ephisomines grunted and licked his lips in a grotesque manner. Resisting the urge to conjure up Meleagros in his place, for that thought would bring him to tears, Nikanoras simply became a statue, allowing the child to play.

CHAPTER 27

The next day at the markets, Nikanoras wore a sword given to him by Ephisomines. Though he wondered if he was allowed to be armed, Nikanoras noticed the Macedonian soldiers eyeing him curiously, but none approached nor took from him his weapon. No one knew the rules obviously, which changed daily. But, he did learn little by little, the native Thebans who fought or kept back their tribute to Philip, were exiled empty handed. It was best to keep silent and bow one's head in such circumstance.

As the men of Philip's army passed, Nikanoras stopped to allow them room on the narrow street. Not a moment after they vanished around a building did he hear a furious roar and the sound of metal unsheathing from a scabbard behind him.

Nikanoras pivoted around in panic.

There, standing before him was the infamous general Persepolos, obviously enraged Nikanoras still walked around a free citizen.

Nikanoras could not believe his eyes, nor his luck at this chance meeting. "General!" he said, causing every head in the area to spin in their direction.

Persepolos' first lunge of his sword passed very close to Nikanoras' right shoulder, almost duplicating the same slice the arrow had made from one of his assassins.

Quick on his feet, Nikanoras ducked out of the way and drew his weapon, very glad he had one. Getting into a good fighting stance, he faced his adversary. But, the moment the weight of the blade elevated passed his waist, his right biceps weakened and burned in agonizing pain.

Dread filled Nikanoras instantly. He had always been able to battle, to defend himself and those around him. The fact that he could not fight, truly alarmed him.

As Nikanoras leapt back and out of the general's reach, a small crowd had noticed their fight.

Unfortunately, lawless murders in the street had become too commonplace in Thebes since their occupation, and Nikanoras knew this was simply one more duel and killing.

Nikanoras searched for something to use in his left hand to deflect his blows. It wasn't going to be possible for him to raise his sword and use it with his right. He had no idea how weak his arm had become, but, it was almost useless in this capacity.

As he hunted for a shield or something similar, Nikanoras yelled, "Still, General? After all this city has endured? You still have my head on your mind? For the love of Athena, General Persepolos. Why?"

The old man grunted and looked blinded with so much anger Nikanoras doubted he could not hear. Persepolos raised his long sword and again brought it crashing down. A perverse curse blasted out of the old man as he lashed out. "You should be dead!"

Avoiding the blade, Nikanoras turned away and smashed into spectators in the process. Nikanoras gripped his own short blade in both hands, hoping at least the strength of the good one would heed the guidance of the weak one. As they squared off, he continued his verbal defense. "How can it be that the mere sight of me sickens you, while the enemy army flood our gates? Shouldn't you be interested in other things? Like salvaging what is left of our beloved city?"

Those words were not meant to pacify the general. Nikanoras knew they would inflict deeper wounds than his saber in this crowd of onlookers.

The humiliation burned in his round, creased face. Through his graying hair and white beard, Nikanoras could see that redness of the general's exertion and rage.

Stalking him, Persepolos had the blade held high once again. "Like a plague, you haunt me. You were all massacred by Macedon, yet still here you are in my city."

He roared, then sliced down the large blade as if he meant to sever Nikanoras lengthwise into two halves.

With both hands holding the hilt of his sword, Nikanoras deflected the powerful blow, metal screeched on metal and the crowd gasped behind them.

The reverberation of the impact burned his sore muscle, causing him to cringe in pain. Through the severe stinging, Nikanoras needed to recover quickly and come back en garde.

Using the last of his reserves, when he thought he had spent enough blood and sweat on Thebes, Nikanoras managed to stand tall and hold that saber steadily. "Your city?" He choked at the absurdity. "Look around you, you fool. You have no city!"

It was as if Nikanoras had only just begun to see Persepolos' hatred rise. As if this were his normal state and he had just begun to grow wild with wrath. The prophetic words of General Deodoras, whom he befriended in the chamber before they were given audience with Philip, came back to him. He had said, *"Why, Nikanoras, do you have so many enemies?"* And added to this thought, Nikanoras asked himself, *Why are these enemies all crazy?*

With both hands to wield his weapon, Persepolos smashed his blade crossways about mid-section in height.

Awkwardly Nikanoras deflected it, but the force knocked him to the ground. He rolled left quickly as Persepolos' blade cut through the grouting of dirt between stones on the street beside him. Nikanoras blinked in awe at how close Persepolos had come to cleaving him in two.

The old man muttered profanity under his breath and scrambled to get his blade upright. Persepolos was on him like a plague of Furies, slashing the air to ribbons, making whistling noises with the steel as he hewed as Nikanoras spun and dodged every slow hammer of the steel.

It was becoming a growing spectacle for the crowd. Bloodshed had always been entertaining, and here was one of the Sacred Band, one who was supposed to work miracles against Macedon on the back foot with an aging general. One can only assume whose side they were on as wagers were made and bets raised in the air.

Had Nikanoras been in top form, it wouldn't have presented a challenge. But Nikanoras had never trained with his weak side. His right injured arm was simply useless. *Useless.* And his left so awkward it may as well have not been attached to his side.

After another menacing blow which almost shattered the tip of Persepolos' long sword as it sparked and hit the paving stone, Nikanoras managed to get to his feet once more. His long mane in his eyes, sweat causing it to stick to his cheek and neck, Nikanoras again had his blade in both hands raised upward in front of him so he could ward off any blow.

He had stopped shouting. It mattered not to Persepolos what Nikanoras had to say. It was just an old score that needed settling.

Seeing his tactic of sword on sword was not getting him any closer to his goal, Persepolos snatched a spear away from an astonished Macedonian mercenary. Unlucky for Nikanoras, this man did not object. The entertainment value was too good.

Sword in the right hand, spear in the left, Persepolos kept pace with Nikanoras' retreat.

As Nikanoras' quickly scanned the surroundings, he wondered who he fought for. Maybe it was just time to give up and meet Meleagros.

Resolved to let go, knowing this type of life was no life at all, Nikanoras stopped in his tracks, stood tall, and lowered his weapon.

A shrill sound of panic emerged from the mob at what he had done.

Nikanoras' senses closed down. That voice came to him again. *"Nikki!"*

Unafraid, staring into those cantankerous old eyes, Nikanoras could see hatred as pure as yellow gold in them. His demise was the general's only aim.

Not caring what Nikanoras had decided, or why, Persepolos may have assumed Nikanoras must have weakened and accepted the general's superior skill.

Nikanoras wondered if those who watched knew otherwise. He was one of the elite warriors of the Sacred Band, and his scars were obvious to all who cared to look.

The general raised the spear, as if he meant to impale him. He took a good strong stance, and drew back for the plunge.

Closing his eyes to not witness his own execution, Nikanoras inhaled, raised his chin high, and held his breath.

When Nikanoras heard a savage shriek he almost imagined it was his own. Blinking his eyes, he found the general on his face on the ground before him. A bloody dagger in his back, dripping with his blood, was still clasped in the hand of what seemed to be Euridises.

Noise erupted from the mob on this turn of events. As Nikanoras' senses caught up, the female with the dagger took the opportunity in the confusion to escape.

"Kyna!" Suddenly, it dawned on Nikanoras who it was.

He pushed his way through a very thick mass of people, to try and catch her. By the time he clawed his way to the other side, she was gone.

As he realized he had lost her, another stark reality hit. The Macedonian soldiers most certainly must deem him a threat. Nikanoras could no longer wander, armed, innocently in their presence.

He had someone angry enough to hunt him down, and yet another willing to murder for him. Nikanoras imaged they thought he must be a very dangerous man, indeed. Add to that 'whom' he was. One of the chosen.

The guard of Macedon, the mercenaries, began whispering among themselves, nodding to him.

Nikanoras knew he was about to be captured and arrested. His sword in his weak hand, he raced out of the marketplace and tried to evade their tail, ducking in and out of the arched columned arcade, shadows as his cover. He paused briefly to catch his breath.

When he was tapped from behind he spun and raised the blade in two hands.

"Nikki!"

Ephisomines was almost killed by Nikanoras' blind fright. As his dilated eyes slowly began to see clearly, Nikanoras lowered his blade and exhaled a deep breath. "I am no longer safe here. I need leave

241

now."

"No. What has happened? Surely this cannot be."

"I've no time to argue." He peered back over his shoulder in fear.

Ephisomines said, "It is just as well. There is another thing I wanted to discuss with you. Maybe the time is now."

In no mood for a chat, knowing the armed guard must be just beyond the bend, Nikanoras said in exasperation, "What thing?" as he looked around to check behind him in paranoia.

Gripping his garment at his shoulder, Ephisomines dragged his ear close to his lips to whisper, "I need you as a spy. You will take information from Athens to Macedon."

At those fortuitous words, his blood washed from his face and drained to his feet. Immediately Nikanoras thought of his father. "A spy? Are you insane?"

Ephisomines stroked Nikanoras' hair back from his face. "No, I am not insane. I am rich from it, and soon you will be too. You need bring some papers to Philip. If you do this, he will reward you. Trust me."

"Papers? Against whom?" Nikanoras shifted his weight from his right leg to left, keenly aware he would die a painful death for this, any of it. "No. I cannot."

"Oh? Are you a fan of Athens after the way they deserted the Sacred Band in war? Come now, Nikki, we have no peace with Athens. And Macedon has the wealth."

Swallowing his fear, seeing behind him only the normal comings and goings of the market and streets, Nikanoras actually considered the request.

In reality, what else was he to do? He had no family. No home. And if he was to be expected to stay with Ephisomines and be his kept boy, he would sooner cleave off his own penis.

"I need to think about it, Ephisomines. Please. Take me back to your home so I may have a moment of peace to think."

"Of course." Ephisomines smiled sweetly, hooking his elbow and escorting him back.

Once inside the palace, Nikanoras felt more secure and better able to concentrate. Ephisomines insisted he luxuriate in a hot bath as he ruminated over the possibilities.

His head resting on the tiled edge, naked under the clear water, an ewer of wine by his side, Nikanoras floated above the steam gently. Dozing in and out of a dream, he thought he imagined Meleagros coming to him, his hands out, beckoning, *"Nikki!"*

Waking with a start, Nikanoras rubbed his face to try and clear his mind, only to see Ephisomines approaching with a servant. In the servant's hands was a tray of fresh fruit and cheese. As he instructed the slave to set the food down on a marble bench, and then leave, Ephisomines delicately sat beside the food tray and smiled adoringly at Nikanoras. "Are you hungry?"

"Yes." He hoisted himself out of the water to sit on the ledge. Nikanoras looked over the tray as Ephisomines lowered it for him to choose.

Picking some figs and dates, he stared at Ephisomines as he stared hungrily back.

"This deed, the one you spoke of." Nikanoras chewed the fruit as he asked, "Is it a one-off?"

"It is as you like. There are no limits."

Swallowing the food in his mouth, Nikanoras wondered what Meleagros would think. As he sat, deep in thought, a hand caressed his damp hair from behind. Knowing if he lingered at this man's side, he'd either grow as lazy as an overfed pet feline, or completely insane from being under his thumb and body, constantly, Nikanoras said in a hoarse whisper, "Yes. I shall do it."

"I knew you would see it was the right thing to do, Nikki." First Ephisomines kissed his head, then he hand fed him another fig.

As Nikanoras took it from his long manicured fingers, he knew the look in Ephisomines' eyes. And no sooner did he finish eating the fruit, did Ephisomines have his lips attached to his own. After the kiss, Ephisomines got on his hands and knees, waiting.

Nikanoras struggled to become excited, since Ephisomines was not anything like his gorgeous brother.

Closing his eyes, recalling the nights he and Meleagros had made love, Nikanoras had to fight his grief and become master of his body.

As Ephisomines waited eagerly for penetration, Nikanoras performed by sheer will and determination, since he felt nothing in his heart.

****

Nightfall came, and the task was explained to Nikanoras. A horse and documents were given to him. Quite simply, he was to ride like the wind to Philip and his son, and hand them the information.

Exchanging his Sacred Band armor for black garments and chlamys he glanced back at Ephisomines only once. His was a face Nikanoras did not want to remember, but, he did owe him a debt of kindness which he was certain his several nights in bed had fulfilled.

"Gods-speed, Nikki. You hold the fate of so many in your hands. If Philip is pleased with us, he will spare us. If not, he will burn our city down and unite with Athens. Go. May the god Hermes be your guide. And when you have accomplished this task, come back. There will always be more information to exchange. And..." he said seductively, "I will miss you."

Nikanoras urged the horse on. Moving slowly at first, so as not to arouse suspicion, he took to the back alleys which he knew well from his childhood.

With visions of his life as a toddler, adored by Euridises, nurtured by her with so much love and kindness, he never knew how much he'd miss it until she was gone.

With heavy thoughts on his mind, Nikanoras passed his father's palace which was lit from within. Eyeing it for the last time, the irony of this deed was not lost on him. The apple had not fallen far from the tree.

But unlike his father, he had no love of Thebes any longer. It was a city of spite and hatred for him. And it was not lost on him at how completely ironic that its fate now lie within his hands.

Alexander had asked the people of Thebes to surrender peacefully. Two men from the council were to be taken as hostage. In return Thebes had asked that they receive the mighty Anitpater and Philotas, two of Philip's right hand men.

Before his ride, Nikanoras read the scroll he carried. He could see it was not about Athens at all, but purely Theban security. He had been lied to yet again. In his hands was the plea from Thebes asking for a treaty. If Alexander did not receive it, he would batter down the city walls, murder as many Thebans as possible, and sell the survivors as slaves.

Grinding his teeth in fury, Nikanoras crumbled that scroll up in his hand.

CHAPTER 28

Once he had passed the temple of Apollo and the city gates, he spurred his horse to run through the mountain pass. The main road was awash with soldiers and mercenaries of Macedon moving in the night to Athens. Though he had information for their king that would benefit them, he dared not stop and tell them this. Instead, he took to the back trails, avoiding their camps and torchlight.

After three nights he arrived at the plain of Chaeronea. He dismounted his horse, unbridled him, and set him free.

In the dimness of the starlit night, the cool December air coming in from the mountain peaks, he could make out the lion monument. Alone in a vast emptiness, he moved to it as if in a trance. Then, after circling the burial mounds only once, he collapsed on the dirt to lean against that stone lion and wait.

****

On the second morning he woke out of a dream to hear the distance sound of an army on the move. Getting to his feet, he could make out the dust and glittering spear tips of Philip's army. Since no word had come to Philip, he was retaliating.

By nightfall Nikanoras could see the flames. Thebes was burning. Six thousand murdered, thirty thousand sold as slaves.

Removing the documents from his kit, Nikanoras knelt on them to stop the wind from picking them up and spiraling them to the heavens. With his flint he struck a spark and ignited it. It burst into flames as the ashes spun and whipped passed his face, like moths to a torch.

When it was completely black like coal, he knelt to the shrine of his fellow comrades and unsheathed his dagger. It was time.

"Oh, great gods of the heavens-hear your humble servant. I am yours now, yours to send into the realm of Hades. Meleagros..." he cried, his eyes watering and running hot tears down his face, the lion in his view, "Lover. Though I thought what I had dreamed of was a simple life of wife and family, I can never be content with it now."

Brushing away a tear, he continued, "They were right, Pelopidas and Gorgidas. Sworn lovers were we. Sworn to live or die together. And my dearest, I cannot live without you." Stifling a wail of agony, his blurred sight never leaving that silhouette of the powerful lion, with both hands he clenched the hilt of his sword.

As his senses dulled, he heard his name whispered again in the wind, *"Nikki!"*

"Meleagros," he answered that invisible ghost, gripping the handle tightly, "I am coming."

He crouched over and plunged the knife quickly into his belly, forcing himself to keep pressing it deeper though the pain was unendurable.

For a moment it seemed nothing happened. Then, he collapsed into a ball, the heat from his blood spilled over his hands, then his knees, steaming in the cold night air.

A ringing came to his ears, then he remembered nothing.

****

As if waking from a dream or a winter's hibernation, Nikanoras raised his head to see his entire regime standing before him. They had waited. Mycandor with his lover, Argos, lovely blond Lysos, hands clasped with his Chasathenes, and his beloved was there.

A beautiful man stepped forward so Nikanoras may see him. His smile endearing and proud, he reached out to Nikanoras. "I have been calling you," Meleagros said.

The tears streaming down Nikanoras' face, Nikanoras drew near Meleagros.

Every one of his comrades were perfect in their shining armor and horsehair crests. There were two hundred and seventy of them there. They would wait for the last thirty, for they would all come as he did, within the year so they could be as one.

Hot tears running down his cheeks, Nikanoras cupped Meleagros' handsome face in his hands. "I have missed you. I am sorry I took so long."

"Shh, Nikki. You are here now." Meleagros smiled affectionately at him.

As the gates of Hades were thrown wide, the men of his Sacred Band were brought back together, *'...that he should have joined lovers and their beloved... a band cemented in friendship and grounded upon love, is never to be broken and invincible-' (3)*

"He is here, Nikki," Meleagros whispered, "Lover, he is here with us."

"Who?" Nikanoras was so enamored with his beauty, he could scarce concentrate on a thing.

"Pelopidas. We are his warriors of the clouds." His smile was impish and delightful. It filled him with so much love and joy, Nikanoras burst with energy.

As Meleagros' words filled his ears like music from a kithara, the men parted to show Nikanoras an old man, dressed in his white robes. It was Pelopidas and his trusted friend, Epaminondas there to greet him.

"And one more surprise, lovely Nikki." Meleagros held him by the waist to turn him to face another direction.

There in flowing white, was Euridises.

Choking in a sob of complete joy, Nikanoras ran to her, lifting her into his arms to embrace and spin around. "My beloved. Oh, my Euridises."

"Oh, my silly Nikanoras. You needn't have suffered so much for me."

"I am sorry. I missed your funeral."

Her cool fingers stopped his words from escaping his mouth. "Shush. None of that matters now. Not here."

As Nikanoras held her hand, he looked back at the warriors of the clouds. They were smiling at him in pride.

"We didn't do so badly, did we, Nikki?" Meleagros tilted his head sweetly.

Tears of joy running down his face, Nikanoras answered, "No. We were heroes, my lover. And we shall be honored and remembered as heroes."

****

So, it was finished. The beginning and the end of their Sacred Band, and yet there they are in the end, sworn to conquer or die...together.

THE END

FOOTNOTES

1. Quote from Plutarch's Life of Pelopidas
2. Quote from Philip of Macedon according to Pausanias.
3. Quote Plutarch's Life of Pelopida

About the Author

Award-winning author G.A. Hauser was born in Fair Lawn, New Jersey, USA and attended university in New York City. She moved to Seattle, Washington where she worked as a patrol officer with the Seattle Police Department. In early 2000 G.A. moved to Hertfordshire, England where she began her writing in earnest and published her first book, In the Shadow of Alexander. Now a full-time writer, G.A. has written over seventy novels, including several best-sellers of gay fiction and is an Honorary Board Member of Gay American Heroes for her support of the foundation. For more information on other books by G.A., visit the author at her official website.

www.authorgahauser.com

G.A. has won awards from All Romance eBooks for Best Author 2010, 2009, Best Novel 2008, *Mile High*, and Best Author 2008, Best Novel 2007, *Secrets and Misdemeanors*, Best Author 2007.

The G.A. Hauser Collection
Single Titles

Unnecessary Roughness
Hot Rod
Mr. Right
Happy Endings
Down and Dirty
Lancelot in Love
Happy Endings
Cowboy Blues
Living Dangerously
L.A. Masquerade
My Best Friend's Boyfriend
The Diamond Stud
The Hard Way
Games Men Play
Born to Please
Of Wolves and Men
The Order of Wolves
Got Men?
Heart of Steele
All Man
Julian
Black Leather Phoenix
London, Bloody, London
In The Dark and What Should Never Be, Erotic Short Stories
Mark and Sharon (formally titled A Question of Sex)
A Man's Best Friend
It Takes a Man
The Physician and the Actor
For Love and Money
The Kiss
Naked Dragon
Secrets and Misdemeanors
Capital Games
Giving Up the Ghost
To Have and To Hostage

G. A. HAUSER

Love you, Loveday
The Boy Next Door
When Adam Met Jack
Exposure
The Vampire and the Man-eater
Murphy's Hero
Mark Antonious deMontford
Prince of Servitude
Calling Dr Love
The Rape of St. Peter
The Wedding Planner
Going Deep
Double Trouble
Pirates
Miller's Tale
Vampire Nights
Teacher's Pet
In the Shadow of Alexander
The Rise and Fall of the Sacred Band of Thebes

The Action Series

Acting Naughty
Playing Dirty
Getting it in the End
Behaving Badly
Dripping Hot
Packing Heat
Being Screwed
Something Sexy
Going Wild
Having it All!

Men in Motion Series

Mile High
Cruising
Driving Hard
Leather Boys

Heroes Series

Man to Man
Two In Two Out
Top Men

G.A. Hauser
Writing as Amanda Winters

Sister Moonshine
Nothing Like Romance
Silent Reign
Butterfly Suicide
Mutley's Crew

Printed in Great Britain
by Amazon.co.uk, Ltd.,
Marston Gate.